Seth thought of Rian, surrounded, wounded, left there to face the punkers alone. Still he kept running. What was the matter with him? This wasn't like him! It was as if someone else had taken over his body. . . .

He slowed, stumbling in the darkness. He had to help his friend! He couldn't let himself be panicked, no matter how bad it was. He turned. . . .

Where was Rian? Where were the punkers? The quiet bothered him more than the commotion had. He used some snow to wipe the blood from his eyes, though it was still flowing. He looked about.

He was standing on a lake. Maybe the ice was sound, but more likely it wasn't.

Cautiously he took a step forward.

Crack!

I don't like this! he thought. If he hadn't panicked, hadn't been blinded by pain and blood, he never would have blundered out here! Still, if he tread softly—

He took another step. There was another crack. . . .

He took a third step—and the ice gave way completely.

PIERS ANTHONY

THROUGH THE ICE

ROBERT KORNWISE

THROUGH THE ICE

This is a work of fiction. All the characters and events portrayed in this book are fictional, and any resemblance to real people or incidents is purely coincidental.

A Baen Book

Baen Publishing Enterprises
P.O. Box 1403
Riverdale, NY 10471

ISBN: 0-671-72113-5

First Paperback Printing, April 1992

Printed in the United States of America

Distributed by Simon & Schuster
1230 Avenue of the Americas
New York, NY 10020

CONTENTS

• One

Trouble

The punkers were high and the jocks were drunk. Periodically a couple would walk upstairs. Every so often the police would drive by, causing a brief nervous hush that dissipated the moment the car departed. It was a typical New Year's Eve party.

Seth Warner leaned back on the black leather couch, mildly interested in the night's events. Drinking and drugs were not his thing, but his friend Rian had wanted them to join the "in" crowd for this occasion, so Seth had done so against his better judgment. He put his feet up on the table in front of him, feigning nonchalance—and accidentally kicked over a can of beer. It was half full, and the liquid spilled across the table in a frothy stream and dripped to the floor before Seth could do anything about it.

Oops. Seth quickly put his feet down and stood up. "I'm sorry about that," he said without much enthusiasm.

"Jerk!" the girl snapped, though she had not shown much interest in the beer before.

Seth moved around the table and walked away, not eager to get into a dialogue that might arouse the girl's rather large punker boyfriend. Avoidance was almost always the better part of valor. This was one good lesson he had learned in the course of his training in martial arts: not to look for trouble.

"Hey, stupid!" It was the boyfriend, who had evidently not had such training. Seth continued walking, not acknowledging the words or the tone. He had after all been at fault; the punker was entitled to his irritation. To an extent. There was, after all, litter and spilled food everywhere; the punkers weren't much on housekeeping.

"Hey, pin-brain," the punker called, stirring. There was a sound that sent a shiver up Seth's back.

He turned, realizing that he was not going to get out of this cleanly. Sure enough, there was a knife thrust into the table: a clear challenge.

The buzz of conversation in the room faded. The others moved with seeming casualness toward the walls, clearing a space. They knew what was coming. The slightest of offenses was enough to provoke a fight, when the liquor was flowing. That was why Seth had tried to get away promptly, hoping that the punker wouldn't go out of his way to start trouble.

"Any problem?" Seth inquired. If the punker demanded an apology, he would make it; if he was required to fetch another beer for the girl, he would do that. He would have offered before, but had feared that any interaction between them would only stir up antagonism. His judgment was being confirmed.

The punker heaved himself out of the chair. He took a moment to get his balance; he was pretty far gone on beer or worse. Not much chance to reason with someone in that condition. He stepped heavily around the table.

Seth slowly brought one foot behind the other in

an almost casual fighting stance, feeling his muscles tensing. He had done his honest best to avoid a confrontation; his conscience was clear about that, at least. He was seventeen, stood six-two, and was in excellent physical condition. He was sure he could handle anything this jerk could throw at him, but he still hoped he wouldn't have to.

The punker walked up, scowling. Seth stood his ground. The punker lunged. Seth brought up his right hand and caught his adversary's arm. He then brought his own left arm up over his attacker, pivoted powerfully, and threw him to the floor. It was a basic technique, and he had used it in an attempt to stop the fight without seriously injuring his attacker. Even a drunk could catch on to the fact that the pickings were not as easy as he had supposed. This should be the end of it.

Seth turned and walked away, but from the corner of his eye he saw movement. He had known better than to turn his back on an opponent without caution. The punker was getting up and grabbing at the table, cursing under his breath. He was, unfortunately, a slow learner.

Seth spun around as the punker snatched up the knife and charged him. This time, he knew, he could not afford to take it easy; he had to finish it quickly and get away.

He kicked the man's hand and sent the weapon spinning across the floor. Then he threw a side-foot kick into the oncoming attacker's chest. The force of the kick was magnified as the punker ran into his foot. He felt the shock of solid contact. There was a splintering crack, and his adversary fell to the ground.

That had been *too* effective! Seth realized that he was hyped up by the menace, and had used full power when a lesser move would have sufficed. If the punker had been moving away, or taking defensive action, it wouldn't have been so bad. As it was, ribs had been broken.

Definitely time to leave! There were more punkers around, and Seth really did not like serious fighting, though he was equipped for it. He was proficient in Ryu Kyu No Te, a form of the martial arts originating in Okinawa, but had hoped never to use it in earnest. Why was it man's instinct to fight? The world would be better off if people could talk out their problems. But as long as there were those who would rather fight than talk, others had to be prepared.

He remembered when he had found a way to meet a challenge without having to fight. He hated people who made rude remarks to or about others. He did not necessarily brood about this in silence. For example, there was a boy who was along on some of the youth group trips he participated in. Somehow he always managed to alienate others without meaning to. He was only a casual friend of Seth's. But when other members of the group became too persistent about teasing him and making him miserable (and not doing much for themselves in the process) Seth had gotten angry. He had stood up and announced that he would have none of this. "Lay off!" They laid off, and it made all the difference in the world for that boy.

Seth had asserted himself on behalf of what he felt was right. That was all it had taken. There had been no violence. In retrospect, he was glad that it had happened, because it had made him realize one of his own values. Every person deserved his chance, as that boy had deserved his.

Seth felt motion behind him. He had allowed himself to become preoccupied at the wrong time!

A hand grabbed around his neck. Seth spun from the hold and jumped back. His friend Rian was standing in front of him. *The fool!* he thought ferociously. To grab him like that, right after he had struck a man down hard! But that was Rian's way; he was often thoughtless, but never malicious. Rian was short, blond and gray eyed, in contrast to Seth's tall, brown and brown, and their personalities differed more than their appearances, but none of that mattered.

"Nice fight," Rian said, nodding toward the punker, who was down to stay, this time. The big difference between Seth and his friend was Rian's unabashed love of fighting.

"We'd better take off before the other punkers realize what I did," Seth said as they walked away. It was their luck that the spectators had not been punkers, or it could have gotten much uglier in a hurry.

"That's a good plan! Are you as drunk as I am?"

"Stupid question," Seth replied. He had not been drinking at all. He respected such things as legal age limits, even if others ignored them. "I'll drive."

They emerged from the building and climbed into Rian's 4x4. Seth fastened his seat belt, started the engine and maneuvered it out of the parking lot.

"Did you meet that girl?" Rian asked. It was evident that he really wasn't intoxicated, despite his remark; still, he had had a few.

"No. I don't think she was there." That had been the other reason to attend this party: the hope that a particular girl would be there, unescorted. Seth really didn't know her, but had hoped to change that. But if she kept company with the likes of the punkers, it wasn't a good sign.

"It's just as well. I don't know what you see in her anyway. . . ." Rian trailed off.

Seth didn't like his friend's sudden quietness. "What?"

"That van behind us is getting a little too close, don't you think?"

Seth cursed himself for not watching more carefully. He was entirely too likely to go off on some stray thought and not watch his feet—or, in this case, his rearview mirror. If Rian was concerned, it could be bad. He looked—and saw the headlights of the van coming up at ramming velocity.

Before he could answer, let alone get the car out of the way, the van rear-ended their vehicle, hard. Seth fought the wheel as the jeep jolted ahead. He tried to bring it under control by braking, but the brakes locked, making a worse jolt. Then Rian's head hit the windshield. He hadn't buckled his seat belt!

Seth jerked his foot off the brake pedal, but was still struggling for control. They swerved off the road and smashed into a tree. All Seth could think of as he saw it coming was how glad he was that by this time they were moving under twenty miles an hour, instead of forty.

He was shaken by the crash, but not hurt. "Rian, are you all right?" he asked, fearing the worst.

"Bruised, battered, enraged, otherwise just fine!"

Rian growled, rubbing his head. Evidently he had braced himself against the final crash. "But those characters are dead! Hand me that bat in the back seat!"

Now Seth, peering through the broken window, saw the van pulling to a stop beyond them. The trouble wasn't finished yet! "Maybe we'd better just get out of here on foot," he suggested. "It's getting dark; they won't be able to see us well enough to catch us."

Rian grabbed the bat. "Not likely! They wrecked my car. I'm going to bash their lousy heads in!" He shoved until he got the door open and scrambled out.

Seth did not care for this situation at all, but he didn't seem to have many options. He couldn't run off and leave his friend, so he had to stay. He doubted that the van was stopping to offer apologies and assistance, but it was possible that this stop was just to verify the damage to the jeep.

It was worse than he had feared. Figures were piling out of the van: about ten punkers, including the one Seth had put down. There was no question about it: they were out for blood.

"Rian, I really think we'd better get out of here and let the police handle it. The bashed bumpers and skid marks will show who's at fault, and—"

But Rian, foolhardy, was already charging; he swung his bat in a wide arc, and it smashed into the nearest punker's skull. Not a killing blow, but the punker landed on the ground with a thud.

Seth knew that any chance at all to avoid mayhem was gone. His friend's recklessness and the punkers' meanness were combining to guarantee disaster. The two of them would be lucky to get out of this conscious, let alone healthy—and even if they did, the mess wouldn't look good at all on their records. What a situation—because of one spilled can of beer!

More cautious, now, the punkers took out weapons: knives, chains, nunchucks, and metal pipes. These were mostly homemade devices, looking crude, but Seth knew how deadly any of them could be. The blades were adapted from carving knives, with special handles. The pipes had tape wrapped around one end for a better grip. A chain was especially effective against an opponent's knife or club, because it could wrap around the hand and disable it. The nunchucks, in the hands of a skilled operator, could be worst of all. They consisted of two short lengths of wood or pipe, connected by a short cord. The attacker held one club, and whipped the other about on its tether, greatly increasing its striking force. This weapon had long since been outlawed, but street gangs still used it, and Seth was frankly afraid of it.

A short punker made a pass with his knife at Rian. Rian dodged the knife and brought the stiffened side of his hand down against the man's wrist, causing the knife to drop. But meanwhile two other punkers grabbed his arms, and then the disarmed one kicked him in the groin. Rian went down in agony, while all three punkers started beating on him.

Seth had been surveying the situation, trying to judge how best to help his friend without merely getting himself beaten up. He had somehow thought that the punkers would attack one at a time, so had been caught by surprise when they piled on Rian. He should have realized that there would be no rules here!

At least that relieved him of his concern about fair play. Seth hurled himself through the air, delivering a flying side-foot kick to the one who had kicked Rian. That one fell to the ground.

No! Seth realized with horror that the punker he had just downed was no male. It was the girl at the party—the one whose beer he had knocked over. She was in a heavy jacket now, and had a cap on; in the dusk he had not recognized her. No wonder her pass with the knife had been clumsy!

Still, she *had* attacked, and *had* kicked Rian. But not quite accurately; Rian was now fighting back with the two who had held his arms, and was making an increasingly good account of himself.

So at the moment two punkers were down: one from Rian's bat, the other from Seth's kick. Two were battling Rian. The remaining six were circling Seth, having recognized him as the more dangerous opponent. All of these were male; apparently the girl had come along because she liked this kind of action, or wanted to prove herself in some way. Seth still wished he hadn't kicked her.

The first of the six charged him. Seth brought his foot up in an arc and delivered a crescent kick to the side of the punker's face. Then he spun in air and scored on a second with a flying reverse kick. The punkers had made the mistake of depending on numbers and weapons; they were relatively clumsy, and almost helpless against truly fast, trained strikes. Still, this was a long way from over!

"Aaaaah!"

Seth spun around and saw one of the attackers thrust a knife into Rian's hip. Blood welled out, and Rian staggered.

Seth stood in shock. Somehow he had still had the notion that it was possible to get through this without serious injury, though all the indications had been against it. It was that spark of faith he nurtured, the faith that no man was truly evil and that there was always a way to come through a problem. He kept wanting to see some redeeming thing about the punkers, even as he fought them. As if at some point they would stop and say "Hey, it's been a good fight, you scored some points, let's quit now and go back to the party." Sportsmanship. Now the obvious had registered: that there was no sportsmanship here, only blind malevolence. The punkers had been primed for a fight, and had grabbed at the first pretext that offered. The beer had hardly mattered.

There was a high-pitched noise. Suddenly he felt the whip of a cold steel chain slashing across his face. He could hardly see, for the blood was flowing into his eyes. Yet again, he had hesitated, he had paused, letting his mind play with concepts. That had let them take the initiative, and thrown away whatever remaining chance he had had.

Blindly, Seth ran, not caring where he went. He heard their shouts and laughter.

Laughter? How could they laugh? They thought this horror was funny? No, of course not. There was no humor here, only derision. They liked scoring, however brutally or unfairly, and they liked seeing their prey hurting, fleeing. It made them feel like big men.

Seth was not a coward, yet he continued to run, not knowing what else to do. Had he been a real fighting machine he would have struck out at the punkers the moment they were distracted by Rian's scream, and reduced the odds. But his heart just wasn't in combat, no matter how good at it he was, and that had made him the victim instead of the victor. Attitude—that was his great weakness. His sensei, the instructor, had told him that, and it was true. "You could be a champ, but you think too much!" All too accurate.

He thought of Rian, surrounded, wounded, left there to face the punkers alone. Still he kept running. What was the matter with him? This wasn't like him! It was as if someone else had taken over his body.

He slowed, stumbling in the darkness. He had to help his friend! He couldn't let himself be panicked, no matter how bad it was. He turned.

A burning blast of heat stung his entire body. What had happened? Had they fired a gun at him? It felt like a flamethrower!

No, it was cold snow! He had brushed by a tree and gotten a load of snow on him, and the cold had seemed hot. He staggered to the side, shaking it off. Now he had stumbled onto ice. He tried to get off it, but somehow got turned around and only got onto more of it.

He used some snow to wipe the blood from his eyes, though it was still flowing. He looked about.

It was now dark, but he saw by the moonlight that there were no trees around him. He had staggered quite a way beyond the one that had dumped snow on him. Where was Rian? Where were the punkers? The silence bothered him more than the commotion had.

He was standing on a lake. Normally that would not matter, in December, for it would be frozen solid. However, it had been a warm winter, thus far, and the lakes had only recently begun to freeze. Maybe the ice was sound, but more likely it wasn't.

Were the punkers watching to see how far out he would stagger before catching on? That would be another fine cruel joke!

He faced the near shore. Cautiously he took a step forward.

Crack!

I don't like this! he thought. If he hadn't panicked, hadn't been blinded by pain and blood, he never would have blundered out here! Still, if he trod softly—

He took another step. There was another crack. No, he didn't like this at all! Ice was treacherous stuff; it could support a person until he changed his mind, then give way. He had to get off this quickly, but didn't dare make a heavy-footed move.

He took a third step—and the ice gave way completely. Seth screamed as the freezing water shocked his body. His head went under, choking him off, suffocating him. He tried to swim up, but already the cold was numbing his limbs and the water made his clothing awkward; he couldn't move freely or efficiently.

Then his head struck the ice—and he realized that he had drifted under the unbroken section. That ice, too weak to support the weight of his body from above, was too strong to let him break through from below. He was in worse trouble yet!

He struggled, but knew he was getting nowhere. The horrible cold and darkness closed in, and his lungs felt as if they were about to burst. Air! Air! There was none.

He knew he had only seconds remaining before it was all over. He had gone through the ice, and if he didn't get back immediately, he would drown. All for half a can of spilled beer!

Yet somehow, now, he lost the urge to struggle. He let the air bubble slowly out of his mouth, and felt himself sinking. An odd tingling feeling intruded on his awareness, and his vision blurred. It was actually becoming comfortable, even pleasant.

Then he thought of his mother, and his ten-year-old sister Ferne with her long brown hair tinged with red and gold natural highlights, and how hurt they would be if he didn't come home. *NO!* he screamed in his mind.

But something was causing his body to spin down, deeper into the water. He made one last effort to fight back, to stroke to the open surface, but to no avail. His body simply would not respond. His family had lost his father; now it was losing him too.

Then, with one last choke, he lost consciousness. He knew he was drowning. He wondered whether Death would appear with a long scythe.

Two

Reincarnation

Seth was acutely aware of the hot sun beating down on him. No wonder—he was in his heavy winter clothes! But it didn't feel like winter here!

Lifting a hand to his face, he felt a long stinging gash. He did not remember being hit. This wasn't from the chain. The ice must have cut him when he fell through, he thought. Through the ice.

Ice? Lying on his side, he opened his eyes. A pearly white beach stretched out under him, as far as he could see. The sand led up to a brilliantly blue ocean, with small rippling waves. This certainly wasn't home!

He sat up and looked the other way. About fifteen feet behind him was a tremendously thick jungle. Although Seth was no botanist, nothing looked remotely like a Michigan landscape. It was, if anything, more like a tropical rain forest.

He looked more closely at the trees. Their bark was not brown. A good number of the trunks were blue, green or white. There was also a peculiar yellow tree which appeared to have no bark at all, and was somewhat disturbing to look at. Most of the leaves were larger than what he was accustomed to seeing. Not quite green, they were almost emerald, with veins of incandescent pink and violet. The overall effect was dazzling.

Where was he? He had just died, so maybe—

"Heaven?" he asked aloud.

"No."

Startled, Seth jumped to his feet. That was not a good idea. Not only was his head hurting, his legs were asleep, and he fell down onto his side, feeling ridiculous. He stretched his legs and flexed them, getting the circulation restored. Then, slowly, he stood up again.

He saw nothing. Had he suffered an auditory hallucination? An imagined voice? That would be no less likely than his presence on this warm beach, after sinking into a freezing cold lake.

"Who is that?" he asked, nervous not so much about his surroundings, as about the state of his sanity.

"Me."

That had definitely been a voice! Seth looked around, and decided that it had come from behind the yellow tree. He walked up and put his hand on the trunk.

What had appeared to be yellow bark felt more like leathery yellow skin. "Hands off!"

Startled, Seth jumped back. The voice was not from behind the tree, it was from the tree itself! He tripped over his feet, almost fainting with the astonishing realization. A talking tree?

"You're going to hurt yourself!" laughed the patronizing voice.

Well, the laughter wasn't cruel. It was better than chains and knives! "What are you?"

"I am a tree, you twit!"

Ask a silly question! Seth tried again. "Who are you?"

"I am Sen-Tree, a direct descendant of the once-powerful Guard-Trees."

Was this a joke? Then who was playing it, and how? Joke or not, this was better than drowning!

"Where am I?" Seth asked. He was almost unable to formulate complete thoughts, much less compound sentences.

"You are on Earth Plane 4, twenty kilometers from the border of the Teuton Empire," replied Sen-Tree.

Seth mulled this over and decided that he must indeed have gone crazy. "How long have I been lying on the shore?"

"A very short time. Two or three days, perhaps."

"Two days! You consider that a short time?"

"I am a tree," the tree said. "I have lived for 379 years, 6 months, and 22 days. It is possible for me to live another 400 years. Thus two or three days is a short period of time. It is all a matter of perspective. You have a problem with that?"

The tree sounded offended. Some of its branches were trembling, and there was no wind. Seth realized that it was time to stop being so concerned about his own situation, and to start tuning into what he was finding here.

"I apologize if I offended you," he said quietly. "It is simply that I am a stranger here, and do not know your ways."

"If you are here, then you are here for a reason," the tree said. "However, if you wish to leave, then you might talk to the Emperor."

He might be crazy to talk to a tree, Seth thought; but crazy or not, he thought it imperative to talk to another human being. If this tree helped him find a man, it was worth it. "Would you be so kind as to tell me how to find him?"

"If you step behind my trunk," the tree said, "you will notice a path which leads to Teutonia. That is where the Emperor resides."

Seth did as he was told. Indeed, there was a path. "Thank you!" he exclaimed.

The tree did not answer him. It was already busy yelling at an amused bird who had landed provocatively on a branch.

Seth set off down the path. A tune was running through his head, and in a moment he identified it: "We're off to see the Wizard, the Wonderful Wizard of Oz!" But this wasn't Oz, or Kansas, or Michigan. This was Earth Plane 4, whatever that was. If he could believe the talking tree. If he could believe in his sanity.

Then he became uncomfortably aware of the sharp pang of hunger deep in his belly. If the tree was correct, he had not eaten in two or three days. His amazement at his situation, and the talking tree, had distracted him from his internal condition, but now it was not to be denied. This was no joking matter!

He looked at the trees beside the path. He spotted what appeared to be a fruit tree with a green trunk and blue leaves. He approached it with caution. The fruit looked good, if he tuned out the color, but it was unfamiliar. How could he know whether it was safe to eat?

Well, maybe this was another talking tree, and maybe it would tell him. It was certainly worth a try.

"Mr. Tree," Seth called, feeling foolish, but not as foolish as he knew he would be to pass up edible fruit while so hungry. "Mr. Tree, is your fruit good? May I take some to eat?"

There was no reply. Seth was relieved. If the tree had talked, it would probably have been as irate as the other one. How could he have been sure whether it would tell the truth about its fruit? It might say it was poisonous when it wasn't, or, worse, say it was good, in an effort to destroy the intruder. It was better to use his own judgment.

He picked a fruit about the size of an apple. Its color, however, was white. It seemed to be ripe, and it smelled like a peach. But, being experienced in outdoor living, Seth did not take a large bite. Mushrooms weren't the only things that could be deceptive! He sucked on a small piece, resting beside the trunk. It tasted much like strawberry, and he found it very satisfying when he closed his eyes so as not to see how clearly it was something else.

After waiting a while and suffering no ill effects, he ate a larger portion. He waited again. This was tedious, but better than taking an unnecessary risk. Again, he suffered no ill effects. Unless this was something like red squill, the stuff used to poison rats without making them sick immediately, this pseudo-apple-peach-strawberry would do.

He ate with greater abandon, but did not stuff himself. Even nonpoisonous food could be troublesome, if too much was eaten on a long-empty stomach. Then he made a knapsack out of his unneeded winter jacket, and packed more of the fruit. This should solve his food problem for the next day or so, and by then he hoped to have found something else to eat. This really did not seem to be an inhospitable region, just strange. Quite strange!

Before resuming his walk, he took inventory. All of his clothes appeared to be on him, except for his scarf, which must have fallen into the lake. Or the sea. He still had no idea how he had come from one to the other. Maybe he had floated down and down through the lake, and somehow that water opened into this other sea in this strange land, and he had washed ashore and lain there, recovering. Certainly he was lucky to be alive, and if the loss of his scarf was all it had cost him, it was a bargain!

He had a few dollars in his wallet, which he suspected would be worthless here. What use would money be to talking trees? Still, he saved them; one never could tell. There was also a pocket knife, which contained a flint and a magnesium rod for starting fires. Seth was no arsonist, but he felt a lot more secure knowing that he could start a fire if he needed to. Finally, there were a few coins: a dime and three pennies. Not much, certainly, but a tangible reminder of home. Somehow he thought it would be long before he saw that home again.

How was his mother doing? His sister? Did they think him dead in the lake? That hurt! He pictured Ferne crying for him, her cheery nature abolished, her brown eyes turning red, and that hurt worse. No more tickle fights! He wished he could tell them that he was all right, in a land that seemed a good deal friendlier than the one he had left. No punkers here! But the image of men dredging the lake came to his mind, breaking the ice to search for his body. They wouldn't find it, but would that give them hope? How could they possibly guess the truth? He hardly believed it himself! Yet maybe, somehow, they would know . . .

Seth resumed his trek, paying careful attention to the scenery around him. A short distance from the path some trees were bending to the sides, as if something were pushing them. He saw no animal, and there was not enough breeze to account for it. What did it mean?

Then he realized that there was a pattern to the motion: the path of moving trees was going to intercept Seth's trail, not far from where he was now.

He thought quickly, then did what came naturally: he climbed the nearest large tree. This one was like a bull spruce, but with a blue trunk and red needles, and the branches were triangular in cross section. He was able to stair-step up them readily enough, and to gain a fair concealment because of their thickness and number. He could peer down, but probably would not be noticed unless whatever it was below looked directly at him.

He saw the creature. It appeared to be a huge purple snake, with a diameter of about two feet. It slithered out of the forest and across the path. It stopped under Seth's tree and opened its mouth—which appeared to be at its tail end. It swung its neck in every direction, then closed its mouth and slithered back into the forest on the other side. The thing was traveling backwards, with the mouth behind and no apparent eyes!

The snake safely past, Seth started his descent. He had remained absolutely still, so as not to attract attention; that serpent might be able to climb! But when he tried to move, he discovered that he could not. He seemed to be glued to the tree.

He controlled his panic reaction; that had gotten him into too much trouble before! Maybe there was sap or something, that adhered to his clothing, fastening it to the trunk. If so, he should be able to work himself free without making a commotion.

He examined himself—and found that little branches or rootlets had grown around him and attached themselves to his clothing. He tried to tear himself free, but could not; the cloth was so closely bound that it seemed to have become part of the tree.

Seth was able to get his right arm free of the sleeve, and to reach into his pocket for the knife. With that he tried to cut the rootlets, but they were tough, and he ended up cutting more cloth than root. He had to climb out of his shirt and Levis and leave them behind, after saving his few other belongings. He did salvage his sneakers, though; apparently the tree could not burrow through their rubber soles or tough upper canvas. He still had his winter jacket, and the fruit that he had been carrying in it. He added his wallet, pen knife and coins to the fruit, as he no longer had regular pockets.

He was alone, and it was warm, but he didn't feel easy about traveling on in his underwear. This wasn't just modesty; there could be predatory insects, though he hadn't been bothered so far. Certainly there were scratchy branches. There was also sunshine in the glades; he could get burned if he was in it too long. He wanted enough body cover to protect him from possibly unpleasant surprises.

After searching the area, he found a tree with ex-

tremely large and tough leaves of a funny color.
Oh—they were green! He cut off several with his
knife. How glad he was that he had not lost this one
tool! He fastened the leaves together with brown
vines from another tree, fashioning a crude skirt.
Then he made an even cruder shawl to protect his
shoulders. As an afterthought he found a suitable
stick and whittled one end into a sharp point. Now
he had a serviceable spear. After seeing the monstrous snake, he knew that this land was not
necessarily friendly, and he wanted more protection
than bare hands and a pocket knife.

He knew that he looked somewhat outrageous,
but he ventured bravely forth. Twenty kilometers
was a long hike, about twelve miles, and it was apparent that he would not cover it on this day. He
would have to spend a night in this strange wilderness. The thought hardly pleased him, but it
appeared unavoidable.

Seth traveled what he figured to be about eleven
kilometers, or a generous six miles in the more familiar measure, and decided to set up camp. It was more
important to have a safe haven for the night than to
make extra distance. With about an hour and a half
left before dusk, assuming that the pattern of the day
here was similar to that of home, he should have time
to build a shelter. Certainly he wasn't going to try to
sleep in a tree! Without his regular clothing on, it
would be his flesh the rootlets found, and they might
like it all too well.

Methodically, he searched the area. He found a
fallen tree of suitable size, and dragged it back to the
path, laying it at a low angle wedged in a V of another

tree. Next he found medium-sized branches which he angled against the tree on both sides. He found a plant with leaves similar to the ones he had made his kilt from, and intertwined the leaves between the branches.

Satisfied, he checked the little hut. An opening at one side was where he would build a fire. If any big snakes came, that should discourage them, he hoped! Seth collected twigs, sticks and branches, making sure to have enough for the entire night.

The fire started in no time, which was good because it was rapidly growing dark. He ate a few more fruits, glad that they were juicy because he had no other source of liquid, then submitted to an urgent call of nature. He picked up his makeshift spear and sat in the shelter, watching the fire. He intended to remain awake all night, so as not to be caught off guard. He had had no experience with the creatures of the night here, and he wanted to see them before they saw him.

He sat silently, feeling more and more tired. His eyes drifted upward, and he watched the sparks from the fire reaching for the sky like aspiring stars.

Suddenly, Seth was no longer sitting in the warm hut, but racing through the snow. He ran through the forest, hearing the punkers laugh. In a fit of rage he turned around. Eight of them appeared, and Rian was on the ground, trembling in pain.

Seth charged the enemy. The first one swung a pipe at his head. He ducked and delivered a front snap kick to the enemy's groin. He inverted his foot and sent a roundhouse kick to the man's face.

There was a loud thud as the punker hit the ground, motionless.

Whirling on the next attacker, Seth saw the glint of a knife. The punker slashed at Seth's face, and he jumped back.

He was not in time. The knife left a stinging gash on his cheek. Rage building with the pain, Seth spun in the air and made a devastating reverse kick, crushing the punker's rib cage.

Three more charged Seth. He moved with blinding speed. The first aggressor met a reverse punch which broke his nose. The second fell to the ground after receiving a side-foot kick that snapped his knee backwards. The third met with a drop-axe kick that broke his shoulder blade and his collarbone.

The remaining two punkers, seeing the way of it, hopped into the van and sped away.

Seth ran to Rian, taking off his scarf and tying it around Rian's wound. He ran out to flag down a car driving down the road. Naturally several cars sped right on by, not wanting to get involved, but then the police arrived. Thank God!

Seth woke, sweating and shivering. He realized that he was in his crude hut, keeping watch against the potential threats of the night. What a weird vision he had had.

The strangest thing about it was the seeming sense it made. That slash on the face—that accounted for the one he had found when he woke on the beach. His lost scarf—he had given it to Rian. In the dream.

Against his best intention, he drifted back to sleep. Now, however, he dreamed of pleasant fragrances, flowers, and the wind playing beautiful music as it whistled through reeds.

When he woke again it was morning. The sun was out and mist was rising off the ground. His fire had burned out. Some alert watcher he had been! He was lucky he hadn't been gobbled by a giant snake.

But there was something strange. He had dreamed of music. Now he was wide awake—but he still heard that music.

• Three

Rame

A soft, lilting melody was drifting to him. Seth shook his head, realizing that this was no dream. Someone was playing nearby!

"Who's out there?" he shouted—and immediately wished he hadn't. He should have kept quiet until he knew more about the other person. Now he had given himself away.

There was no answer, but the music stopped. This was not a good sign! Cursing his thoughtlessness, Seth reached for his spear. He had been foolish, but he didn't have to make it worse. This was no time to panic!

He assessed his situation. He was in a hut, and there was someone or something somewhere outside. It wasn't necessarily hostile. It had been singing, after all.

The other could have known that Seth was in the hut all along. It could have been watching him all night. Not good—not good at all! Yet it hadn't attacked, so this might not be bad either. There was no way to be sure.

First things first: if he stayed in the hut, he was an easy target. Better to get out quickly. At least he would be ready to defend himself, then.

Seth burst out of the hut, uttering a harsh cry, so as to surprise the other and scare it back. And crashed chest to chest with a gorgeous girl. She screamed and fell on the ground, her bright purple skirt spreading in disarray to show her lovely legs.

Seth, so well braced for trouble, had not been ready for this! Why hadn't he realized that it was a girl playing the music? The tune had been light, after all. He had been so worried about the danger that he hadn't really listened.

He felt terrible. He extended his hand to her, in a gesture of conciliation.

"Aaayyyeeee! Rame, help!" she cried, scooting away in panic.

Startled, Seth retreated. He was embarrassed about almost attacking the girl, but alert for danger. It had been a girl who had gotten him into trouble back where he came from, after all. With his peripheral vision he noticed movement about a hundred feet up the path. He whirled.

He heard a whooshing sound, and another. One arrow flew past his left shoulder, and one past his right. Fortunately both had missed.

Or had that been bad aim? The bracketing was so neat and swift that it could be a warning. Seth hesitated.

Suddenly his neck was caught by a rope. His hands came up reflexively, grabbing it before it tightened further, but the rope was already pulling hard. His head was jerked back, and he was hauled off his feet.

For a moment he swung wildly, his feet pedaling air, his hands trying desperately to keep the noose from becoming a garrote. Then his back smacked into the trunk of a tree.

The arrows reappeared, going in opposite directions, circling him. *Circling him?* Even caught as he was, Seth gaped at that!

Then he realized that they were tethered arrows. In fact, the two were tied together. Like the business end of a bola. They circled around the tree, coming closer with each pass, until each slapped into the bark beside his head.

Seth didn't breathe much of a sigh of relief. Despite his effort to hold it off, the rope was like nylon cord, and was cutting uncomfortably into his neck. He sagged against the tree, and it tightened further, cutting off his breath and blood. He could have held his breath for a time, but when the pressure cut off the blood he blacked out instantly.

Seth woke to the sound of music, again. Cautiously he opened his eyes. He didn't want to knock down any more pretty girls and incite any more devastating attacks!

He was in a cave, lit by torches. He lay on a mat on the floor. Standing beside him was the most beautiful girl he had ever seen. The one he had encountered before. Her hair was long and silky blonde, her eyes were stunning green, and her figure made the term "perfect" seem inadequate. She wore the same bright purple skirt and brown blouse, and on her this seemed the ideal decor.

The girl looked at him and saw that he was awake. This time Seth did not extend a hand; he knew better. Instead he slowly shifted his body, rolling toward her. "My name is Seth," he rasped. "What is your—"

"Aaayyyeeee!" she screamed, exactly as before.

Startled, Seth sat up. He shouldn't have. He

banged his head into a stalagmite and blacked out again. He seemed to be spending a good deal of time unconscious!

Once more Seth woke. This time there was no music. He cracked open his eyes and saw in front of him a man of about his own age. The man had reddish brown hair, shaggy pants, wooden shoes, pointed ears, and horns.

Seth blinked. Yes, horns. And those shoes weren't wooden after all, and they had no toes. In fact they weren't shoes at all. They were hoofs.

Standing before him was the mythical creature known as a satyr. Horned, with the upper body of a man, and the lower body of a goat.

"Hello!" the satyr said. "Glad I didn't kill you. The name is Rame. When I heard Malape scream I thought she was being attacked, and I'm afraid I acted without looking. I shouldn't have; she's a nymph, and they tend to be jumpy when there's no reason. Are you all right?"

Seth reached up to touch his head. He had a bruise there, but there didn't seem to be any blood. The same was true for his neck. He had a dull headache, unsurprisingly. Concussion? "Nothing that some aspirin and a few days rest won't cure, I think," he said hoarsely.

"Asp run?" Rame asked, perplexed.

"You don't know about aspirin?" It was still an effort to speak; that rope had bruised his larynx.

"I see you are in pain. The hamadryad can help with that." He turned. "Malape, this person is not a danger to you. See if you can heal his head."

The girl approached timidly, her face and bosom poised for a scream at the first sign of trouble. Seth had the sense to remain absolutely still, this time. She put her cool right hand on his forehead, and immediately he could feel the sting of his bruises easing and his headache fading. She put her left hand on his neck, and his throat eased. It was like magic!

Magic? Here he was in a strange land, where trees could talk or grow instantly into his clothing, talking with a satyr. What was so odd about magic?

"Uh, where am I?" he asked, bewildered, hoping his voice wouldn't spook the girl again. Her touch was so wonderful! Already his voice was improved, as the power of her healing hand spread down through his throat.

"You are not from this area?" Rame asked.

"I don't think I'm from this planet! Incredible as it sounds, I talked to a tree and it told me I was on Earth Plane 4." Seth didn't mention that it seemed just as unlikely that he should be talking to a mythical satyr; that might be undiplomatic.

"Talking to a tree is not unusual, though it is frustrating at best," Rame said. "You are, however, on Earth Plane 4."

"What am I doing here?" Seth cried desperately. The nymph flinched, but did not remove her hands, to his relief. He had to be careful how he spoke; he had good reason not to disturb her!

"Perhaps if you told me how you arrived, we can find out why you are here," Rame proposed.

"I'm really not sure. I remember falling into a lake in my world, and waking up by the ocean in this world. I talked to Sen-Tree, and he told me to follow the path to the Teuton Empire. I spent a night in the wilderness, and now I'm here." Seth looked at the satyr, half expecting him to laugh at this preposterous story.

"It is possible," Rame murmured. "Have you encountered any other creature?"

"Nothing. Oh, I did run across a big snake moving backwards."

Rame looked alarmed. "Did it see you?" he asked urgently.

"I don't think so. I was hiding. It didn't seem to have eyes, anyway."

"It sees where it has been, through an eye in its mouth," Rame said. "It could be deadly to your cause. If my guess is correct."

"We're in luck, then. I climbed a tree, and got into other trouble, and—what cause?"

"It is not my place to tell you the specifics," Rame said soberly. "I don't think I know them all, as it is. You must avoid all serpents, dragons, snakes and lizards. They are all the eyes and ears of Nefarious the Sorcerer."

"I have no idea what you're talking about!" Seth exclaimed, and the girl retreated nervously. However, his head and neck felt completely relaxed; her touch had been better than any medicine! "Dragons?"

"Dragons! I realize this makes it sound very bad, but that is all I am able to tell you for certain. Before we leave, we shall feast, if your head is well now."

"It is much better! I never felt such a healing touch!"

"Yes, of course. Malape, fix a meal for our visitor."

Then he looked puzzled. "I'm sorry, what is your name?"

"Seth. Uh—leave?"

"Yes, very soon."

"We?"

"I would not send you alone."

"But you were shooting arrows at me!"

"A misunderstanding, as I explained," Rame said. "But I didn't shoot at you; I shot to confine you without hurting you."

Seth had to admit that this was so. His worst hurt had been from his own banging against the stalagmite. Now he discovered that not only was his pain gone, so were the scrapes on his head and neck. Malape had truly healed him!

"The girl, Malape—you called her a hamadryad?—what is this power she has? All she did was put her hand on my head—"

"Malape isn't a girl. She's a wood nymph—a creature who shares her life with a tree. Like all her kind, she is beautiful, and she has the power of healing minor scrapes, but she's very timid and not incredibly smart."

"A nymph of a tree," Seth said, amazed. "But you are treating her like a servant!"

"No, I merely tell her what I want, and she is glad to do it. In return I protect her and her tree from harm. When she screamed, I acted—too quickly, I now see. It is a fair exchange. It would be a burden on her to have to make a decision about a stranger. She knows I will not betray her interests, and that I have reason for what I ask of her."

Seth looked at the nymph, who was now gathering

things for the meal. Her skirt and blouse, he now saw, were fashioned of bark and leaves, somewhat like his own but far better fitting. Actually they were hardly more than slip and halter, with most of her torso and legs bare. There was only one term that properly described her, and that was luscious. "She does anything you ask, without question?"

"Well, not anything. She won't leave her tree, for example, and no nymph is any good for intellectual games. But it is not necessary to spend the night in the open, as you did, if you are on good terms with a hamadryad."

What would a satyr do with a lovely and completely obliging nymph, during the night? Seth decided that he didn't need to ask. This wasn't his world, after all.

Malape fixed a magnificent meal, consisting of many different types of fruits and vegetables. Yet when he bit into them, they did not all taste the way they looked. Some had the taste of meats, and others of fish, and others of pasta and many other foods whose nature was foreign to his domesticated palate. Seth started to eat hesitantly, afraid of the effect of the alien food on his body. Soon, however, he felt no further need to be cautious, and ate with the hunger that his body had built up over the past two days. The fruit he had eaten before had not been enough; he realized that now.

"You seem to enjoy our food," Rame commented politely.

"It's fabulous, thank you!" Seth sputtered between bites of a fruit that tasted similar to ravioli.

Once the edge was off his hunger, Seth ate more slowly, and talked with Rame. He found himself coming to like the satyr. There was no evidence of the horrific sexual appetite that legend claimed for this species; indeed, Rame paid little attention to the nymph.

Rame explained that the tree that had stolen his clothes would not have hurt him; it simply had a taste for fabric. The snake creature he had seen was called a Synops. It was not generally a threat, unless annoyed or hungry, except for the matter of its connection to Nefarious.

They finished the meal. Seth would have liked to rest and digest it, but Rame gave him no time for that. He showed Seth out of the cave. It turned out to be in a hillside beside a huge tree of uncertain type, perhaps a variety of oak. The great purple roots came down to enclose the mouth of the cave, while the spreading brown foliage shaded and concealed it. Indeed, Seth realized that what he had taken for wooden shoring was merely the network of roots enclosing the cave. The nymph had really not left her tree!

As an afterthought, he noted that the hamadryad matched her tree, by no coincidence: her brief skirt was from its bark, and her blouse was made of its leaves.

"Malape," Rame said sadly, "it is time for Seth and me to go. I will return as soon as possible, though I do not know when that will be." He took her in his arms, kissed her lovingly, and let her go. Suddenly Seth realized that the bond between these two was not lust but love; he had been too free with his private conjecture.

Malape dissipated and faded into her tree. At any

other time, Seth would have gaped, but he was coming to understand some of the ways of this world. She was truly the spirit of the tree, human only in appearance. It was the tree, really, that had healed his injuries.

Rame turned to Seth. "Now," he said with a deadly serious tone, "we must travel. However, it would be extremely helpful if you had some way to protect yourself. Can you use any weapon?"

Seth realized that he certainly hadn't covered himself with any combat glory, here! Yet if he had had a better notion what he faced, he could have avoided the arrow-bola and perhaps given a better account of himself. He thought back to his karate training with the Boken, a wooden practice sword. He had gotten pretty good with it. That might be a good choice. "Can you get a sword for me?"

Rame walked back into the cave. After a few seconds he came out carrying a long wooden box. "This will be your weapon for the time being. I found it in the cave, and saved it until I could find a proper use for it. It is magic."

Seth opened the box and lifted out a broad sword. It was a breathtaking weapon! The steel glistened in the sunlight, beautifully polished, with a design on the blade. The handle was equally stunning; it appeared to be made of gold. A white tassel hung from the hand-guard, completing the effect.

There was a black scabbard with a harness that Seth realized fitted on his back. He sheathed the sword, got into the harness, and adjusted it for comfort. He would be able to reach over his shoulder and draw the sword without much hesitation.

"But I can't just take this!" Seth protested, realizing that the sword was worth a king's ransom even if never used. "I realize I'm only borrowing it, but— can I make you some sort of trade?" He found his collection of personal things, which was undisturbed. The money was pointless, but the pocket knife might be suitable. "This little folding knife?" He showed how the blade came out.

Rame was amazed. "A knife that folds in half!" he exclaimed.

"It also can be used to make fire," Seth said, demonstrating the flint and magnesium rod.

"Such magic!" the satyr exclaimed, delighted. "Let me trade in turn! Here is a magic dagger of mine, whose blade is always sharp."

"But you've already lent me the—"

"No, that is not mine to give. This is."

Seth nodded. He would return the elegant sword when he parted from Rame. They traded knives. He felt good about it. The satyr evidently felt the same.

"Why can't you explain to me what's going on?" Seth asked, perplexed, as they began to walk down the path.

"The truth is, I'm not quite sure," Rame replied.

They walked in silence for some time. Rame was surely thinking of Malape, who might not be bright but seemed in every other way to be a fine figure of a woman. Seth was thinking of home. How was his mother doing, and his little sister Ferne? He tried to tell himself that he shouldn't worry about them, because there was nothing he could do, but he *did* worry. They would have no way to know that he was all right—and even if they did, who was doing the chores? There was snow to be shoveled, a house to be maintained—his mother had to work, so was gone most of the day, and Seth normally drove Ferne to her music lessons after school. His absence would be causing serious disruptions!

Finally Seth found the silence unbearable. He simply had to talk, to take refuge from his own thoughts. "I may not know this world, but satyrs were mythical, nonexistent creatures on my world. They were supposed to be very mischievous sprites who frolicked with others of their kind, and were, uh, very free with women. This doesn't seem to be true about you."

Rame nodded. "I suppose we will be spending some time together, so we may as well talk. I prefer to think of myself as a faun. The appearance of fauns is identical to that of satyrs, but our behavior differs. Your description of satyrs is accurate, but to my way of thinking there is no point in the mischief they create. The Elders warned me that if I failed to change my ways I would be exiled. Instead I chose to leave Clan-Satyr on my own volition, because I could not conform to their ways. Leaving was almost as bad as being exiled; the members of the Clan vowed not to cast their gaze upon me, and I was stripped of my magic."

Seth listened, and decided that he really liked this person, whether he was a man or a creature. "I doubt that it matters, but I feel you were right in your decision."

"You would, you're human," Rame said. Then, as an afterthought, "Thanks. Anyhow, I traveled about twenty days before finding the cave in which I now live. I met Malape in much the manner you did: when I was tired and hungry to the point of collapse, because foraging and survival was much harder without my magic. Hamadryads are normally rather shallow, but she had been around for some time— you saw the size of her Tree!—and was willing to learn new things. She will never be able to travel or to harbor complicated concepts, but she has her virtues and was kind to me. She put her healing hands on me and brought me food, and kept me safe among the roots of her Tree until I recovered. We learned how to get along together: she is most comfortable when I simply tell her what I want with no ambiguity, but she does it because she wishes to please me, not because she has to. When something threatens her Tree, I do what I can to protect it, not from any debt to her but because I want to please her. After a while I grew to love her—a feeling that no true satyr would have."

Seth did not know what to say, and thought it best to remain silent. How wrong he had been, when he had thought Rame was treating Malape as a servant!

They walked for quite a while. The forest was getting thicker around the path. The foliage overhead had grown so dense as to let only slivers of sunlight show through. It was as if they were moving into a deepening cave. Seth was nervous about this, not sure what monsters might slither through such reaches, but Rame seemed unconcerned. Since the faun knew this world much better than Seth did, Seth was reassured.

Rame took a reed whistle out of a pocket on his quiver and put it to his mouth. From it came the music Seth had heard when he had awakened in the morning. So it hadn't been Malape after all!

It was beautiful. The melody was new to Seth; he had never heard it before this day. But it made him feel whole. It seemed to have a rejuvenating quality to it. His fatigue from the hiking was easing; it was as though Malape were putting her healing hands on his feet. Rame had said that he no longer had magic, but it seemed his whistle did!

"AAAEEEEEEEE!" came a scream from above their heads.

Rame stopped his music, grabbed Seth and flung him out of the way. A black furry ball with a gaping mouth and yellowish-brown fangs dropped with a splat to where Seth had been standing.

"What is that?" Seth cried, instinctively reaching over his shoulder to draw his sword.

"That is a Hebetudinous, Hebe for short," replied Rame. "They hunt in packs."

"AAAEEEEEEEE!" came another scream from above Seth. This time Seth jumped to the side on his own. Another black furry creature bit the dust next to him.

"Don't move!" Rame shouted. "The Hebes are only dangerous if you walk or remain standing directly under them when they fall, mouth open, on top of you. They would be more dangerous, except for the fact that they always scream before jumping."

"Always?" Seth asked nervously. "Don't they realize that this gives them away?"

"Yes, they are stupid to warn their prey that way. I am not sure why some ground-walking creature doesn't tell them that."

Seth smiled. He liked Rame's sense of humor, too! Imagine the hairy predators losing out because their prey did not tell them how to improve their attack! This was a conspiracy of silence he would gladly join.

They moved on, each of them jumping out of the way every time there was a scream above. Seth looked back. It was almost pathetic: about fifteen furry balls were lying face down on the path. "Are they dead?"

"No, they are tougher than that. They play dead until they are sure that no one is watching them, and then they somehow climb back into their trees. If you thought one was injured or unconscious, and tried to pick it up, it would chomp you, and get you that way."

That made more sense! If the monster missed, and the prey felt secure and tried to take advantage, the monster would win after all. Probably more chomps were made by that route than by the initial drop. Again he had been too quick to assume foolishness on the part of another creature. That tendency of his could get him into trouble!

After passing the Hebe herd, they came to a stream which ran under a bridge across their path. Seth was quite thirsty now, and stooped to take a drink.

"Stop!" yelled Rame. "The stream may be unclean."

"But there shouldn't be pollution here in this wilderness!" Seth protested. "The water is clear."

"There can be danger in what looks clean." The faun leaned over the stream and blew into his reed whistle, and a foul note came out. "Indeed it is unclean, I dare say deadly. Walk further; we will eventually run across another stream. There, if it is safe, we shall drink and eat."

Seth's thirst had dried up. He did not want to learn what this world's poison could do to his body!

In due course they did come to another stream; this time when Rame blew into his whistle a lovely note issued forth. "We can drink here," the faun said, unnecessarily.

Seth knelt at the stream's edge, bent forward, and touched his lips to the cool water. Ahh, he thought, as he swallowed the refreshing liquid. He really hadn't had much to drink in the two days of his travel, other than the juice in the fruits he had eaten, and the pure stream water tasted fabulous.

He looked up—almost fell into the water. Could he believe his eyes? Rame was playing the reed whistle, and fruit was appearing out of the air before him!

"Magic?" Seth asked, bewildered.

"Naturally," Rame responded. "Magic is the driving force on Earth Plane 4."

"But I thought that the Clan satyrs took away your magic!"

"That they did! This magic, however, is not mine. It is the magic of the reed whistle. You could perform it also, if you knew how to play."

That was interesting. Seth made a mental note: if he ever wanted to try doing magic himself, he would have to find a magic whistle, or some other magic object. He wasn't sure he believed in magic, but the evidence for it was certainly convincing, here.

Seth ate some of the fruit. It was delicious, just as the fruit of Malape's feast had been. Could this be more of the hamadryad's fruit, perhaps plucked and set out by her, waiting for Rame's whistle to conjure it at need?

After their meal, they rested briefly, then resumed their journey. Rame did not rush things in so many words, but he didn't waste any time either. Why was it so important to get to wherever they were going? As far as he knew, Seth was just a drowning teenager who had somehow landed here; he had no value to whatever powers that existed on this world.

Well, he would surely find out soon enough. Probably it was some misunderstanding, just the way the American Indians had a misunderstanding about the nature of the Spanish Conquistadors, supposing them to be gods. What a costly confusion that had been, to the Indians!

The foliage began to thin; then it faded out entirely. There were hardly any trees, just long grassy weeds. The ground was hardening to rock. The hard surface made it tougher for the faun, because his hoofs were adapted to the soft ground of the forest. To make matters worse, dusk was setting in, and they needed to find a somewhat sheltered area. Were there other hamadryads here who might provide it? That seemed unlikely, because there were so few trees here, and they were so scrawny.

"Draw your sword," Rame whispered. "We are in danger!"

Quickly Seth reached back and drew his weapon. Something was wrong: the tassel which before had been pearl white had turned jet black. There was no time to consider the tassel, though, for in the dim remnants of daylight Seth could see figures crawling out of the ground and charging toward them.

"Trolls!" Rame screamed. He had already skewered one of the creatures with an arrow.

Seth stood paralyzed with fear as approximately ten of the most hideous monsters imaginable charged him. They were vile-looking creatures, each about the size of a small man, with lumpy gray skin, huge callused hands, and a disfigured lump with brown teeth and red eyes for a head. If they had been human punkers, perhaps he would have had a better notion what to do. But these—how could he fight horrible magical things?

Rame shot another. Soon, however, he would be in trouble, as the trolls were coming too close to combat effectively with arrows. That jolted Seth out of his horrified trance; he couldn't let his friend be overrun!

He charged forward toward the ugly beasts, leading with his sword. The first troll jumped through the air, and Seth easily lifted his blade, impaling the monstrous body upon it. Dark blood flowed across the weapon as the troll died. Seth lowered the point, and the hulk slid off.

Well, that had turned out to be easy enough! Now if he could just keep his gorge down. . . .

Glancing to the side, Seth saw Rame holding off two trolls with a dagger. He was truly an expert fighter.

There was no time to get sick. More trolls were coming at him. Seth swung at the next, who had a heavy wooden club.

The club connected with the sword—and knocked it out of Seth's hand. What a blow! For a moment all Seth was aware of was the numbness of his hand.

Then two trolls charged into him and knocked him onto his back. He fought desperately, knowing that if he didn't he would be done for. He was wrestling with the troll who landed on his chest, while the other troll bit into his leg. Ouch!

In a fit of pain, Seth closed his fist, leaving open two fingers, and violently thrust them into the red orb of the troll on his chest. The creature appeared shocked, but seemed not to feel too much pain, for it kept fighting. Seth brought his hands around its neck to feel for an area of soft tissue. He found it. Drawing back, he stabbed into the creature's throat. The troll fell off his chest, clutching at the caved-in part of its neck.

The other troll continued to bite into Seth's leg. Groping to his sides, Seth found a hefty rock; with a surge of strength he heaved it into the air and slammed it down on the troll's head. He scrambled up, knowing that more would soon be attacking.

Seth looked toward Rame, who had apparently dispatched all but three of the trolls. Two of these were trying to drag him to the ground, while the third was biting his ankle.

Seth looked about and saw his sword. He ran to fetch it, glad that while the troll who had bitten him had penetrated deep enough to hurt, it had not done serious damage; he had no trouble on his feet. He picked up the sword and charged Rame's attackers.

Hearing his approach, the two trolls pushing Rame turned around. Seth did not hesitate. With one lethal swing he sliced through the necks of both trolls. The dark blood spouted, and they pitched over, their heads rolling away.

Rame, now having two free hands, reached into his

quiver, grabbed an arrow, and drove it through the neck of the last one, who was still gnawing his ankle.

All was quiet. Seth noticed that the tassel on his sword was once again white. He stared at it. What was going on?

"The tassel," Rame explained, "turns black when the person possessing the sword is in physical danger. Since it was on your back, I saw the color change before you did."

Rame took out his reed whistle and played a powerful, lively melody. Seth watched in amazement as the bite on his leg and the one on Rame's ankle healed themselves with a visible speed. The pain, however, did not go completely away. There must, he thought, be limitations on the good the reed whistle could do. Malape's touch had alleviated the pain as well as the injuries.

"Let us go," Rame said briskly. "We must find shelter. We will need to spend one more night in the wilderness before we reach the Teuton Empire."

By Seth's judgment, according to the advice of Sen-Tree, they should have been there already. But they weren't going directly, and he suspected this was because the faun was taking them the safest way. The unsafe way would surely be no pleasure!

They walked on until they reached a wooded area where they were able to build a shelter. It seemed that his own strategy for spending a night was valid here, where there were no lovely and friendly nymphs.

They ate mostly in silence. Then Seth watched as Rame slept. He would wake his friend when he couldn't keep alert any more.

He tried to figure out what was happening to him. Again he felt sorrow in his heart for his family. If they thought him dead—

As before, he drifted without realizing it into sleep. Again, his dreams were of home. This time, however, Seth was not a participant. He was watching his family, and someone was there who was pretending to be him.

- **Four**

The Chosen

Seth woke, blinded by the brilliant rays of sunlight cutting through the tree tops and slanting into the hut. Rame was up, and he motioned for Seth to join him outside the shelter. There was a vaguely familiar aroma.

"Is that bread?" Seth inquired.

The satyr was tearing a large brown fruit off a plant. "It is not bread made from grain. It is, however, a fruit which tastes very much like it."

"Why pick it if you can conjure it?"

"Observe." Rame picked up his reed whistle and began to play a very compelling melody. The fruit began to quiver. It shook, until it was practically jumping. With the last staccato note, it vanished.

"What happened?" Seth asked, dismayed.

"Nothing negative. I could not conjure this fruit because I had never before encountered the plant, other than in satyr text books. Once it is in my instrument, however, I can conjure as much of it as I need."

Rame played again, and the fruit reappeared. "Oh—like doing a cut and paste on a computer!" Seth exclaimed.

The faun gazed at him blankly. "We shall cut it, but we have nothing with which to paste it to anything, if that were desirable."

Seth laughed. "I'm sorry. I used a—an expression from my own frame. A way to make copies of something by removing it from one region, and restoring it to another, as many times as one wishes."

"Yes, that is correct. I did not know that you knew how to do that."

"I don't. It requires a machine—a pretty fancy one at that. And it doesn't work on physical things, just text. That is, writing."

"That does not seem extraordinarily useful," Rame said doubtfully. "I do not mean to be unduly critical."

"No, you're right! What you can do is much better!"

With that, Seth and Rame sat down to eat breakfast. After a light meal of bread and a fruit tasting like peaches, they set off on the last leg of their journey. There were no hazards, and eventually the path came to the top of a hill. The other side of the hill dropped off into a huge valley, and in this valley was a city.

The city was awesome. The streets were red cobblestone, the stone houses had thatched roofs, and standing out for all to see in the center was an enormous castle. The castle had gray stone walls topped by bright red parapets, and on top of all four towers were white flags with red emblems.

"What do the emblems signify?" Seth asked.

"I have never before been to the actual city," Rame said. "But I know that the flags show that it is the capital of the Teuton Empire. Whether they mean something more than that, I don't know."

"Where do we go?"

"There." Rame pointed to the castle.

That was what Seth had both hoped and feared. He still did not know what this was all about, but that castle looked important, and that was encouraging— and alarming. He needed answers to his questions, and they were more likely to be provided by the leaders of this realm. But he was not at all sure that he would like the answers that came.

Slowly and carefully they descended into the valley. Seth had to slow down to help Rame, whose hoofs were not made for climbing any more than for hard rock. This surprised him; he knew that goats were sure-footed, and these were like goats' feet. But appearances could be deceptive.

As they reached the level ground and walked through the town, Seth noticed the townsmen staring. "Are they not used to seeing fauns?"

"My friend, it is a human man, in a skirt made of leaves, wearing white covers on his feet, that they are not used to seeing," Rame replied politely.

Seth looked at himself. He did indeed appear ridiculous. What the townspeople were wearing looked rather silly to him—but of course this was their land, not his. And, he had to confess, even in his own land he would have been quite strange in his present outfit! Had he gone among those punkers in a costume like this—

"I guess it is a matter of perspective," Seth said, thinking back to his encounter with Sen-Tree.

Soon enough the huge castle towered before them. It was surrounded by a moat which they had not seen from the ravine. There was a rather large creature with even larger teeth swimming in it. Rame signaled to Seth, and they walked to another side. Here there was a lowered drawbridge, with two guards armed with swords.

It turned out to be no ceremonial post. The guards were alert, and they moved immediately to bar the way. "What business do you have with His Majesty?" one demanded, while the other stood back with his hand on his sword hilt.

"This man may be a Chosen," Rame responded.

"A what?" Seth asked, thinking he had misheard.

Rame did not answer. The guards, tough and experienced as they evidently were, seemed incredulous. The near one reached into an alcove in the drawbridge housing and brought out a box. "Hold out your hand," he ordered, in a we'll-abolish-this-nonsense tone.

Seth did not trust this. He did not move.

"Do it," Rame said tightly.

Seth extended his hand. The guard held the box under it. He then waved his hand over Seth's. There was a tingling sensation, and Seth's forefinger began to bleed. Only a drop welled out, but that was amazing, for there was no cut. The drop fell to the box and turned white.

The guard stared. "It's true!" he exclaimed.

"I thought it might be," Rame said. "That's why I brought him here."

The guard recovered from his surprise. "Now you," he said to Rame.

"Oh, I'm only his guide!" the faun protested. "When I thought he might be a Chosen, I had to bring him immediately. Anyone would have. As soon as I see him safely recognized, I will return to my forest."

"I don't care who you are," the guard said firmly. "I am required to test anyone who might be a Chosen." He held out the box.

"Do it," Seth said, with half a smile.

Rame shrugged and put out his hand. A drop of red blood welled out similarly, and fell to the box— where it also turned white.

The faun stared. "But I never—I couldn't be—"

"Thank heaven the last are here," the rear guard whispered, impressed.

The forward guard spun about. "Please follow me, Chosen."

A confused Seth, and even more confused Rame, followed him. They crossed the bridge and entered the lavishly decorated castle. The town was beautiful, but it paled before the interior of this edifice. Apparently Teutonia was a wealthy empire. The stone floor was crystalline, and the walls were hung with elaborately woven carpets showing scenes of action. The ceiling of the entrance hall was arched so intricately that it resembled a church.

The guard brought them to a room closed off by curtains. News of their presence had evidently already spread, for a servant was ready with new clothing for them both. They were obliged to don brown knickers-type pants, and black jacket tops with numerous pockets.

The next chamber had four chairs, two of which were already occupied. Seth and Rame sat down in the other two. The people in the other chairs appeared to be a few years older than Seth, though still young enough. One was a husky, rugged-looking man; the other an attractive woman with oddly striped hair. Both were clad in outfits similar to those of Seth and Rame. Seth wondered whether the woman had had to change in front of the guard, as he and Rame had, and what her reaction might have been to that. Not that it was any of his business.

The room was lit by a kind of glow that seemed to have no source. Magic, Seth thought, finding it easier to accept this than it would have been a few days ago. He glanced at Rame, who seemed to be as bewildered as himself. So the faun had thought he was merely guiding a potential Chosen one—and turned out to be one himself! Whatever it was to be Chosen.

The glow dimmed. The man who had given Seth his clothing entered. He stood before the four for a moment without speaking. Suddenly he did not seem like a servant.

"We realize that you are wondering why you are here," the man said. "I assure you that in due time your questions will be answered. My name is Turcot, and I am the Emperor's top adviser. The man you are about to meet is the current ruler of the entire Teuton Empire, of which this city is the capital. I suggest that you give him the respect that you would your own leaders on your own worlds. Consider this expedience if you prefer; it is best to honor the forms until you understand them well enough to violate." He smiled briefly, and Seth got the very strong impression that there was absolutely nothing humorous about this. There was a new glow at another door.

"All rise for His Majesty, Emperor Towk," Turcot said loudly.

All of them obliged, as much from confusion as respect. The Emperor entered. He was an old man, who had a look of sternness and benevolence about him. He was ordinary physically, yet something about his presence took Seth's breath away.

"Tirsa, Vidav, Seth and Rame," the Emperor said abruptly, "you have been brought here for reasons of extreme magnitude. You are the Chosen."

Seth was amazed. How had the Emperor known their names? The two others might have been known before, but neither Rame nor Seth himself had given their names. This was growing stranger by the minute!

"After hearing what I say, you may choose whether to participate in a quest," the Emperor continued. "If you do not participate, all of our worlds will suffer dire consequences. If you do, you have no guarantee of survival. Regardless of your choice, you will not be able to return home."

The four Chosen sat in stunned silence. The Emperor was pulling no punches! He seemed to know all about all four of them—and knew that they were from different worlds. That they were some sort of key to some world-shaking project. Seth could tell by the reactions of the others that they were as amazed as he was.

"Before I tell you exactly what your mission is, let me give you a little background information. First, we are all from the same Earth; a different awareness, but the same planet. There are, as far as we know, four separate planes or levels of awareness of Earth. Each is governed not completely but partially by a particular force. Earth Plane 1, where Vidav comes from, is driven by physical strength. Tirsa, who ar-

rived at the castle first and already has some idea of
what is going on, comes from Earth Plane 2, governed by mental ability. Seth comes from Earth
Plane 3, where the driving force is science. Rame is
from this plane, Earth Plane 4, where the governing
force is magic. You are obviously not here accidentally. Your presence is needed for the welfare of all of
the planes."

At this point the large man named Vidav stood and
said, "Erxvq naqstx zet tzas argqynofskx!"

"One moment," the Emperor said. He gestured to
Turcot, who handed each of them a small pill. "Swal-
low this. It will allow you to talk in the language of the
person or group to whom you are speaking, as I am
doing now. Rame does not need one, for all intelligent life on Earth Plane 4 can communicate with all
other intelligent life."

Seth found that hard to believe. The Emperor had
been speaking in English! How could a pill affect
anything other than the body? Language was something of quite another nature.

But he saw Vidav and Tirsa taking their pills. The
woman was so well proportioned that she made even
the strange clothing look good. Her hair, which had
seemed odd at first glance, now seemed appropriate
to her; apparently it grew naturally in black and
white tresses. Her eyebrows echoed it, being similarly
zebra striped. If what the Emperor said was true, she
was from another world, or at least another aspect of
the one he knew, and spoke a completely foreign language. He wanted to understand her when she
talked! So he took his pill, deciding to trust in what
the Emperor said, even if it was nonsense.

Vidav repeated his sentence. "What do you mean, we can't go home?" Apparently he had been too shocked by the news to ask the question immediately. That much Seth could understand; he should have asked about it himself!

"There is a delicate balance, an equilibrium, in and between every plane," the Emperor said. "All creatures born in a particular plane stay in that plane; the balance of their world requires this. There is, however, a time immediately before death when a person is in a state of limbo, and not in one definite plane. Magic is a very powerful force, that extends into the state of limbo. By using magic we were able to draw you out of limbo just before your deaths. You were not dead; that would have been too late. Not only would it have stopped us from bringing you here, it would have made it pointless had it been possible. You were, in a sense, split. While in that brief period of limbo you were recreated by magic."

He paused to gaze at them a moment. "I see you are having difficulty with this concept. That is hardly surprising! Let me put it another way: you are doubles of yourselves. Both you and your doubles look exactly alike, and your doubles are all alive in their respective planes, except in the case of Rame, who needed no such translation. By keeping one set of you on your own planes we have not disturbed Earth's balance. You have actually been borne to this world without harming our balance."

He paused again. This time there were no questions. All four seemed stunned. Certainly Seth was; he had tackled the oddities of this new existence with the assumption that it was temporary, and that at some later date he would find a way to return to his own realm. To have that assumption so bluntly refuted—no, he just couldn't accept that!

"I understand your concerns," the Emperor continued. "But do not worry. Your friends, your lives and your families will be treated by your doubles exactly as you would have done. The doubles are *you*." He oriented on Vidav. "Let me try to explain why you cannot return home, in this situation. In order for any of you to return, your double would have to enter limbo once again by the threat of death. We cannot arrange that; it must come in its own fashion. Your doubles could all very easily live long lives, dying of natural causes later than you do. Only sheerest chance could set it up to enable you to return—if we knew exactly when to act. We do not; we are not clairvoyant."

"Now wait a minute!" Seth exclaimed. "How did you know to bring us in now?" Despite his resistance to the idea, he found himself accepting it. Certainly it explained a lot that otherwise would remain a mystery.

Turcot's face turned grim. "You must not address the Emperor in such a tone!"

But Emperor Towk made a gesture of negation. "They are new to our culture, and we expect much of them. The forms are the least of our concerns." Then he faced Seth. "This is an exceptional situation," he responded evenly. "We had no clairvoyance, but we did have an ancient prophecy. We did not actually fetch you; we knew only that the concurrence of four Chosen would be available at this time, three from the other planes, one from this one. We knew the instant to act, and we extended the full force of our magic at that prophesied moment. This enabled each of you to split, so that you could not only survive, but come to us here. But that exhausted our effort. We had no knowledge of your precise points of crossover, and no resources to search every cranny of the Empire to locate you. You had to find your own separate ways here. Because you were strangers to this plane, we hoped that your presence would soon be evident; all citizens of the Empire were instructed to assist any obvious strangers to come to this spot, as Rame knows."

"But I did not know that I was to be the fourth Chosen!" the faun exclaimed. "I'm not even human!"

The Emperor smiled. "We did not know either. But we did know that the Chosen from this plane would feel the urge to come here, after the magic signal went out, so the guards were ordered to test all who approached the castle on any pretext. Because the special magic, which affects all Chosen, not merely the ones from other planes, causes the blood to turn white when tested in a certain way, we had a sure way to identify each of you. Thereafter we used incidental magic to obtain the immediate facts about each of you—your names, languages, and so on. What is in your hearts we do not know; magic does not extend to the depths of human or near-human nature."

His gaze lifted to cover them all again. "Regardless of your preferences, you will need to remain here for some time. For a while, because you and your doubles were created from one, you will be able to see your world when your active consciousness relaxes. When you dream, you will be seeing through the consciousness of your other selves. However, in time, we believe those dreams will fade, and you will be completely of this plane."

Seth thought back to his dream about Rian. Thank God he was all right, and thank God that someone, even a clone, would take care of Seth's family. "You have explained how we came here. Now tell us why!" Seth demanded. He spoke more vehemently than he had intended; he had been profoundly disturbed by what the Emperor had said. He was pleased to note a supportive reaction from others of the small group, especially the woman Tirsa. They might be from different worlds, but they were united in their abrupt separation from all that they had known before.

"Please," Emperor Towk said. "I was getting to that. Although the four planes are different, there are various similarities. A buildup of evil in one plane is a direct result of a buildup of evil in one of the other three. The situations are bad on each plane, as you are aware on your individual bases. We cannot be sure which is the originator and which the follower; perhaps they feed on each other. But we do know it is becoming perilous for all the planes."

Seth thought of the nuclear arms buildup and the war in which Russia and the United States had recently "unofficially" fought each other. That had been just one in a long chain of similar episodes across the world. The populations of some small nations had been decimated, and in spite of a brief hopeful time things did not seem to be improving. A buildup of evil? Yes, it was fair to call it that! He looked at the faces of Rame, Vidav and Tirsa, and knew that their worlds also faced serious problems.

"In our world the cause of evil is Nefarious, an extremely powerful sorcerer. The situation here has been thoroughly assessed, and it is our conclusion that no one from our world can stop him. The Empire itself is helpless against his magic; our magic is puny compared to his, and our economic and military powers cannot compete with magic of this nature. If he cannot be stopped here, then neither will the evil in your worlds, because of the linkage. It will be your task to do what the Empire cannot, and eliminate the threat that Nefarious represents to all our planes."

For the first time Tirsa spoke. "Forgive me if I seem dull, Emperor Towk. But is it reasonable to expect a rough man, a cultured woman, a faun and an impetuous youth, most of whom are ignorant not only of magic but of the ways of your world, to accomplish what your no doubt competent minions can not?"

Seth loved the sound of her voice, which was melodious, and appreciated her reasoning, which was sound. But he hated that reference to "an impetuous youth," partly because he could not deny its accuracy. He would have to settle down and try to give a more mature account of himself. Meanwhile, he had noticed that even her eyes were striped, in their fashion: they had concentric light and dark patterns. The effect was eerie—and intriguing.

The Emperor smiled. "You are hardly dull, Tirsa! You have cut to the very heart of our problem. I must answer no, it is not reasonable to expect this, and indeed we have no certainty of the outcome of this struggle. All that the prophecy guarantees us is a chance; it does not indicate which side will be victorious. But since we seem to have no chance otherwise, we must take what offers, however unlikely it may seem, and that is the Chosen.

"Your group may seem small. Certainly it is, and for excellent reason. We have ascertained that we can not attempt it with more than four. A large group could readily be detected by the evil sorcerer's spies. The operation must be done in the utmost stealth, for if he knows where you are he will destroy you. I ask you not to doubt me in this: he has the means to obliterate you, from any distance, once he knows precisely where you are and what your nature is."

"But with such power, he will be able to locate us very soon," Vidav said.

"Perhaps not. To an extent, his power is his liability, in this case. He has, among other things, the ability to sense people by their magic. Because of this, an attack on him by the people of this world who possess magic would be impossible. He would always know where we were, and would eliminate us at his whim. But all of you, Rame not excepted, lack the ability of self-driven magic. Therefore he will not be able to detect you by your natures, and you will be able to approach him and surprise him. But he knows of your existence, so will be alert, and his spies will be everywhere. You must avoid them or, if discovered, kill them, to maintain your secret—but even that is not good, because his spies surely report in regularly, and he will soon know if any disappear. So this will be a great challenge—but you do have resources, and perhaps you will be able to succeed. Rame knows the terrain, and also understands the nature of Nefarious. The rest of you have been Chosen, not randomly, but by a prophecy and a spell related to it. You will not be unprepared. Every possible item that can help you will be at your disposal, and if you survive, you may live your lives here in whatever manner you desire. If it is possible to defeat Nefarious, you are the ones who can do it."

"We may not be unprepared," Tirsa remarked dryly. "But it might be an overstatement to refer to us as prepared."

"Accurately put," the Emperor agreed. "I said before that you have a choice; once again I must state how important this choice is. It will determine the fate of this world—and your own. Circumstances require haste; please, if you wish to leave, do so now. There will be no penalty; we know that you must do this of your free choice, or failure is assured."

Seth realized suddenly that this choice was upon him, and the others. He had either to object now, or go along. The thing was of course crazy; he had only the word of a man who claimed to be an Emperor that the mission was important, and no assurance that he would survive it, let alone be successful. It was no good, to let himself be stampeded into such a dangerous undertaking on a strange world!

The room was quiet. None of the others were leaving. Were they each waiting for someone else to make the first move? Rame, beside him, was absolutely still; what was he thinking? He glanced at Tirsa, and realized that whatever she did, he would do too. He knew her even less than he knew this world or this mission, and cursed himself for a fool. But he would not leave if she didn't.

Emperor Towk nodded. "I see that the prophecy was correct and we have chosen wisely. I thank you, each and all, for this commitment. You have brought hope to the planes."

Commitment? Seth was ashamed. He had merely waited to see what the others would do, especially Tirsa. His was the commitment of indecision!

"We will feast, and then you will be shown to your rooms," the Emperor said. "There is much to be done tomorrow!"

The four Chosen were escorted to a huge dining room, where they met the Empress, a gracious lady in a surprisingly ordinary gown. Evidently this world wasn't much for fancy clothing.

They sat down to feast. This time it was not simply fruit; meats and pastries of all kinds were served, together with delicious, sparkling beverage that, he realized belatedly, was somewhat intoxicating. He was enjoying himself greatly, and only hoped that he wasn't making a fool of himself because of his light-headedness. He noticed that Tirsa hardly touched her drink, after the first sip; she had been too smart to gulp it down the way he had. Her plane featured mental ability, after all. Meanwhile, Rame conjured many new foods into his reed whistle, perhaps more than he actually ate. Vidav ate slowly and steadily, his mood hardly lightening.

Aside from the music of the faun, they ate in silence. Tomorrow, perhaps, they would talk.

After the dinner, each guest was shown to his quarters by a rather pretty maid named Domela who seemed to be assigned to them. She had lustrous auburn hair and eyes to match. Seth wondered whether they had selected the prettiest maid for the most honored guests, to encourage a positive attitude.

Seth knew he should clean up, but first he tested the bed. He sank into the soft, fluffy surface and closed his eyes for a moment—and didn't open them again. Plenty of time to worry about this world tomorrow! Tonight he slept.

- **Five**

Training

There was a sound in the far distance. Seth tried to ignore it, for it disturbed his sleep, but it persisted. Finally he woke and sat up—and the sound was gone.

Relieved, he lay back in the darkness, and soon he was back asleep. But the sound returned to pester him.

Again he woke, irritated, and again there was nothing. It was like a mosquito that zeroed in on him only when he wasn't alert. He hated that!

This time he turned on his light, which he could do merely by speaking to the switch, and checked the room. There was nothing, only the bare walls. He realized that he had fallen asleep in his clothes, so he got out of them and went to the lavatory to wash himself. That made him feel better; he did not like sleeping grimy. Then he lay down again, leaving the light on.

He was soon unconscious. As part of his martial arts training he had learned how to relax, deliberately, so as to focus only on the immediate lesson, or to proceed further to sleep. He remained tired, and knew he needed a good night's rest.

The sound returned. *Go away!* he thought.

Instead, it became louder, like a mosquito homing in on a succulent earlobe. Seth wrenched himself out of sleep and sat up—to silence. The light remained, but not the noise.

Angry, he lay back yet again. This time he did not relax; he feigned sleep, hoping to catch whatever it was unguarded, so that he could identify it and deal with it. But the sound did not return.

Well, at least he had gotten rid of it! He relaxed, and once more slept.

Whereupon the sound returned.

Seth was aggravated but not stupid. Realizing that obvious consciousness banished the sound, he schooled himself to wake slowly, this time tuning in on the distraction. He did not move, he only listened.

The sound grew steadily stronger, until it was like the noise of a mighty engine, steady yet melodious in its fashion. Becoming intrigued, Seth focused further, trying to understand it. He was now fully awake, but lying quite still, his eyes closed. Would opening them banish the sound?

He cracked one eyelid open. The light was bright, but the sound did not fade. He opened the other eye, moving no other part of his body. Now he was staring at the ceiling, and the sound remained. He had fooled it; it had not fled with his awakening.

There was nothing in the room. Indeed, the sound did not seem to come from anywhere outside. It seemed to be in his head. This was no mosquito!

What are you? he thought, addressing the sound.

To his surprise, he got an answer, of a sort. *Who?* It wasn't exactly a sound, but an aspect of it, a questioning.

I am Seth, of course! he thought, becoming quite

interested. *Who are you?*

Seth! It was more like a voice, now, though not exactly. *I am Tirsa.*

"What?" Seth exclaimed, jerking up his head.

He was alone, and the sound was gone. He had blown it!

Still, he had determined that it was not his sleeping state, but his relaxation that made it happen. Now he knew it was Tirsa, using her mind to contact him. The Emperor had said that she was from a plane governed by mental ability. That had not meant much to him at the time, distracted as he had been by everything else, including her appearance, but he had assumed that it meant she was especially intelligent. Now he realized that it could mean something else entirely: telepathy!

She was using telepathy to contact him? He was delighted by the prospect! He lay back, relaxed, and opened his mind.

The sound came quickly. It was no longer a noise, but seemed more like a carrier beam for a signal of communication. Soon it seemed to fade, as he searched for the meaningful part of it.

Seth—did you answer? the thought came. *If you receive me, do not speak or react. Answer with your mind only. Focus your thought and I will tune it in.*

He concentrated. *I hear you. I am answering. Do you hear me?*

I receive you, she responded immediately. *Not with the ears; there is no sound. With the mind. Your thought is crude, imperfect; focus it more.*

He tried. There was a quality about her thought that was not present in speech; it was more rounded, less defined, yet more meaningful. It was as though he were receiving a radio signal directly in his head, fraught with nuances, only a few of which he could interpret. He did his best to emulate it, feeling clumsy. *You are beautiful!*

The freighting of nuances doubled. *This is appreciation or impertinence?*

Yes, he agreed, marveling at his audacity. He had intended to formulate a routine communication, but his mental image of her had expanded as he tried to focus on her as receiver, and somehow he had sent that instead. Now he was embarrassed.

In your plane, such opinions are not expressed? she inquired.

Not to strangers, he returned. *In my plane we cannot read thoughts, so we think very freely. I would not have spoken such a thing to you, but it is a true thought.* He hoped that would mollify her.

I am not antagonized, merely curious, she returned, again reading more than he had intended. *I am of course beautiful by human physical standards; this requires no statement. I assumed you had a motive for expressing the obvious; now I understand that you were not aware you were expressing it. You are doing well in your communication, and this is excellent practice.*

Thank you, he thought sincerely.

You are very quick to adapt, considering that your plane does not do this. You may be impetuous, but you are also clever.

Thank you, he thought again, deeply pleased by the compliment.

But you must learn to distinguish statements of fact or opinion from efforts to please or displease. Now that we have established contact, you cannot hide your thoughts from me, so it is best to keep them in order.

He could not hide his thoughts from her? That bothered him. Suppose he thought something negative—or, worse, erotic?

Precisely. It is not good to burden other parties with undisciplined thoughts. Treat the matter as you would spoken things in your own plane.

Certainly he would not go around telling every attractive woman he encountered how sexy she was!

I asked you not to do that, she thought reprovingly. *I have as I explained no interest in repetition of the obvious.*

Brother! He concentrated on the basic times-tables, trying to blot out any thought of the way she looked.

No, this is uncomfortable for me, she protested. *I do not care to rehearse your mathematics. Simply direct your thoughts appropriately.*

I'm trying to! he thought. *But I'm an impetuous youth!*

True. I shall make an allowance. Now I must try to alert the others. You may sleep now, so as to provide no further distraction. Remember: do not express this matter verbally.

Why not? I think it's a great thing, communicating telepathically!

Because I have sensed hostile elements within the castle. I presume these are agents of the sorcerer we are to oppose. Our physical expressions may be monitored, but I think this is not so for our mental ones. If we are to succeed in our joint mission, we must not only develop such a linking, we must conceal it from those agents. I have ascertained that the Emperor himself is not aware of the precise nature of my mental ability; it would be best to keep that private.

That made so much sense that Seth had no further question. *But I don't know how to tune out,* he thought.

Now that telepathy is possible, I'll be thinking of it constantly. How do I sleep?

I will help you. Use your relaxation technique for your body, and I will pacify your mind.

Seth attempted to do that, fearing that it was impossible. He told the light to turn off, and relaxed his individual muscles, but his mind was raging with excitement. Then abruptly he felt her presence, like a bath of warm oil, and before he knew it he sank out of awareness.

He woke refreshed, to the natural light of morning. What a dream he had had! Tirsa, telepathy—what could have sent him off on such a notion?

He had to smile. It required no psychoanalyst to fathom that he had met a beautiful and intelligent woman who was as much a stranger to this weird magic world as he was himself. Naturally he was interested in her! She was a sharp contrast to the teenage girls he had encountered on his own plane, and of course wouldn't have been part of his social world even if she had lived next door to him. But here she was like a beacon, an ideal figure, and he couldn't help thinking about her. What was more natural than dreaming that she had made secret contact with him? He loved the idea of telepathy; he had always been interested in ESP and the study of paranormal powers. It would be a dream come true to be able to practice it himself. Especially with such a person as Tirsa, whose mysteries became more intriguing as they were explored.

But he had always schooled himself to know the

difference between dreams and reality. A dream might be of the perfect woman; the reality was that if such a woman did exist, she would hardly be interested in an impetuous youth. So he could dream all he wanted to, at night, but by day he would deal with reality. It had always been that way, with dreams that had become increasingly fanciful as the reality turned increasingly grim. The dreams were, he realized, his way of compensating for a life that was not living up to expectations. That was all right, as long as he never confused the two.

Yet what a turn reality had taken! He had been about to drown—and then turned up on a world where magic governed. Now he was committed to a quest whose nature he knew virtually nothing about, except that it would be dangerous. Now that he was here, his main desire was to return to the dull world of his origin. Emperor Towk said he could not do that—but perhaps the Emperor merely wanted him and the other Chosen to undertake the mission, and knew that they would not do so if they had a real choice. If they succeeded in dealing with Nefarious, it well might turn out that there *was* a way for each to go home, that the Emperor had somehow forgotten.

He had been dressing as he considered these things. Now he touched the door panel, and the door slid open to admit him to the hall which led to the main chambers of the castle.

The others were already having breakfast, served by the buxom maid Domela, though they did not seem to have been there long. He should have paid more attention to his preparations, instead of lost in his thoughts. Rame greeted him with a smile, but both Tirsa and Vidav ignored him. What else should he have expected?

He ate quickly, catching up, hardly paying attention to the odd appearance and taste of the fruits. The Emperor had promised that there would be much to do, and Seth believed it; he wanted to be ready.

The Emperor's adviser Turcot appeared. "First we shall instruct you in the use of some of the magic items we have prepared for you," he said.

The items were impressive. There was a miniature tent that could fit inside a pack; when invoked, it expanded to become a full-size tent for four, complete with sleeping bags and insect netting. There was a stove that was just a foot-long rod; when stuck upright in the ground and invoked it radiated enough heat to warm the tent, even in a snowstorm. There were tools that expanded similarly: a shovel, axe, heavy hammer, and an assortment of knives. There were boots that greatly facilitated walking; in fact, each step in them was the equivalent of thirty paces of the mundane kind.

"Caution," Turcot warned. "Never invoke these inappropriately. If you invoke the stove-pipe while it is in your pack, it may set your pack on fire and destroy everything else that is in it. If you invoke the tent while you are within it, it will close to its small size around you. This could be awkward. It will not actually harm you, but it will tear and destroy itself in its effort to complete its imperative. These are only items; they have no human discretion."

The four nodded. They would be very careful about using such artifacts!

They were taken out to a nearby countryside, where they rehearsed their travel technique. Each in turn had to invoke all of the magic items, and practice using them. They had to don their boots, which had magically perfect fits, but which were as awkward as skates or stilts to use the first time. "Take small steps," Turcot warned.

Seth took what he thought was a small step—and abruptly found himself almost crashing into a tree. That tree had been fifty feet away; now it was close enough to touch! He would have to watch where he was going, if he didn't want to bash his head in! But once he got the hang of them, he found the boots marvelously competent. They did not exactly speed him up; it was more like matter transmission, with his body phasing from the rear foot at one location to the forefoot as much as a hundred feet away. There could be, he learned to his surprise, trees or even houses between the two spots; it didn't matter. Just so long as there was no tree at the spot he landed! He would not, it turned out, actually merge with the tree; his body would be shunted aside, by a protective spell associated with the boots. But the effect would be like slipping on a banana peel, as he was abruptly set down where he hadn't planned to be.

Rame was very quick to become proficient with the boots. His goatlike hoofs disappeared into them, and it looked as if he had normal human feet, which was strange. But his natural agility enabled him to adapt rapidly, and in moments he was stepping from region to region, without passing through the spots between.

Tirsa had no trouble about banging into things,

because she took very ladylike steps and did not go far, but that was a problem in itself. "Farther, woman!" Turcot directed. "You must keep up with the others." She frowned, and forced herself to take a giant step that would have been disastrous in a skirt, but wasn't in the pantaloons. She got there, but did not seem comfortable. Seth could have sworn that her hair-stripes were more intense than before, as if they reflected her concentration.

Vidav, accustomed to carrying his own weight, did not want to use the boots. "I can keep up," he protested, and demonstrated by running at a rate that dropped Seth's jaw. The guy was like a two-legged racing car!

But Turcot was unimpressed. "Keep up with them as they cross that ravine," he suggested, pointing.

The others obligingly took three steps each, crossing plain and forest and ravine without effort, to stand on a knoll and look back. Vidav ran, but could not match their magical paces, and had to stop completely at the ravine, which was about forty feet wide and hundreds deep. Grudgingly, he donned his boots, took a step—and wound up way beyond them. He had put far too much power into it.

By the day's end, they were all reasonably proficient with their magical devices. Seth was exhilarated but tired, not so much from the physical effort, but the mental: accepting and using things which he had once thought to be impossible. Those boots—not exactly seven leagues, but plenty to handle anyway.

He cleaned up, noting the darkening beard on his face. Well, Vidav was bearded; that seemed to be be the best way, here. He lay down and slept almost instantly.

The sound came. Abruptly alert, Seth tuned in on it. *I am here, Tirsa,* he thought.

I tried to reach the others last night, but could not, she thought. *Their minds are not as open as yours.*

Thanks, I think! Anything I can do to help? He did not question the contact; if this was a dream, he wanted to stay with it.

Yes, you may be able to help. But you must not dismiss this as fantasy. It is not magic, it is direct mental contact.

Why wasn't there any during the day, then?

Because of the need for secrecy. I cast about, and verified the presence of at least three spies. I did not want you to betray the nature of this communication, so did not contact you.

You don't have much confidence in me! he protested, hurt.

I have asked you before not to restate the obvious. I fear your impulsive nature. You could have reacted in a manner that the spies would have noted, and thereby done irreparable damage.

Well, maybe it's that same impulsive nature that enables me to accept your thoughts when the others can't! he retorted.

True. So you must join with me in making the attempt. Linked, we shall have enhanced power of communication, and this may suffice.

Seth decided that he would much rather be linked with her, than neglected by her. *I'm game.*

Please reduce the romantic implication, she thought. *It is a nuisance when there is something important to be done.*

He had been caught by the broader aspect of telepathy again! If he hadn't known before that she had no interest in romance, she had certainly put him straight. *I'll try.*

That is not true. I am interested in romance, but not with you.

He ground his teeth. *I got the message. Now if we can cut out the irrelevant nuances . . .*

This time her laughter caught him, making him laugh too, involuntarily. Then they settled down to business.

She could not describe exactly what she wanted him to do, but it seemed like pushing a car out of a mudhole, so he pictured himself doing that. He heaved and heaved—and the car began to move. Tirsa seemed to be in the driver's seat, steering it, but pushing too.

What is this? a gruff thought came.

Tirsa. Open your mind, Vidav, so I can communicate.

Get out of my mind, alien temptress! I have no need of a succubus!

Seth suppressed a laugh. A succubus, he remembered, was a demoness who came to men in their sleep, seducing them to evil. Vidav had no more interest in Tirsa than she had in Seth!

Must I remind you yet again about stating the obvious? her thought shot back, feeling irritated.

Seth couldn't help it: he liked that irritation. She had been served as she served him.

But she was already addressing Vidav. *Please keep your crude interpretations to yourself. I know you are married and committed to your wife and children. But you will never return to them unless the four of us who have been Chosen succeed in working together. There are spies in the* castle who mean mischief for us. We must be able to coordinate without alerting them. Now focus on me, and learn to speak with your mind alone.

Vidav was unimpressed. *It is the nature of empires to have spies. Have you identified them?*

Do you wish their names or descriptions?

Descriptions.

She sent a mental picture of one of the scullery boys they had seen. Then another, of the maid Domela. A third, of a noble to whom they had been briefly introduced.

Now Vidav was impressed, as was Seth, both by her visual imagery and her apparent alertness. She had obviously been checking every person with whom they came in contact. If her effort had not been evident to the Chosen, it surely wasn't known by anyone else.

I wondered about that noble, Vidav thought. *He had a smell about him. And that maid—the way she keeps smiling at me, and bending forward in that low dress. I thought she was interested in—but no wonder, if she's a spy! Then, after a pause: You read about my family, in my mind? Have you no honor in the use of your talent?*

Tirsa was stung; Seth felt the backlash of emotion. *I found myself in an alien land with a strange language and odd customs, thrown together with others with whom I was to work closely. I used my ability to separate potential friend from potential foe. What would you have done?*

Vidav considered. *I apologize, woman. I would have done what you did. But I ask you not to snoop further on private matters.*

I can read only those thoughts and feelings which are uppermost, and those I cannot avoid, she responded. *Your*

*family has been much on your mind, and your guilt about
deserting it. If you do not think so much of it, I will not be
able to receive it.*

How can I not *think of those closest to me?* he demanded, and now Seth felt the pain of that
separation. But he also picked up that guilt she had
mentioned; there was something out of alignment
here. Vidav, who had seemed so gruff and strong, was
quite another person, mentally. He was tough, but
his feeling was great. Seth understood it well enough;
he felt love and guilt for his own family and his seeming desertion.

I can no more not receive than you can not think, Tirsa
pointed out. *I do not seek your secrets, but when I attune to
you, I receive only what is there.*

How is it there was none of this before? Vidav asked.

I can read any mind on which I focus, Tirsa explained.
*But that is passive. It is more challenging to send to that
mind, especially when that mind has no experience with
mind talk. There has to be interaction. Your mind was
closed to my approach. Now it is open, and that is much easier for me. We four Chosen must work together, and be able to
talk with each other when others do not know. Only in this
manner can we avoid the spies, and hope to accomplish our
mission.*

You make sense, woman, Vidav acknowledged. *It is a
distinct tactical advantage to have secret communications.*

*Yes. Do not make any indication of this ability by day.
Others cannot read us, but it is best if they do not even suspect we are linked.*

Agreed. Now let me sleep.

Seth slept too, at that point, whether from fatigue
or her sleep-thought he wasn't sure.

He also still wasn't sure whether this was dream or reality. He would have to try telepathy in the daytime.

The next day they trained in combat. "Nefarious has minions among both human and nonhuman creatures," Turcot explained. "You must be able to defend yourselves from attacks by types which may be unfamiliar to you."

"Body armor and a good sword can do much," Vidav asserted.

"Not against a cloud of poison mites. For that you need magic, or proficiency with a net."

Vidav nodded, yielding the point. He would train with a suitable net.

Seth, meanwhile, was trying to fathom whether his dreams of the night had any reality by day. *Tirsa!* he thought. *Do you read me?*

She gave no sign that she did. Either she was playing some kind of game, or there was no telepathy.

They practiced with the nets against neutralized poison mites. They were tiny flies that hovered in a cloud, not flying strongly, but the bite of a potent one would, Turcot assured them, numb the region near the bite, and multiple bites would bring unconsciousness and even death. The nets had very fine mesh, magically enhanced, so that they could trap the mites. It was just a matter of sweeping them through the air. But any mites that were missed could be deadly.

They also drilled against other types of creatures, any one of which could be handled, but only if the proper technique was known. Some were likely to be encountered individually; others always came in packs or swarms. Some had to be fled, while others could generally be bluffed. It was confusing at first, but Seth knew how important it was to get it straight.

"Two mountain trolls, charging from either side," Turcot announced. "What do you do?"

They had learned what to do. Seth leaped to join his closest companion, who happened to be Tirsa. They stood back to back, swords lifted high. That was all that was required; seeing no ready rear approach, the trolls would give it up as a bad job and forage elsewhere. They were fearsome when they thought they had the advantage, but cowardly at other times. Seth remembered the fight he and Rame had had with the smaller valley trolls, who had thought they had the advantage because of their numbers. He didn't want to run afoul of big trolls!

You are doing well, Seth, Tirsa thought.

You mean it's real? he responded. *We really can communicate telepathically?* He had no concern about giving himself away in his surprise, because he was supposed to be nervously watching for trolls; any expression would be in order at the moment!

Certainly! Why should you doubt?

Because I tried to reach you this morning, and got nowhere.

That was because I was not attuned to you. I am telepathic; you are not. I must orient on you, and read your thoughts.

You mean I wasn't really sending? he asked, disappointed.

Not in the way I do. Perhaps in time you could achieve that, but you have not had your full life to develop your power, as I have. It hardly matters; I will link you with the others whenever necessary.

But I helped push you into contact with Vidav!

True. You made an effort, and I drew on it. But the ability to do that was mine, not yours; your effort was undisciplined.

Then they had to move on to the next exercise. They separated, and she tuned out. While what he had learned had not been entirely heartening, still it confirmed that his experiences of the past two nights were real, not dreams.

The exercises were becoming routine, and Seth mastered them readily, because his training in martial arts had disciplined him for such drill. His thoughts drifted back to his home plane. He wondered if Tirsa saw him the way he had seen a girl of his class. She had been plain, and so not in demand for dates. When a turnabout dance came up, she had asked him. Surprised, he had accepted, though he did not expect to enjoy it the way he might a date with a pretty girl. But he discovered that appearance was deceptive; the girl was lively and an interesting conversationalist, and he had a great time. He had learned something then: not to judge by initial impressions. Sure, beauty was great—but there were other things, and they could be more important. He had accepted the date only as a favor to the girl, but he felt that in the end he had done himself one.

Then he saw Tirsa looking at him. Ouch! Had she read his thoughts? He threw himself more vigorously into the exercise, hoping that his exertion would hide the flush on his face.

That night they went after Rame, and finally managed to hook him into the network. It wasn't that the faun resisted it, but that he was not fully human, and it was hard for Tirsa to find the key to his mind. Once she did, Rame was happy to participate.

In the following days' training they began linking mentally, and it made them into a remarkably effective team. They worked so well together, in fact, that they had to start making some deliberate mistakes, to avoid arousing suspicion. Even so, Turcot was amazed. "Perhaps we do have a chance," he muttered.

There was one thing that bothered Seth increasingly, however. Their mission was one of murder. They would have to seek out Nefarious, and kill him. Maybe the Sorcerer was an evil man who deserved to die. Maybe he would destroy the planes if he had the chance. Maybe he would gleefully kill the four Chosen. But those were all maybe's. One thing Seth was sure of was that he was not a cold-blooded assassin. But he was the most proficient one of them in combat; their drills had made it clear that his physical coordination and prior experience made him their expert. He was the one most likely to deliver the killing stroke. That made the ultimate decision his.

He brought it up when Tirsa linked them in the evening. *I have trained in martial arts on my own plane, and I am training here,* he thought to the others. *But I am not a killer. I can't just go out to kill a man I don't know, just because someone else tells me it has to be done.*

I agree! Rame's thought came. *I can kill when the need arises, but I must be the judge of the need.*

It is right that you do so, Vidav thought. *No man takes*

delight in killing, or does it carelessly.

Seth was surprised and gratified by this support. He had come to know the other Chosen physically during the past few days, and mentally during the nights, but this subject had never come up. He had thought that Vidav would kill without compunction; now he saw that this judgment had been hasty. He was glad.

Certainly I do not support casual killing, Tirsa thought. *We shall have to make a judgment when the occasion arises, on this as in other aspects of the mission.*

Other aspects? Rame asked.

There is much I do not understand about this situation, she explained. *It seems to me that we four came onto the scene quite conveniently. Perhaps it is as the Emperor says— but I am not certain that we should take that on faith. Prophecy is treacherous business—and how can we be sure it is a true prophecy? The three of you I have come to know well enough to trust, but I think I trust none other here.*

Agreed! Vidav thought, and Rame and Seth echoed the sentiment. They would go on the mission, but they would make sure of the facts before doing anything final.

- **Six**

Dreams

It seemed in one sense only a moment before they sat before Emperor Towk again, and in another sense a year. Physically they had hardly changed, but mentally they had shifted from individuals to a tightly knit group. They looked like four quite different people, but Tirsa linked them so that they were constantly sharing thoughts.

"It is time for you to set out on your mission," the Emperor said. "Turcot advises me that you have learned the use of the tools and weapons we gave you very well, and that you are as well prepared as any group can be. We have shown you on the map where Nefarious's castle is, but you must not approach it directly, for he would quickly intercept you. You must choose your own route, known to no others, and come upon him by surprise. I cannot overstress the importance of your mission; you are the Chosen, and if you fail, the four frames are lost."

Standard peptalk, Seth thought, not with disrespect. The others agreed. They kept their faces straight, giving no sign of their private interchange.

There were formalities, but Seth hardly paid attention. He was already pondering their course of action, with input from the others. They intended to drop out of sight, not only from Nefarious, but from the Emperor as well. But how were they to do that, in a countryside where every peasant farmer would recognize them instantly? They had some notions, but had refrained from discussing them; it was enough of a job just to complete training and master the telepathy.

They started off at noon, with a fanfare: the Empire Orchestra was there for the occasion, with its strange and magical instruments. A great crowd of townsmen turned out; they had evidently been granted a holiday. Domela, under the pretext of bringing Vidav an item he had forgotten, managed to sneak in a kiss, to his evident disgust. But Seth picked up enough from his linked mind to know that his disgust was mostly that she was a spy. Otherwise she could have been tempting indeed. However, this was quickly left behind, as they took steps with their traveling shoes; in moments they were out of sight of the castle, far down the main highway.

First one who sees a green insect, take the lead, Tirsa thought. That was their way of making their travel essentially random. Each of them had worked out a possible route to Nefarious's castle; since there was no way to tell who would first see the insect, they could not know whose route would be used. If they themselves did not know, how could anyone else? If Nefarious had analyzed their personalities and abilities—as surely he had!—he would have come to a conclusion about their likely course, and set his trap somewhere along it. This would nullify that, for they were not taking a sensible, agreed-upon course. They were taking a haphazard one.

I see one, Rame thought. His eye was excellent for natural things. *Lock on me.* This was a technique they had developed by secret experimentation: they tuned in to his awareness, and let his mind guide their actions.

Rame turned north and stepped toward the forest. They matched him in virtual lock-step. Two steps brought them to the trees. Then Rame took baby-steps, that moved him only about ten feet at a time, so as to be able to move between trees without overlapping any. Anyone observing from a distance would have seen them enter the forest, and perhaps would have assumed that they were proceeding in the same direction, at the same speed through it. But Rame turned at right angles, skirted the clearing, came to the edge of a large field, and took a giant step across it. They followed precisely.

In this manner, what Seth thought of as baby/giant stepping, they took such a devious course that no one could have followed them physically. The faun tried to keep to the cover of trees, always moving rapidly across open spaces in one, two or three steps, never pausing. It was a bit wearing, staying with him, but their mental rapport made it possible. They were doing an excellent job of losing any possible pursuit. They were fortunate that Rame was the one in charge, because he was by far the most skilled in this type of thing.

Seth was hardly aware where they were, because he was busy staying with Rame, who was pursuing an incredibly intricate course generally north. Forests, fields, lakes, mountains, miscellaneous ravines and bogs—he hoped the faun knew where they were going, because Seth certainly didn't!

As the day grew late, they came to a small mountain lake. They slowed to baby-step rate and approached a village whose dwellings seemed to be fashioned from woven animal hair. As they came close, Seth saw that the houses were small. What kind of folk lived here?

In a moment he learned the answer. They were gnomes: manlike creatures about half normal human height, and furry all over their bodies. *Let me make contact,* Rame thought.

The three paused, while the faun went ahead to the edge of the village. The Fur-Gnomes came out to meet him. They talked, then Rame's thought came back: *I talked with Cotan, their chief. They will let us camp here for the night, and will not betray our presence to the enemy, but we must do them a service. They have had bad fishing; can we catch them a batch?*

Tirsa concentrated. *I pick up many fishly minds, deep in the water where they have gone to feed.*

I know net-fishing, Vidav thought.

Soon they were busy fashioning a large net from strands provided by the Fur-Gnomes, following Vidav's instructions. They weighted the corners of the net with stones and tossed it into the section of the lake where Tirsa sensed the fish. When it sank to the right level, Vidav hauled on its lines, closing it around the fish and bringing it toward shore. It was a hard job, but Vidav seemed tireless; he kept hauling it in, hand over hand, until it came to the surface before them.

The net was bulging with trapped fish. The Fur-Gnomes pounced gleefully on them and bore them away. Before long the net was empty—but the village problem of food for the week was solved.

There was a feast of baked fish that evening, which the Chosen shared. The Fur-Gnomes, originally reserved and wary, had become quite friendly when they saw the fish, and a number of them came up to introduce themselves. Their men were stout and strong, their women slender and pretty, and their children were bundles of joy and mischief. The gnomes put on a show for the visitors: a firelight dance whose intricate motions were hypnotic. Seth was reminded of the patterns of the marching bands of his plane. Even the smoke of the fire was beneficial: it kept the003 thronging nocturnal insects at bay.

The Fur-Gnomes, Chief Cotan explained, were sometime allies of the fauns. That was why Rame had sought them: he understood their ways. They had no use for Nefarious, but also not much use for the Teuton Empire; they preferred to be left alone. "Both of them want to tell us what to do, and take our folk to be their servants," the chief explained. "But we die if we go too far from our native haunts."

If we eliminate Nefarious, do we make it easy for the Teuton Empire to exploit these folk? Seth thought.

We must take care in what we do, Vidav thought in his gruff manner.

Yes, Rame agreed. *There are many free folk who are best off without the meddling of human empires.*

When the feast and dance concluded, the Fur-Gnomes retired to their homes. That was fine with Seth, who was tired. Rame drew the miniature tent out of Vidav's pack, chose a suitable spot beside the lake, and invoked it. The tent expanded until it was full size, complete with sleeping bags and stove-pipe.

At this Seth realized that they would have to share the residence. It had always been a four-person tent, of course, and he had known it, but during their training at the castle this hadn't quite registered. Each of them had had separate rooms for the night. Of course the three males would be all right, but what of Tirsa?

What of her? Tirsa's thought came. *Am I not to share our residence?*

Seth's thoughts went into a jumble of confusion. Of course she was entitled to share—yet if she wanted to change or wash up, what then?

Enough of this foolishness, Vidav thought. *I shall swim before I sleep.*

Good idea, Tirsa thought. *I will join you.*

We all will, Rame thought.

Vidav began stripping his clothing, tossing it down beside the lake. It was dark, of course, but the telepathic linkage make it clear that he was naked. Tirsa was doing likewise. Rame did not have to strip, as his fur was his clothing.

Seth held back. To swim naked with a woman— how could he do that?

The same way you share thoughts with her, Tirsa's thought came. *Secrets lie in the mind, not the body.*

Suddenly he realized that she was right. All his foolish notions about romance, which she had chopped down so methodically, were a far greater embarrassment than such a swim would be. After the first couple of nights he had found that he no longer embarrassed himself with untoward thoughts, because there was no ambiguity in their relationship. He had heard it was the same at nudist camps: when no one wore clothing, its absence wasn't sexy, it was routine, and there were no titillating mysteries of the body. Minds open to each other brought greater understanding and trust—and a far more accurate appreciation of the acceptable limits of behavior. Just as he wasn't afraid of falling when in an airplane, because he trusted its mechanism, he wasn't afraid of embarrassment in the mind linkage, now that he understood and trusted it. He had passed over the hump days ago; now such things as changing, swimming and sharing a tent hardly mattered.

He scrambled out of his clothes and splashed into the lake to join the others. It was wonderful in the chill water, after the nervousness and effort of the day's travel. Except for one thing: he remembered the ice. The ice that had almost killed him.

He found himself struggling desperately. *No!* Tirsa's thought came. *This is not ice! You are not alone! I will help you.* Suddenly she was there, putting her arms around him in the water, helping to hold him up. *I am sorry; I did not realize that this was the way you died. I misunderstood your hesitation.*

"You didn't misunderstand!" he gasped verbally. "But thank you. I can make it now."

She let go, and he resumed normal swimming. However, he decided he had had enough, and soon returned to shore. What an ugly surprise he had had!

It is better not to speak in response to a mental communication, Vidav thought. *Someone might be listening.*

He was right; Seth should have kept his mouth shut. *I'm sorry; I panicked. It won't happen again.*

You were thrust into a situation similar to that of your death, Tirsa thought. *This can cause a reaction.* She emerged from the water, her body glistening in the moonlight. *I will sleep beside you, in case you need comfort.*

Seth started to protest that there was no need, but stifled it. He *had* been severely shaken, and her power of telepathy was strongest when she was closest. Her help would be welcome, if he needed it.

She shook herself dry and went to the tent. The sleeping bags were laid out two by two. They took the two farther from the entrance, so that the others would not have to scramble over them when they came in from swimming.

Only after he was lying down, about to sleep, did he realize that he had never thought of romance or sex after entering the water, despite getting quite close to a beautiful and naked woman. He was making progress; a month ago it would have been a completely different story!

Yes, you are learning, she agreed. *Just as you learned about the plain girl.*

He stood near the lake, soaked. Behind him the icy water churned, the broken plates of ice grinding against each other as if the lake were gnashing its teeth in anger at losing its prey. He was shivering, but he was alive!

It was dark; he could hardly see a thing. He staggered away from the lake. His foot turned on a stone, and he lost his balance. His arms windmilled, and his outflung hand touched/

/the dank stone of the tunnel. It was too close; how could she get through? She wanted to scream, but knew that would be both unladylike and futile. There was no one to help her; she had to make it on her own.

But the rock closed in yet closer. Her hips wedged,

scraping skin, but would not pass. Yet there was no salvation in retreat; this was the only way out. She *had* to make it through!

She struggled, but knew she was only getting caught worse. The air was running out; she was panting for breath, though it did no good. She was losing control, mental as well as physical. She tried to scream, while condemning herself for this foolishly primitive and pointless exercise.

A hand squeezed hers. *It's only a dream! Snap out of it! It's all right, Tirsa!*

Who? she thought, unable to make sense of this.

Seth. I am holding your hand. Come—I will draw you out of it.

Seth! Then she remembered. She clung to his hand, and he drew her out of that dark tunnel and into the better darkness of the tent. *Oh, Seth! I sought to comfort you, but you comforted me instead!*

You helped me too. When your hand caught mine, it snapped me out of my bad dream and into yours.

Dreams! This must be a siege!

What?

We must rescue the others! Quickly—you go for Rame and I'll go for Vidav! She scrambled out of her bag, toward the other end of the tent.

Seth didn't argue. If the two of them had had bad dreams, the other two might too. He didn't understand why, but evidently she knew something. She had mentioned a "siege." Was that some enemy plot?

He reached Rame. The faun was moaning and clinging to his sleeping bag as if afraid something was hauling him out of it. What was he dreaming?

Seth found Rame's hand and clasped it with his own. "Wake up, Rame!" he said. "It's not real! It's only/

/The storm caught him like the blast of water from a fire hydrant. It picked him up and whirled him around. It was a tornado!

He saw trees, upside down, and realized that he was being spun in the cone, sucked up into the maw of the terrible storm. He reached out, trying to catch at a branch, anything, though he knew that a tornado could rip whole trees out of the ground and strew their parts across the landscape. It seemed like a futile gesture, yet anything was better than being hauled into the sky!

He missed the branch. The ring of inverted trees seemed to rise—which meant that *he* was rising, being carried above the level of the forest. He felt the vertigo, and his stomach roiled. He seemed to have no hope of escape.

No! This wasn't his dream, it was Rame's! He had come to help his friend, and instead had allowed himself to be sucked into it. What kind of a rescuer was he? Ashamed and angry, he struck back in more effective fashion. *Link with me, Rame! This is a mental attack! Hold my hand, come out with me! It is a dream, and we can leave it!*

Now he felt Rame's hand. There were two of them whirling upside down in the storm. *A dream!* Seth repeated emphatically. The storm continued, but with less force. The winds still howled around them, but had less effect. They were becoming transparent, untouched by the storm.

Then the dream faded, and they were in the tent,

clasping hands. "Just a dream," Seth repeated. "But you don't have to face it alone, with mind linkage."

"Thank you, friend!" Rame gasped. "But the others—"

"They're here. Tirsa is seeing to Vidav. We all dreamed, I think."

"A sending by Nefarious!" Rame exclaimed. "But are the others safe? You drew me out, but—"

"Well, let's see," Seth said, realizing that there was neither physical nor mental contact with the other two. "All we need to do is take their hands."

They reached across and scrambled for hands. Seth found Vidav's/

/The flames reared up in front, forcing him back. He turned, only to find more flames behind. He was in a burning building, and there seemed to be no way out. His skin was blistering, and he was choking from the smoke.

It's a dream! he thought. *It's not real! I have your hand, follow me out!*

Then, slowly, the flames faded. The four of them were sprawled in the tent, hands linked.

Thank you, Seth, Tirsa thought. *I could not pull him out! The flames were overcoming us both.*

Rame helped, he replied. *With two of us helping, it wasn't hard to end the dream. But what did you mean by a siege?*

We can return to our own bags now, she thought. *I shall maintain the linkage, and will explain.*

Seth crawled back to his sleeping bag and got in. In a moment Tirsa's thought came again:

I believe that this is a sending by Nefarious. He is not telepathic, but he can project crude emotion, such as fear.

He knows we are coming for him, and when his spies were unable to keep track of us, because of our unpredictability and Rame's clever dodging, he tried to scare us away by broadcasting fear. I have encountered this type of thing on my plane, though never as powerfully. He sent the elements—water, earth, air and fire—and each of us reacted according to the one we related to. My greatest fear is of being trapped in the deep earth, of being suffocated and crushed, because that is the way I was dying when I was transported here. Seth's is of water—dark, icy water, drowning him. Vidav's is of fire; he was on the verge of burning to death when we came here. Rame's— She paused, reading the faun's thought. *Is of air, a violent storm. He suffered it in life, I think, at the same time as the others of us suffered our traumas. We all verged on dying, and so when the sending came we all relived it.*

That makes sense! Seth agreed. *It would be too much of a coincidence that we all had bad dreams simultaneously. You must be right: Nefarious doesn't know where we are, so he sent out a scare-broadcast, a siege as you call it, and we feel it because we are scared of what almost killed us.*

I did not realize that my encounter with the storm was connected, Rame thought. *It came up so quickly I was caught before I could flee it, and I thought I was about to die. But then it passed as suddenly as it came, and dropped me unharmed to the forest floor. Malape soothed me and healed me. I put it out of my mind as a fluke—but I see now that the fear of it remained.*

It is natural to fear what almost kills one, Vidav thought. *Yet this fear must be resisted.*

With that they all agreed. *But if Nefarious could do this to us this time, by a blind sending, can't he do it again?* Seth asked.

Surely he can, Tirsa replied. *But probably with diminishing effect, because we have overcome it this time. If we remained linked, we can withstand it. Then we will be proof against both his spies and his mental siege.*

Can we remain linked while we sleep? Vidav asked.

Yes, as long as I focus on it. I could not do it continuously, but for a night or two I can.

With that they slept, linked.

And regretted it. Seth found himself standing where his prior dream had left him, beside the icy lake. This time the ice wasn't threatening him directly, it was threatening the town. He saw a monstrous glacier approaching, grinding toward him at horrendous velocity, for ice. It seemed to tower miles high, and to cast its shadow far ahead.

I don't like this dream! he thought, trying to break out of it. But he could not; he seemed to be trapped. The mental linkage, instead of freeing him, locked him in to the horror.

He ran, not to save himself, but to warn the town, which seemed oblivious to the threat. "Beware the ice! Beware the ice!" he called, but no one woke.

He ran to his own house. "Get out of there," he cried. "The ice is coming!" But no one emerged, while the glacier ground closer. In minutes it would be too late.

He yanked open the door and rushed in. The house was silent. He took the stairs two at a time and burst into his sister's room. There was Ferne, ten years old, asleep on her bed, her friend and confidante teddy bear beside her. "Ferne! Wake up! The ice is coming!"

She did not stir. Her pretty face was perfectly composed, framed by her brown hair, with no flicker of animation. She remained so still that it alarmed him. He touched her shoulder. "Ferne!"

Then he became aware of something. Her shoulder, under the pink frill of her nightie, was rigid. In fact, it was cold—freezing cold.

He touched her hand. It was as stiff as an icicle. He clasped it in both his own, horrified, trying to warm it—and felt cold liquid. Aghast, he stared.

Her hand was melting. It was nothing but ice.

"Ferne!" He reached across to touch her face. It melted in the pattern of his fingers, becoming misshapen.

She had turned to ice!

He lurched up and ran to his mother's room. She lay similarly, and he knew without touching her that she too was frozen. The shadow of the glacier had fallen across her, and enchanted her into ice.

It had turned the whole town to ice.

Then he felt the shudder of the glacier, as it overran the town, crushing the buildings. The town was lost, but maybe he could still warn the world. For somehow he knew that the ice was destined to bury all of it, unless they rallied and stopped it immediately.

There was a short-wave radio transmitter in his room, from his hobbying days. He rushed to it. If he could call out, alert the hams, so that some sort of resistance could be organized—

The house shuddered. The ice was right up against it, pushing over the building! The power cut off, and the house began tumbling over, slowly.

Seth scrambled out through a shattered window, dropped to the ground, and ran clear just as the house collapsed. But there was nowhere to go! Mountains of ice surrounded the town, and the remaining houses were being crushed. He couldn't get away! He couldn't warn anyone! His world was being destroyed, and he couldn't do anything about it!

But at the same time he knew that this didn't make any sense. This wasn't the Ice Age! A whole world couldn't be destroyed like that! Even if there were enough ice, it would move so slowly that there would be plenty of time for action. This was a dream, and he knew it—but it still terrified him.

He reached out to the others. *Get me out of this!* he thought.

He felt a hand clasp his, and/

/The sky was turning red, like sunset, but this was no normal closing of day. Something was coloring it. There was a tremendous amount of dust aloft, as if the worst sandstorm of history was in the making. The red was reflected in the roiling surface of the nearby lake, beyond the vague outlines of houses.

Seth squinted, to keep out the blinding dust. He sighted along his own arm to see what was beyond, because he still held someone's hand.

It was Tirsa. "Oh, no!" he exclaimed, the dust seeming to muffle his words as they emerged. "I got out of my dream—and into yours!"

She became aware of him. "Oh, Seth, I'm so glad you're here!" she cried. "Pull me free!"

"I can't! My dream is just as bad! Ice is destroying the world!"

"But look at this!" She used her free hand to point.

Seth looked up—and saw what was causing the dust. There was a planet in the sky, a monstrous ball of rock that loomed larger even as they watched. There was going to be a collision!

Her nightmare of being suffocated and crushed, deep in the earth. This was similar, but enlarged to encompass the whole world! Just as his dream of the icy lake had became a dream of a glacier destroying the whole town, and the world. They had not escaped the awful sendings! In fact, their mental linkage only seemed to expand the scale of disaster.

He had drawn her out of it before—but could he do it again? He had to try!

"It's a dream!" he said. "We're in our tent! All we have to do is wake! Concentrate with me, and step out of it!"

They tried. He felt her effort, as a surge of emotion, and he joined in with his. But nothing happened. They remained standing in the swirling dust, while the sky reddened further, and the oncoming planet swelled larger yet, its craters and cracks manifesting. Now it filled a third of the sky—no, two fifths—and it was growing faster.

"We can't escape it!" Tirsa cried, appalled. "My world is to be destroyed, and I can save neither it nor myself!"

"I couldn't save mine either!" Seth admitted. "Everything was turning to ice! But I called to you, and caught your hand—"

"And joined my world, no better off!" she finished. "It is to be crushed under rock, a collision!"

Somehow they both knew that when that happened, it would be over for them, in reality as well as in the dream.

"But maybe we can catch another hand!" he said. "There has to be some way to wake up, before—"

"Before we get killed in our dreams!" she finished. "Nefarious is doing this, I'm sure! Trying to kill us in our sleep!"

"We won't let him!" he said, but it was bravado, for they seemed to be powerless against this awful thrust of the distant sorcerer. "Maybe if the four of us can link again, we'll be too strong for him."

"Yes! We must link up!"

They concentrated. Seth's free hand flailed, but swept through nothing but dust, while the onrushing planet filled half the sky. He felt the awful tug of its gravity, and knew that the end would come much faster than the beginning.

Then Tirsa connected. "I've got a hand!" she exclaimed. "I think it's/

/They were back in flames, but not as close as they had been when they had rescued Vidav from his prior dream. This was Vidav's vision, surely; Tirsa had caught his hand and drawn them into the other dream.

Seth looked. He was holding Tirsa's left hand, and her right was holding Vidav's left. They formed a line of three, standing on the pavement of a city street.

It was the surface of the world, but it was burning. There was a forest fire in the distance, beyond the city. But the houses were burning too. Columns of smoke roiled up, thinning, merging above to become one huge dark haze that smudged out the sky. Seth had seen the fringe of a forest fire once, and it had been something like this: hell on Earth.

"The lake!" Seth cried, somehow knowing that the layout was the same as on his own world. It had been the same in Tirsa's dream, he realized: the town, the lake, the forest. They were all from the same place but different planes. "We can get away from the fire there!"

They ran for the lake, hands linked. They knew they had to stay together, and their physical linking in the dream was the only way they could be certain of their mental linking beyond it.

But already the fire had reached the lake, and was spreading across it. No—it was the water itself that was burning, Seth saw with amazement. And, at the edge, the ground itself! This whole world was burning!

"I know it's a bad dream," Vidav said. "Crafted for me, bringing the fire I fear. Nothing will put it out; it will burn our flesh too, as if it is dry wood. Something else I could fight, but how can I fight when my weapons and flesh burn too?"

"We have to escape the dream," Seth said. "That's the only way we can fight—to unite, and in our strength defeat Nefarious!"

They concentrated again, as the fire closed on them. Seth extended his left hand, seeking Rame, who he knew had to be close. As close as a nearby sleeping bag. Somewhere, not visible here, but in the adjacent plane of the dream—

He brushed something. He moved his hand back, and found it: another hand. He clasped it, and/

/The wind smote them with gale force. Rame's dream was of air, a storm, a tornado, sweeping the faun away.

But this was worse. The wind was rising rapidly, sweeping up not only dust but sticks and bricks and water. The lake was being scooped out as if by a giant hand, its water splashing into the sky. The bushes and trees beside it were being ripped out of the soil. Buildings were flying apart. The wind was not circular in the manner of a tornado; it was moving straight across. This was a wind that was passing across the entire world!

Seth did not need to question Rame. He knew that this was the faun's dream of destruction, an extension of his fear of the air, the storm that had nearly killed him. They had thought it enough just to escape their prior dreams, but Nefarious, having zeroed in on them, was now giving it all he had. This wind would rise until it blew away the land itself, and made of the planet nothing but a great cloud of dust, a nebula in space.

"Now we are linked!" Seth cried. "Now we must make our stand—together! We must fend off this sending and wake, and that will save us!"

"But how can we do that, when Nefarious controls our very dreams?" Rame asked, the wind making him almost inaudible.

"Well, united we have four times the strength we have separately. That may be enough to overcome his power."

"Yes," Vidav said. "Unity is strength. We are four, and he is one. We must overcome!"

They curved their line into a circle, Vidav and Rame clasping hands to complete it. The wind battered at them, but they drew together, concentrating. "Wake, wake!" Seth cried.

"Wake, wake!" the others chanted.

But the wind only tore at them harder, threatening at any moment to sweep them off their feet and throw them into the sky along with the other debris. It wasn't working.

Seth struggled to think of something better. He had honed his martial arts ability to a fine degree, both on his home plane and here in training. What was a person to do when confronted by superior strength?

That gave him the answer. "Yield to it!" he cried. "Make it worse!"

"What?" Rame asked, dismayed.

Seth didn't have time to explain. "All of you—concentrate on intensifying your dreams! Destroy your planes! But keep linked!"

Tirsa started to protest, then read his intent. "Yes! Make it worse! Do your utmost!" she cried.

Vidav and Rame exchanged a glance, then shrugged. "We're doomed anyway," Vidav muttered. "Might as well make it fast."

They concentrated, each on his or her own horror. Seth pictured the glacier not only covering his world, obliterating everything on it, but piling up so high that the very planet was offbalanced and spun out of orbit, wobbling toward the sun. He knew this was impossible, in real life, but this was his dream, and he could dream what he wanted. Maybe the ice would overrun the sun itself! "Flaming iceball!" he cried. "Frozen nova!"

"Burning cosmos!" Vidav agreed.

"The stars blowing away!" Rame cried.

"Crushed universe!" Tirsa exclaimed.

There was a jolt. The dream-framework shuddered, then flew apart. Fragments of ice and rock mixed with windblown fire, swirling erratically.

"It's off balance!" Seth cried. "Now push it back! Back where it came from!"

"Ah!" Vidav cried, comprehending.

They concentrated again, willing the dream, full-strength, back toward its origin. It was as if it were a world-size medicine ball; when they pushed together, it moved, slowly, then faster, until they heaved it away from them. It would fly back to the one who had sent it, Nefarious, who would then have to deal with the destruction unleashed within it.

They had overcome the dream, not by opposing it directly, which was beyond their ability because it had been formed of their own fears, but by pushing it the other way. Like an aggressive man who, braced for action, suddenly finds no resistance, it had stumbled, losing its bracing. Then they had pushed it back, and it had gone. They had, almost literally, gotten around it.

Seth knew they had won. Their effort might not hurt Nefarious directly, for he surely had ways to deal with his own sendings, but it signaled their effective counter to his attack. If he sent another sending, he would get it back in his face, like a huge stone that bounced back at the thrower. His chief weapon against them had been countered.

Thanks, Seth. It was Tirsa's thought, suffused with genuine relief and a certain dawning warmth.

He sank gratefully to sleep, knowing that this time his dreams would not be horrors.

• Seven

Breakdown

It seemed only minutes from the time of the dream to the time Seth woke, but the sun was beginning to rise. The others were still asleep, and he could understand why; it had been a most adventurous night, even if their bodies had not moved at all after the first siege of dreams.

He climbed quietly out of the sleeping bag, crawled past the others, and walked outside. The day did not seem as nice as the prior ones, but he realized that this might be because he was no longer in the comfort of the castle. There were numerous clouds, and a cold wind was rising. Or was it an echo of the wind of Rame's dreams?

Seth peered at his reflection by the lake's edge. He looked awful! He had hardly looked in a mirror during the last week, and he was now working on a burly beard. It was time to do something about that.

He reached into his pocket for Rame's knife. It was magically sharp, though it never cut the pocket itself, and would probably suffice for shaving. He knelt down at the edge of the lake and dunked his head in the chill morning water. Hoo! What a sensation! If he hadn't been sure whether he was awake before, there was no doubt now!

He brought the knife up to his cheek and began to shave. The impromptu razor stung, but it felt good to clean off the beard.

"You have a lovely face," a voice said behind him. "I never knew there was one, under that hair."

Seth looked through the ripples in the water at Tirsa's reflection. The alternate bands of her hair were overlapping as the water moved, but then they became clear. What a pretty sight she was, even in morning disarray!

How many times must I chide you about the obvious? But the current of annoyance was muted this time, if not actually playful. Her prior aloofness had eased significantly.

"Good morning," he said, continuing with his uncomfortable task. "Are the others ready to leave?"

"After we eat." *What do you think it meant?*

Seth had to keep straight what was spoken and what was thought. He doubted that there was any spy to listen here, but he appreciated her caution. It was best not to speak aloud of their experiences of the mind.

I'm not sure, now that I'm truly awake, he thought. *We all dreamed of the destructions of our individual worlds. This couldn't really have happened, because something just as bad would have occurred here. Anyway, Rame dreamed too, and this is his world. So I can't take it literally. But I can take it as a warning, or as Nefarious's effort to kill us in our sleep. Something like it well may happen if we don't succeed in our mission.*

Mentally she agreed emphatically. But her spoken words were on a different subject. "I have been wondering how we are supposed to defeat a sorcerer that an entire world can't stand against. Maybe we're hidden from him now, but he will certainly know of our approach to his lair, because anyone who sees us there will tell him."

Seth sat silent, uncertain now how they could win. After all, the dreams had almost taken them out. What did Nefarious have waiting for them at his lair?

"We were chosen for a reason," Vidav said as he emerged from the tent. "I couldn't tell you what that reason is. I only hope we come across it before we meet our enemy." *But I think we have already met him—and fended him off,* he added mentally. Tirsa was linking them, but within that framework each had private control.

Seth nodded. They were expressing their doubts openly, for the benefit of any possible spies in the Fur-Gnome camp, but they had private experience that suggested that Nefarious was indeed worried about them.

Rame was last to emerge from the tent. He brought out their weapons and the back pack with the medical supplies. Then he faced the tent. "Invoke," he commanded.

The tent quivered, then folded in on itself, until it was once again small enough to fit in Vidav's pack. The others picked up their weapons while Rame conjured breakfast. After eating, the four Chosen walked to Chief Cotan's hut.

The Fur-Gnome leader was awake and active. He greeted them heartily. "I am glad our village was able to assist you in your journey," he said. "The best wishes of every creature that is good are with you."

Aptly put! Unfortunately, they were headed for the stronghold of bad creatures. "Thank you," Tirsa said, with a smile. She did not smile often, Seth realized, and only when she meant it, but it was worth waiting for.

They bid goodbye to the Fur-Gnomes and continued on their way. They used one of the Fur-Gnomes' magic paths until it veered from the direction Rame had chosen. According to his map, there was an elf village ahead, and the elves were good folk. It would take a day to reach their village, even with the magic boots.

Seth looked at the sky. It was going to be a nasty day! He realized that in the three weeks since their arrival it had never once rained. The rain must be pretty solid when it came, and of course it would come on the least convenient day. "Some things must be the same on every plane," he muttered wryly.

"If you're talking about the weather, you are probably right," Vidav replied, looking into the sky himself. Then, abruptly: "What is that?"

They saw an enormous creature flying low in the sky toward them. "I'd say it was a dragon," Rame said. "A very large one. It may have been sent by Nefarious to locate us. We'd better hide from it."

Good idea, Tirsa thought. *But don't talk; I understand dragons have good hearing as well as eyesight.*

They ducked quickly into the nearby bushes and watched as the creature flew overhead. Seth was tense; that dragon was huge, and he had little notion how to fight it, despite their training. The best advice of the Empire trainers had been simply to avoid dragons. He relaxed as the monster passed them and started to flap away.

There was a flash from behind him. He looked

back. A break in the clouds had let a ray of sunlight shine through and reflect against Vidav's shield. What a bad break!

The dragon caught the flash. It circled back and gazed down, its head cocking to one side and then the other. But they had retreated deeper into the bush and covered up the moment the creature started turning. They were well hidden now, but the dragon had an idea that something was down there. Possibly it smelled them, though their swim in the lake should have reduced their odors somewhat.

The dragon rolled its neck back and then shot it forward, issuing a strange blast of noise. Then it flew off as if looking for another sign of them.

I think it knows we are here, Tirsa thought. *I tried to get into its mind, but it is too alien. I can handle only human minds well. But it's aware of something.*

Then why did it leave? Seth asked.

It may not be able to land in this heavy concentration of trees and bushes. I'm worried that its shriek was to alert other creatures.

That gave Seth an unpleasant chill. Of course the dragon would signal its allies that it had found something!

Listen! Vidav thought.

Seth heard a distant clicking sound, coming toward them. His chill got worse. What would make a noise like that?

I think we should leave, Rame thought.

Yesterday! Seth agreed.

The group took off, with Vidav in front, using his great strength to plow a course through the vegetation. They did not dare take giant steps with their magic boots, for fear of careening into trees, so had to run more or less hobbled; Vidav's effort really helped. Even mincing, they were zooming through the forest at eerie velocity, narrowly missing collisions. It was hard to imagine how any creature could keep up with this magic-assisted rush.

Yet the clicking sound grew louder. Whatever that thing was, it was fast! Unless the terrain changed and allowed them to make full use of their magic boots, they would be overhauled. That would solve the mystery of the pursuit, but Seth dreaded the answer. Running did not seem to be the solution.

"I think we will need to fight!" Rame shouted. "They are coming too fast!"

"My thoughts exactly!" Seth replied. Since the pursuing thing or things obviously knew where they were, speech made sense; it would be suspicious if their little party organized for defense without any dialogue to set it up. But their real plans would have to be silent. *I'll climb a tree and try to spot whatever it is first,* Seth volunteered. *The rest of you can set up an ambush, if we have to fight.*

The others agreed. While Seth climbed, placing his boots very carefully so that they would not send him sailing up out of the tree, Tirsa, Vidav and Rame nocked their arrows in preparation for battle. They were all good shots, thanks to either their prior skills or their recent training. But would arrows be enough?

Seth strained his eyes. All too soon he glimpsed something. *I see a patrol of about eight creatures,* he thought. *They appear to be large lizards, but I can't make out what kind.*

Listen to the clicking, Rame thought. *Does it follow a pattern of several in a bunch, with brief pauses?*

Yes, just like that. You recognize it?

They sound like Sateons, Rame replied. *The clicking comes from their legs, which are armored. They are intelligent creatures who follow Nefarious. They normally foray in packs of eight, and usually attack with poison darts. This won't be an easy fight!*

Ouch! That meant that one puncture or scratch could mean disaster, even if it seemed superficial. The tree would be no protection when they came close. *Why didn't the Emperor drill us on combat with Sateons?* he asked.

Because he was sure we would lose, Tirsa responded. *I read the concept in his mind, once. He wanted us to flee from any creature too dangerous, such as dragons and Sateons.*

And here they were trapped into battle, not properly prepared! Seth knew that a danger could not be thwarted by ignoring it; that was fundamental to his experience. But the Emperor wasn't versed in combat; he was a civilian general.

Seth jumped out of the tree as the first Sateon came into view. The creature paused, lifting its arm. Rame let his arrow fly in that moment, and it scored between the creature's eyes. Seth saw the thing spin about and fall, as he himself did something similar as he hit the ground and scrambled for cover.

Then four more creatures appeared. Immediately they fired their darts: two at Seth, and two in the direction from which Rame's arrow had come. The Sateons were alarmingly quick and apt!

Seth jumped behind a tree. The others were already hidden, not giving away their positions. But the

Sateons were advancing, and soon would reach and circle the trees. Their noses twitched; they were sniffing the scent of their prey. There was no way to avoid a fight.

Vidav stepped out and shot an arrow, but the Sateon saw his motion and dodged to the right. Seth stepped out, hoping to catch the creature while it was dodging the first arrow, but another Sateon oriented on him first. Those things might look like reptiles, but there was nothing slow or stupid about the way they reacted!

Seth jerked himself to the side. There was a zap, and a dart hit the tree next to him. That had been a perfect shot; only his desperate effort had saved him. But he had been trained in similar combat; even as he dodged, he was aiming his bow and loosing his arrow.

The large lizard tried to dodge again, but its inertia from the prior dodge slowed it, and Seth's arrow struck it on the leg. There was a clang as the arrow bounced off the creature's armor. His shot had been wasted after all!

Then he realized that there were only five creatures in front of him, including the one Rame had killed. Rame had indicated that there should be eight. Where were the other three?

Seth spun around. The Sateons had outflanked them, and the other three were somewhere at their backs. Then he saw them, about twenty feet behind his friends, and loading their tubes. *Look out behind!* Seth thought in warning.

Vidav turned and saw them. His tree was no protection against this! But he didn't flee. Instead he put his bow away and took hold of a small tree, hugging it. What was he doing?

Then the tree was ripped out of the ground. Seth stared; he had known Vidav was strong, but not *that* strong!

The Sateons also stared, forgetting for the moment to aim their dart tubes. Vidav hurled the tree, trunk, branches, roots and all, at the three Sateons behind. It crushed two of them immediately. The third managed to step aside. It put its mouth to the tube, but Seth was quicker, and scored on it with an arrow. This time he aimed for the face instead of the armored legs. The creature let out an ear-piercing scream before it fell dead.

Seth ran to the side of his tree, where he was shielded from the darts. The battle appeared to be a stalemate. The four remaining Sateons had retreated behind rocks and neither the Chosen nor the Sateons could hit each other.

"CHCHCHCHCH!" It was a loud noise coming from the Sateons behind their barriers. It was answered by a repetition of the sound in the distance.

"They are calling for reinforcements!" Tirsa yelled.

They were indeed, Seth realized. There were at least two sets of answering clicks, in different directions, which meant two other parties of eight. There would soon be about twenty Sateons to contend with! They would have to run, or face odds that would surely finish them. But as soon as they ran, they would be shot down.

Could they hold their shields to their backs while they fled? That might work for a while, but if they encountered a creature in front of them, there would be more trouble. Also, they had tried running before, and the lizards had gained on them. How could they get away and stay ahead? The Emperor seemed correct in his judgment: if they encountered Sateons, they were lost anyway, so there was no point in training them for this. But Seth couldn't accept that.

Time was running short. The clicking of the two other contingents was getting louder.

Then Seth had an idea that might save them. Quickly he conveyed it to the others, mentally. They weren't certain, but agreed that it seemed to be about their only choice.

They acted together. Rame threw his shield to Seth, and Tirsa threw hers to Vidav. Holding one shield to cover the back of his upper torso, and the other to cover his lower torso, Seth ran to Rame. The faun continued to fire at any Sateons who showed their heads, preventing them from charging. Tirsa covered Vidav similarly as he ran to her. Then the four of them joined, with Rame in front of Seth and Tirsa in front of Vidav. The two with the shields served as barriers to the enemy darts, while the two with their hands free were able to aim and fire their arrows from that moving cover.

They retreated, keeping their alignment. They had to move in lock-step to stay together, because of the way the boots magnified their forward motion. But when they got beyond arrow range, the Sateons jumped out and gave chase. At this point one of the other Sateon patrols arrived, and a barrage of darts hit the shields. The lizards would soon flank them and start making their darts count from the sides; there were too many to avoid for long.

Rame and Tirsa put their bows over their shoulders and drew their swords. They tried to chop at small trees and vines to clear a path, but this wasn't any better; the Sateons could still outrun them. If only they had been able to make it to a clear region, where their boots could have full effect!

Vidav swung his top shield to the side. The sharp edge of it clipped a small blue tree, felling it. There was an angry hiss behind as the tree crashed down on the pursuers, and the Sateons lost some ground. But in a moment they had scrambled around the tree and were gaining again.

Vidav felled another tree, this one larger, chopping through it with his shield. Seth was amazed again at the man's strength; it was beyond anything that normal flesh or bone should have been able to generate. Maybe it was akin to magic, following its own rules.

The second tree crushed several Sateons, and this slowed the pursuit of the group. Seth glanced at Vidav's back as they ran and realized that what he had presumed to be luck was not; the Sateons' darts had scored on Vidav when he moved the shield. But they had hit his backpack instead of his body.

Where are we headed? Seth thought to Rame, who had sheathed his sword and was now running with the map and compass. *We can't keep clear of them much longer!*

We should encounter a river soon, the faun responded. *We were going to have to cross it anyway, and it may just save us. These creatures will drown in the water because of the armor on their legs. They won't follow us across.*

Seth certainly hoped so! The clicking was getting louder. The Sateons had learned, and were now running to the sides instead of directly behind them. Vidav could no longer fell trees on them, only on the ones close behind, if they didn't dodge. Soon the ones on the sides would be able to start a crossfire of darts.

Then Seth heard another noise. It was a roaring sound: the river! The others heard it too. They increased the pace of their lock-step, encouraged.

The trees cleared and the river came into view. Seth's heart sank. It was a fairly wide stream with raging rapids that looked deep as well as swift. *We can't cross that!* he thought. *We'll be washed away!*

Not so! Vidav responded.

They came to the water's edge with the Sateons close behind. Seth gave Rame back his shield and Vidav returned Tirsa's.

"Rame!" Vidav shouted over the roar of water. "Give me your spool of rope!" The faun quickly obliged.

Vidav grabbed the rope and ran toward a large gray tree. "Cover me!"

The other three fired their arrows indiscriminately at the Sateons, sometimes having as many as ten arrows in the air at once in order to keep the lizards from taking aim at Vidav. They were using up their supply at a foolhardy rate. Under that cover, Vidav ran to the tree and tied the rope around the trunk. They had each been given fifty of the slender arrows in their quivers, but now they were running low. They could not continue this way; they would soon run out and be overwhelmed.

Vidav had lowered his shield as he worked on the rope. As the covering arrow fire eased, the enemy fire increased; evidently the Sateons had plenty of darts. One of them scored on Vidav's shoulder. Not stopping his work, he ripped the dart out and hurled it back at the Sateons. Then he used the edges of his shield to chop through the larger roots radiating from the tree. Finally he put his arms around the tree, heaved, and ripped it out of the ground.

The Sateons scrambled back; they knew what a tree that size could do to them! But Vidav wasn't aiming for them this time. He swung around and heaved the thing across the river. *Play, Rame!* he thought.

Rame, catching on, began to play his reed whistle. This caused the rope to expand and lengthen. The tree landed with a loud thud on the far bank of the river. Vidav grabbed the near end of the rope, made a quick lasso, and dropped it over a boulder about ten feet out from the shore. The Sateons would not be able to untie that!

The tree now on the opposite side was heavy, so they would be able to pull themselves across. Seth marveled again at Vidav's feat; it should have been impossible for the man to uproot such a tree simply by standing beside it, even if he had infinite strength: his feet would have sunk deep into the ground, being much smaller than the trunk of the tree. So it had to be akin to magic. Vidav had always said that strength could do a lot, but he hadn't demonstrated the full extent of it until now, and Seth had thought he meant just normal human strength.

They entered the rushing water. Vidav went first, forging through, followed by Tirsa and Rame. Tirsa was almost swept away by the terrible current, but Rame caught her, and Vidav tossed them the leftover end of the line and pulled them in. Seth brought up the rear, holding his shield behind him to prevent anyone from getting hurt. It was nervous business, because of the hail of darts, but the figures were bobbing constantly in the water, only their heads exposed, making difficult targets.

The Sateons ran to the water's edge, and for a moment Seth thought they would jump in, but they stopped at the brink and fired their darts. It was true: the Sateons couldn't handle the water.

"CHDCHDCHDCHDCHD!" the Sateons were screaming again. Surely, Seth thought as he hauled himself along the rope one-handed, if there were Sateons on the other side, they would not hear the call over the rage of the river. So the devastating current posed a barrier not only to the lizards' physical pursuit, but to their signaling system. He was getting to like this angry river!

Then he heard flapping, despite the noise of the water. Flying toward them was the dragon who had been searching for them before. The Sateons had not had to chitter across the river, just back the way they had come, and they had summoned their airborne ally!

Their group was only about a third of the way across. The dragon would reach them soon. *Look out above!* Seth thought to the others.

They tried to move faster, but the current was simply too strong for speed. The dragon had no such problem! There was a whining noise like that of a dive bomber as the dragon came down on them.

Get down! Rame thought unnecessarily.

Seth ducked under the water as a jet of flame issued from the dragon's mouth. When Seth came up again for air, there was steam rising from the top of the water where the fire had struck. The dragon was now beyond them, being unable to turn on a dime in mid-dive. Seth expected it to turn around for another strafing run, but it kept flying. Was one burst of flame all it could muster?

The dragon flew to where the rope was tied to the thrown tree, and shot a jet of flame. The rope caught fire and burned in half. Suddenly the monster's course made sense! They had lost their anchorage, and could not complete their crossing.

The four of them were carried downstream because of the broken rope. One end of it remained tied to the rock, but the rope no longer provided support, and they were dragged under by the raging current.

Let go of the rope and try to swim! someone thought. That made so much sense that Seth wondered why he hadn't thought of it himself. He let go, and stroked downstream, and in a moment his head broke the surface.

Already the swift current had carried him a good distance downstream. The Sateons and dragon were out of sight. Maybe they thought he was dead, so were no longer pursuing him.

Him? What of the others? They all knew how to swim; there had been a water session during training. But not in water like this! They were in no way safe, even if the enemy had forgotten all about them.

Seth looked around, but saw no other heads. The

current was too powerful to make it easy to swim to shore. He had to ride it out until the rapids ended, conserving his strength. He had been in rapids before, and knew that he should keep his feet up and float mainly on his back in order to prevent a leg from getting caught on the rocks. He might get his rear bumped, but that was a lesser evil.

He tried to float calmly, but the rapids threw him about, and the water was constantly in his eyes. He tried again to locate any of the others, but still couldn't see them.

Help! Was that Tirsa's thought? Where was she? He would try to swim toward her, but he had no idea of the direction.

Where are you? he thought, but got no answer. That gave him a chill that wasn't of the water.

Then he heard a louder roar above the rapids. Oh, no! He wiped the water from his eyes and peered downstream. He saw the water abruptly end. It was the dropoff of a waterfall!

Now he tried to stroke for the shore, urgently. But it was no use; the current was carrying him swiftly along. In a moment he was at the brink, and then he was over. His stomach seemed to fly into his throat as he fell, arms flailing. Was this the end?

Then he splashed into deep water about thirty feet down. What a relief! It was shallow, rocky water that was dangerous; deep water was fine.

He was drawn to the bottom by the surge of falling water. He did not try to surface, but simply held his breath and rode the undertow. When it eased, he dragged himself along the river bottom by grabbing onto whatever rocks he could find.

His lungs began to burn. He had to try to surface! His phobia of drowning in icy water was redeveloping. He would panic soon, and he knew that was no good. Pushing off the bottom, and praying that he had moved far enough away, Seth surfaced.

The waterfall was behind him, and the chaotic water near it did not extend this far down. He could float safely, now. But the current remained swift, and was still dragging him along. It was pointless to fight it.

Seth looked ahead and thought he saw calm water. What a blessing that would be!

But in that moment of his distraction, he let his feet sink. He heard his own cry of anguish before he became aware of the pain in his leg. It was wedged between two rocks! His body was abruptly stopped, and the current at his back forced him under.

He tried to kick free, but his leg was firmly stuck. He could not surface because the water bore him down. He needed leverage, to lift his head to breathe, and to move back upstream just far enough to free his leg. But he had no leverage. He was helpless.

Again his lungs were aching. Was he to drown a second time? No, this time he wasn't trapped under the ice, he reminded himself, and he had his sword. The bow and arrows had been washed away, but the harness for the sheath for the sword was worn around both arms, and the sword itself was strapped in.

Quickly Seth drew the sword and swung it through the water in front of him. He set the point on the riverbed and pushed straight down. But instead of giving him a good push upward, the blade sank into the soft muck of the river bottom.

He fought off his panic. He pulled the sword back, and moved it more carefully. He found a rock, and set the tip against it. Then, fighting hard against the current, Seth pushed himself to the surface. He sputtered for air. What a relief!

But he still had a problem. His leg remained wedged between the rocks, and he was using both arms to hold himself up. If he tried to change his position, he might be back the way he had been, drowning.

But he had one free foot. He moved that, feeling for the rocks that were holding his other foot. He managed to push himself backwards against the current, until at last his foot came out of the crevice. It was bruised and hurting, but he was free!

He quickly brought his legs up to the proper position, lifted his sword, and floated through the rest of the rapids. He had indeed seen calm waters, and soon he reached them.

Seth dragged himself to shore. Were the others all right? Were they even alive? He wanted to search for them, but as he stood his fatigue manifested overwhelmingly. He reeled, and collapsed on the ground.

Seth woke as a drop of water landed on his face. He pulled himself up against a tree—and felt a sharp pain in his right ankle.

Carefully he sat down and bent his knee so that he could inspect the ankle. It was swollen, but he could move it; it probably wasn't broken. He hadn't felt the pain as he staggered out of the water, but obviously the rocks and current had done some damage, and now that he wasn't struggling for his life, he really felt it. He didn't have any cloth suitable for tying around his ankle, so he looked for a stick to use as a cane. He had to do it on hands and knees, which wasn't much fun either.

After crawling around for a while, he found a branch with a V at one end to put under his arm. It was slightly long, but he cut off the pointed end a little with his sword. It would do until he found something better.

Using his new crutch, Seth stood up and looked around. If the others were alive they were probably between him and where they all had entered the river. After all, if they hadn't gotten out sooner, they would have climbed to shore where the rapids came to an end, which was right here. So they should be on the bank, upstream.

Unless they hadn't made it, and their bodies had been carried on downstream. . . .

But he refused to accept that notion. He would search for them and find them; that was all there was to it.

It had been starting to rain. He hadn't noticed before, but of course it had been one of the first drops on his face that had wakened him. Now the wind was picking up, and the drops were fatter and thicker. They rattled against the leaves of the nearest trees. His clothing remained soaking wet from the river, but was still helping to keep him warm; that was its magical effect. But he felt quite uncomfortable in spite of this, perhaps because of his memories of the icy lake in his home plane. He wished he could be back in the warm tent, with Tirsa holding his hand. Against his better judgment, and her discouragement, his feeling for her was growing.

Seth set his jaw and began to walk up the river. *Tirsa!* he thought as powerfully as he could. *Tirsa!*

There was no answer. He fought off the dread that came. First he had lost his family; he couldn't lose his friends too!

He began to run, clumsily, painfully, slightly panic-stricken at the thought of the others possibly being dead. What if they were? Would he continue the mission, or give up?

The rain was increasing. It was now quite a downpour. That made him think of home again. The Emperor had told them they could never return, but that had not quite penetrated the deeper levels of his belief. There had to be a way to get back!

His crutch slipped on the wet ground. His ankle sent a horrendous jolt of pain as he came down on it too hard, and he fell. How he wished he were home!

Seth, are you all right?

Joy suffused him. *Tirsa! Where are you?*

I'm with Rame. He found me unconscious, caught in a fallen tree that was hanging over the river. I just now got organized enough to re-establish the telepathic connection. Are you well?

I'm all right. Possibly a sprained ankle, but I can manage. His relief at receiving from her was pouring through, he knew, but he tried to keep it business-like. *How is Rame?*

Rame is fine. But I'm worried. I can't contact Vidav.

So three of them had made it through—and one

was in doubt. *He's so strong, he must have made it! Maybe he's out of range.*

I should be able to receive a faint signal anywhere on the planet, she responded. *On my home plane there are so many mental contacts that the signals become hopelessly jumbled with distance; it's a function of the number of communicants per unit of geography. But here there are only the four of us, and I am the only linker; there is almost no interference. There should be something from him!*

Now her alarm was coming through. Seth feared she had cause, but he knew that they had to be steady. He tried to broadcast a reassurance he did not feel. *We must get together; then we can concentrate on Vidav. He may have been knocked out, and a physical search will find him.* That made so much sense that he was encouraged himself.

Yes. Where are you?

Ask Rame if he saw a waterfall.

There is one near. We can hear it.

Then walk in the direction of the waterfall. I'm below it.

Below it? You went over it? Her alarm came through again.

The water was deep. I wasn't hurt. Then I caught my ankle in a crevice between two rocks, and almost drowned. He made a mental laugh. It would have been ironic to die in such a minor way, after getting past the main threat unscathed.

That's not humorous! she thought severely, picking up his private thought. Now there was a concern for him so genuine that he was flattered.

Seth got back to business. *Go toward the waterfall, and I will do the same. Which side of the river are you on?*

The side we were trying to reach.

Good. So am I. Keeping walking. Maybe one of us will find Vidav before we meet. He hoped!

Seth began to run despite his injury. He looked to right and left, hoping to spy an unconscious but living figure.

Soon he came to a cliff, the one where the water was cascading down. Rame and Tirsa were descending it. "You didn't see Vidav?" he asked verbally, knowing the answer.

"No." There were worry lines between her eyes. "We have to find him before it gets dark. Rame says there are nocturnal predators. That's why he brought us to the Fur-Gnome village last night; it was protected."

Seth trusted Rame's information! If Vidav was unconscious, he would be easy prey for anything that sought blood. But it was already beginning to get dark, and periodic claps of thunder suggested that the lull in the storm was temporary. There would be a torrential downpour!

They walked back the way Seth had come. Tirsa and Rame had checked the region above the falls carefully, and found no indication of Vidav's presence. He must have been carried over the falls, just as Seth had. He could be farther downstream, on either side.

Rame brought out his reed whistle and played it. For a moment Seth was irritated that the faun should be so cheerful in this dreary situation. Then he felt the healing in his ankle. Rame was playing a healing tune! Soon his leg was good enough to enable him to walk without the crutch, which was a wonderful feeling. "Thanks, friend!" he said.

They spread out so that they could cover a wider swath. Vidav might still be in the water, or washed up on the bank, or he might have crawled under a bush farther from the river. Seth was the one closest to the river, and he spied nothing but water.

"There!" Rame exclaimed, pointing.

It was Vidav, sure enough. He was walking slowly along the shore, downstream.

"But there is no mental contact!" Tirsa said, bewildered.

"Vidav!" Seth shouted. But the man did not turn around.

Seth began to run after him. "Seth, wait!" Tirsa shouted. "Something is wrong with him. I'm concentrating on his mind, and there is something there, but I can't read it."

"Maybe I can find out what's the matter," Seth called back, continuing to run. She had once called him an impetuous youth; he was being true to form!

He caught up to Vidav and grabbed his shoulder. "Hey, friend, remember me?"

Vidav turned, and Seth rocked back in horror. The man's face had a purple hue and his eyes were blank white, with no animation at all. Vidav opened his slack mouth in an effort to speak, but nothing came out other than a bit of drool. Then he collapsed.

"What happened?" Rame asked as he came running up.

"I don't know. Look at him! His heart is still beating but he doesn't seem alive. He's like a zombie!"

"He was hit by a dart, remember," Tirsa said, arriving on the scene. "We were so busy we hardly noticed, but I remember that he pulled it out and continued as if unaffected. Rame, do you know what type of poison the Sateons use?"

"They have more than one kind, depending on their need. For hunting they usually use one that stuns, so they can keep the meat alive for a while and prevent it from spoiling. But in combat they use the kind that kills almost immediately. I can only assume that the strength of his body, and the short time the dart was in, caused a partial effect. That might kill him slowly. Maybe my pipe can help him." He brought out his whistle again and played it diligently, but Vidav did not stir. It was obvious that it would require something more specific to cure this malady.

"Where is his backpack?" Tirsa asked.

"It's not on him," Seth answered. He started checking around the area. "If he had it when he came from the river, he might have dropped it by the bank, but it doesn't seem to be here. The river might have ripped it off him and carried it away. Our medical supplies were there; how can we help him without them?"

Rame ceased his futile effort with the whistle. "We shall have to get help. The elves might know what to do."

Seth's compass was still in his pocket, and Rame's map was still readable, so they were not lost. They could find the elf village.

The storm, however, seemed to be getting even worse. The rain had eased at times, but seemed to be only teasing them, for it always came back stronger. It was almost pitch black now.

"What should we do?" Seth asked. "We could press on, but we could get into even more serious trouble in this blackness."

"I agree," Rame said. "I can find my way by day and often by night, but this is unfamiliar territory and the storm makes it worse. I vote that we stay here, and tomorrow in the daylight we can go for the elf village."

Tirsa considered. "We must make a shelter, and eat, and Rame must resume playing, in case the effect is slow."

"First I will conjure some food," the faun said, and to that they agreed emphatically. Hunger had been forgotten during the crisis, but they did need to eat.

Seth took his sword and cut branches and saplings to fashion a crude shelter. He found large leaves and overlapped them to make an almost watertight covering. Then Rame conjured a good meal for them all. It was too wet to try building a fire, and in any event the smoke might have attracted the attention of the Sateons or a dragon. Rame was disappointed; he had wanted to try the "magic" flint in the pocket knife Seth had traded him. So they huddled together under the lean-to and ate, while the rain poured down just beyond. Vidav lay farther back; they had dragged him into the most protected part. Between bites of food, Rame played his whistle, sending the healing toward the unconscious man.

"At least he isn't getting any worse," Tirsa said. "Perhaps it is doing him some good, inside, and after a while he will be able to throw off the effect of the poison."

"I wonder whether it could have been the stunning kind," Seth said. "Is it possible that they had orders to capture us instead of kill us?"

"I really don't see why Nefarious would want to capture us," she said. "The moment we are dead, the only threat to his power will be gone."

Seth nodded. There didn't seem to be much point to capture. "I think we should maintain a watch during the night, so that nothing comes on us unawares. I'll take the first shift while the two of you sleep, and one of you can relieve me after a few hours."

"Yes, this is sensible," she said. "I will take the second shift, and then wake Rame for the third."

The other two crawled back and lay on either side of Vidav, their bodies helping to keep the unconscious man warm. Seth sat in front, at the fringe of the pouring water.

He had thought that the storm had reached its ultimate, but it grew yet another notch in intensity. The winds swooped in, catching at things, threatening to ruin their shelter. Jagged spears of lightning struck close by. Suppose lightning felled a tree and it crashed down on their heads, Seth wondered nervously. Ordinarily he would not have given such a notion a thought, but now it was easy to believe.

There seemed to be one benefit of the storm: no creatures appeared to be out hunting. Evidently they did not like this weather any better than the human party did.

Suddenly there was a crash in the bushes a few yards in front of him. Seth jumped up and drew his sword, moving slowly toward the noise. It was probably just a fallen branch, not worth waking the others, but he was not about to take a chance. One of the frequent flashes of lightning should illuminate it for him.

Now there was a commotion. Something seemed to be tangled in the brush. Seth raised the sword, ready to strike out immediately.

The lightning flashed, and he saw a wing flapping. That was no lizard! It seemed to be a large bird.

"Are you friend or enemy?" he asked, not expecting an answer. If the sound of his voice reassured the creature, he might be able to cut it free and let it fly away. He had always liked birds, and other non-hostile wild creatures.

The commotion stopped. The bird moved its head up to peer at Seth. He could see the faint glistening of its moist eyes. "I am unarmed. Please do not kill me," it said.

Seth almost dropped his sword. Then he remembered the background he had been given: some birds here were intelligent, and did speak the human tongue. Perhaps it was that the potion they had been given at the castle enabled the Chosen to understand the language of all creatures, not just men. "You're a friend?" he asked hesitantly.

"My kind is neutral to your kind," the bird replied, "but I sought to help you. The storm blew me out of control and into this snag bush. Please help me out of it. I will depart and leave you in peace after I have done what I came to do."

"No need, if you are friendly," Seth said, still marveling at this development. "We have shelter and food which you may share if you care to. We seek only to pass the night safely." He stepped forward and used his sword cautiously to cut the vines entangling the bird. His eyes had adjusted, and he could see just enough.

Now he thought to look at the tassel on his sword. It was white, indicating no physical danger. Why hadn't he thought to check that before?

"I thank you, Man. I am a Fleigh, and I accept your kind offer, as I prefer not to risk myself again in flight through this storm."

A Fleigh. Now Seth's memory focused on what he had learned, and it was as if he were opening a book to the correct page. This was a civilized creature that lived in colonies, loosely allied to humans. It was about as tall as Seth himself, with a wingspan of about ten feet and beak and claws that could do a lot of damage when it chose to. But the word of this bird could be trusted, he remembered.

He unhooked the last of the barbs that were caught in the creature's wings. He had to work carefully, because the feathers were delicate and the barbs were cruelly sharp. The Fleigh stood quite still.

"The storm is pretty bad," Seth remarked. "But I wouldn't think it could blow such capable creatures as your kind is off course. You must have been flying very low."

"I was. I saw you today when you were under fire. I was flying to my home to get armed help, but when I saw a dragon coming I had to hide on the ground for fear of being burned out of the air. The dragon saw me but did not attack; it flew toward you four. I flew up after it passed and saw it flame your rope. After the Sateons and the dragon left I flew down the river hoping to find you."

"Hold it," Seth interrupted. "Do you mean to say you know who we are?"

"Of course. Your weapons and clothing are those

of the Emperor's Royal Guard, and the Fleighs are allied to the Emperor. I did not find you then, but I did find this.'' The bird indicated something behind it, that had before been hidden in the darkness.

Seth stared in amazement. The Fleigh had brought them their Vidav's pack, with the tent and stove! But there seemed to be little point in trying to set up the tent now; the lean-to was doing the job.

"I continued to search the area in the hope of finding you, but when the storm got this bad I began to fly back. I tried to carry your bundle, but it bore me down. The wind buffeted me, and caught the bundle, and that threw me off. I could have recovered, had I not already been flying so low and had the rain not interfered with my flight. That is why I crashed.''

"We aren't the Royal Guard, you know. We're the Chosen.''

The bird spread its wings slightly, surprised. "Then it is even better that I found you, even if by accident! Take your bundle.''

Seth eagerly took the pack. The top strap had broken and the shelter and stove-pipe had fallen out. Ouch! He felt the bottom, and found one container of medicine. That was what they needed!

Seth, where are you? What's going on? It was Rame's thought.

Important news! Seth returned. *I have found a friend!*

"Come and meet the rest of our party," Seth said to the Fleigh. They walked together back toward the impromptu shelter. The rain was entering another remission, but he didn't trust it.

Tirsa was also getting up. "This is a Fleigh, who

brought us Vidav's pack, and there is medicine in it!" Seth said, keeping it verbal so that the bird would not catch on to their secret mode of communication. There was no point in being careless with their secret. "And these are my companions, Rame and Tirsa."

Rame took the pack. "Is this all that was left?" he asked, taking out the medical kit. "It is one of the weaker versions, and may not be enough."

"The rest fell out," Seth said. "But half a loaf is better than none."

"Half a loaf of what?" Tirsa asked, perplexed.

"I mean that little is better than nothing," Seth explained. Something else was bothering him. Something the bird had said. Why would the Emperor have them dress in clothing that would make them easily recognized?

Then he thought of something else. "Rame, play your whistle over the medicine."

"Why? I can't conjure that sort of thing."

"I'm curious. Please humor me."

Rame shrugged and played his reed whistle. A foul note sounded. "That can't be!" he exclaimed. "It's poison!"

Seth nodded as things fell into place. "The Emperor sabotaged our quest. He gave us bad medicine that would kill us instead of curing us when we got in trouble. He also garbed us in clothing and gave us weapons that would immediately let our enemies know who we are. We are marked."

Rame stared, astonished and appalled. "But why?"

"It couldn't be the Emperor," Tirsa said. "When I first arrived I was reasonably suspicious, and I checked the Emperor's thoughts thoroughly. They were complex, and I couldn't read all the levels, but I am sure he wants us to be successful, even if he doubts that we will be."

"Could he have stopped you from finding out the truth?" Seth asked. "You said that on your plane it could be done."

"It is true that mind blocks can be established. But he is not from my plane, and does not know telepathy. He had no mind block, only such a complicated mixture of emotions relating to the Chosen that I could not fathom it all. If there has been sabotage, it must have been someone else."

"One of the spies!" Rame exclaimed.

"No, they did not do anything, they only observed; I read that in them," she said. "Except for that maid, what's her name, Domela, who had a passion for Vidav, because she is impressed by strength. But I suppose that if there is someone high up, who might benefit if the Emperor's plan fails, he might have done it."

"So he could take over!" Seth said. "If the Emperor was discredited!"

"Yet the Emperor saw us in our Empire clothing," Tirsa said. "He felt no alarm over that. Why should he set us up so foolishly?"

"Maybe he had bad advice," Seth said. Yet he wondered. Who could have given that advice, except Turcot—who surely was loyal? Something remained odd, here.

"I do not understand," the bird said. "If you did not wear the Empire clothing, how would we know you?"

"Could it be that simple?" Tirsa asked. "It never occurred to them that what made us identifiable to the friends of the Empire also made us vulnerable to its enemies?"

"That doesn't explain the poison medicine," Rame responded grimly.

"But that could have been done separately, by a spy," she said. "I did not think to check for that, in their minds, and might not have been able to fathom it anyway."

"In the morning we should camouflage our clothing," Seth said. "The two of you should cover any distinguishing marks on your swords." He glanced at Rame. "Since you gave me this sword, Rame, I won't need to cover it."

"I still don't understand," the bird said. "How does Empire clothing make you vulnerable? It should frighten the enemies of the Empire."

"Excuse me," Seth said. "What is your name?"

"I am Brieght."

"I will answer your question, Brieght. If we wear the Empire clothing and weapons, our friends will know us, true. But we are going into enemy country, and so our enemies will also know us. Our friends won't kill us, but our enemies will. Indeed, they almost did! So we need to be anonymous."

The bird's eyes widened. "Oh, I see! That is true!"

"Do you think you could fly to your village in the morning and bring good medicine for our friend?"

"He was the one shot by the Sateon?"

"Yes. A dart hit him, but he pulled it out."

"Then I am afraid that any medicine we have would have little or no effect. The Sateons use powerful poison that we cannot combat, as we have learned to our sorrow. He is lucky to be alive. To where are you going tomorrow?"

"The elf village."

"They may be able to help you. They fight the Sateons. One of their number is a wizard and could possibly help your friend. If you like I will fly above you and scout for enemies while you hike."

"That's not necessary," Rame said. "You've helped us enough, and if you are with us Nefarious could spot us easier."

"I won't be with you, I will be flying above you. I insist, it is the least that I could do for the Chosen."

"Then we thank you," Rame said. "Seth, it's about time for me to take over the watch so you can sleep."

That was right! He had forgotten about the watch. "Thanks."

Seth, Tirsa and Brieght went farther into the shelter, settled down around Vidav, and went to sleep.

He walked up his front steps. His key was out, and he put it to the door. It did not fit. He tried to turn it, but nothing happened. Yet he knew it was the right key, the one he had always used.

He heard a scream from inside. Seth ran over to the window and peered in. His mother was screaming, backed up against the wall. There was a man with a flowing black cape in the house, his back to Seth.

What was going on? Why couldn't he get in to help his family? Who was the man in black?

Seth woke in the lean-to. The storm was still going full thrust. Tirsa had taken over the watch from Rame; the faun was asleep, as was Brieght, his head tucked under a wing. It looked as if it was getting closer to morning, for a reluctant grayness was nudging at the blackness at the front of the lean-to.

He lay back and returned to sleep.

Seth charged the front door, put his shoulder hard against it, and burst open the lock. He crashed into the house.

His mom was sitting on the kitchen table with her head in her hands, crying. But before Seth could investigate that, he heard a scream from upstairs. That was his sister!

He turned and charged up the stairs. His sister's room was at the end of the hall. He ran, but the hall was too long; it continued interminably. He kept running. The doors flew past on the sides, but he was no closer to his sister's room than he had been when he reached the top of the stairs.

Then Seth stopped running, but the walls to the side continued to move past faster and faster. He was getting dizzy at the speed of this impossible movement. He seemed to be on a conveyor belt, being carried along at a racing pace no matter what he did. How could any of this be happening?

Suddenly the walls came to a stop. Seth's body was thrown forward. He slammed into the door of his sister's room, knocking it open.

Ferne was sitting at her desk with the desk lamp on, doing her homework. Seth, dizzy, walked slowly over to her. He was half afraid that she would turn out to be made of ice. But this was a different dream, wasn't it?

The door slammed shut behind him. Seth spun

around, but no one else was in the room. He turned back, and his sister was gone. What had happened to her? She hadn't melted, for there was no puddle of water. Had she been a ghost?

He returned to the door and tried the knob, half expecting it to be locked. It wasn't; it opened readily.

Two scaly clawed hands grabbed Seth's neck. They tightened and lifted him off the ground, gasping. He stared into the twisted face of the man with the black cape. But it was not a man, it was Nefarious!

Seth struggled to free himself from the deadly grip, but was helpless against this powerful creature. His feet dangling in the air, his body limp, he lost consciousness.

• Eight

Trek

Seth woke and looked out of the shelter. It was still raining, though the storm had died down considerably. Tirsa was on watch, and the sun was beginning to rise over the horizon—or so the foggy patch of light to the east suggested.

Apparently his bad dream had been routine, not a sending, because he had come out of it on his own and the others did not seem to be suffering similarly. His concern about the possibility of betrayal by the Emperor must have sent him into it. But it did seem more likely that the Emperor was straight, and that a spy had sabotaged the medicine.

Seth climbed over Rame's sleeping figure and crawled over to Vidav. The man's face remained purple, but when Seth pulled up his eyelid he saw that the pupil and iris had returned to normal. That was an improvement!

Rame woke, and also took a look at Vidav. "I'm afraid he's not looking much better, but at least he's no worse. We will need to reach the elf village today, and get help there but how will we move him?"

"I may have an idea," Seth said. "You and Tirsa camouflage yourselves, to prevent easy recognition, and I will work on the problem of moving him." Seth and Rame left the shelter and told Tirsa of Vidav's condition; then the three set about their specific jobs, eating fruit on the run.

After submitting to a call of nature, Seth searched about for an appropriate plant. In a few minutes he found a tree covered with fairly strong orange vines. He took the dagger Rame had given him and cut a vine into fifteen sections, each about three feet long. He tied these branches together with the vines about five inches apart from each other, and then carried it back to the others.

Tirsa and Rame had chopped vines off the snag bush and hooked them into their clothing. They had also taken mud and smeared it over their jackets, pants and faces. Seth did the same, then helped to cover Vidav.

Rame found a use for the poison medicine: they spread it on their clothing, and it repelled the insects that now sought to attack them. "It's an ill wind!" Seth remarked, and then had to explain that for the others: this ill wind of the poison had brought them a bit of good after all.

They ate breakfast with Brieght in a hurry; there could be no time wasted if they were going to keep Vidav alive. Seth showed them how to carry Vidav using the improvised stretcher. They placed him on the stretcher and picked it up. Seth put a branch on each shoulder, with the stretcher behind him, and Tirsa put a branch on each shoulder with the stretcher in front of her. This made the carrying much easier. Even so, Seth was glad that Tirsa was a pretty strong woman, for Vidav was one solid weight.

Rame walked in front, with the map and compass. There was no need to draw his sword, as Brieght would warn them of any approaching danger. Rame would switch with Tirsa when she became tired, and Tirsa would switch with Seth when he became tired. This rotation, he hoped, would allow them to travel without resting too long. Delay could be fatal, to Vidav and perhaps to them all, if another dragon spied them.

They set out. The river crossing hadn't washed them far off course, and if they kept a good pace and hiked partially into the night they should be able to reach the elf village. Vidav's weight slowed them down, while their magic boots speeded them up, and this resulted in an approximately normal walking pace.

The rain finally stopped, but the clouds hung overhead, threatening more at any time. Could this be the mischief of Nefarious, he wondered, invoking the weather itself to hamper their effort? That seemed fantastic yet in this world of magic, it might indeed be possible.

Relieved of the beat of rain and the restricted vision the fog had caused, Seth noted the splendor of the forest. They were beginning to see more animals, wildlife, and plants not found in civilized regions. A number of them were intriguing, but not because of their alien quality. In fact, some of the smaller animals came incredibly close to looking like some of the smaller Earth animals he knew, such as rabbits and squirrels. Did that suggest that in its natural state, this plane was closer to his own world than it had seemed?

"Is your Earth as lovely as this?" Rame asked.

"Mine is," Tirsa said. "But it is also very different."

"My Earth is also beautiful," Seth said. "But not

everywhere. Some of the places that used to look this way have been destroyed for reasons that can't be justified."

"Such as war?" Rame asked.

Seth scowled. "War is one reason. There are others."

"You know," Tirsa said, "even if we destroy Nefarious, his minions will probably still wage war."

What of the Teuton Empire, Seth thought. *Isn't it warlike too?*

"Yes," Rame said, acknowledging both the spoken and mental comments. "Earth Plane 4 has never seen a war with the magnitude that this one promises. There are of course minor skirmishes, such as those between villages, but the outcome of this war could be very damaging, to say the least."

"Is it possible that if we destroy Nefarious a war can be avoided altogether?" Seth asked.

"It's hard to say. If we destroy Nefarious, then the human species and its allies will have a good chance for victory. But avoiding war? I doubt it. The tension between the good civilizations and the corrupted civilizations has been building for centuries. Both sides have armies primed and ready for battle, but both sides have been waiting and looking for some clear advantage. Nefarious is now that advantage."

"Nefarious has been alive for quite a while," Tirsa said. "Why is he an advantage to his side only now?"

"Until a year ago the Teuton Empire had a sorcerer of great talent," Rame explained. "He was not as strong as Nefarious, but his help in battle would have been significant, so that there was no clear advantage on either side. He was killed by a spell

brought into his house by one of Nefarious's creatures. At least, that is what we assume."

"You assume?" Tirsa asked. "You mean you aren't
sure whether Nefarious sent the creature?"

"We aren't sure that he is dead. His home completely vanished, and he with it. So the spell either
destroyed him, or transported him to some place
where he was helpless. Certainly he hasn't been seen
since."

"Why then," Seth asked, "didn't Nefarious attack
a year ago?"

"I really don't know. It may be because though he
is powerful, he could not destroy the allied forces
alone, and the evil ones are unorganized, often fighting among themselves, as most evil creatures do. He
had to take the time to make alliances, and to organ-
ize and train the armies."

"No enemies in sight!" came a call from Brieght.

"Thank you, friend!" Rame yelled. "Keep up the
good work!"

"Seth!" Tirsa exclaimed. "Stop walking. Vidav just
moved his hand!"

Seth hadn't seen Vidav, as he was carrying the front
of the stretcher. They stopped and put the big man on
the ground. Seth became aware of the burden he had
been carrying as he got free of it; Tirsa hadn't com-
plained, but she must have been sorely fatigued. Of
course their magic boots had been helping, supplying
extra lift instead of forward motion, so that they could
all carry far more than otherwise. Still, this was no fun
excursion!

Vidav was indeed looking better. The purple hue
seemed to be fading, and his eyes looked normal.

"Can you talk to him through your mind power?"

"No, I've been trying, but his mind is still not functioning," she said. "I hope that this is merely because his body is healing first, and that his brain will recover in its turn. The poison may have stunned it without permanently damaging it."

"We had better keep moving," Rame said. "Tirsa had the last break; I'll switch with you this time, Seth."

"That's fine," Seth agreed. "I'm not that tired, but I'll take the lead." Yet he had been tired enough to have forgotten that they had been switching out, and his shoulders were turning leaden. He knew he needed the rest.

Rame and Tirsa picked up the stretcher again. Now Seth saw how worn Tirsa looked; facing forward, he had not been able to observe her before. She was sweat-soaked and grimy, and her hair hung in straggles, the luster of its zebra striping lost. The weight had to be worse for her than for him, yet she had not let on. She was some woman, and not just because of her appearance (which wasn't much, at the moment) or her intelligence and telepathic ability.

Please spare me the obvious, she thought at him, but there was tired humor in it.

Somewhat guiltily, he faced forward, taking the lead. But he felt compelled to maintain a dialogue, perhaps to put something between them and his embarrassing thoughts of a moment before. "Tirsa, what about war? I mean, is there a lot of fighting in your plane, even with the mental contact?"

"No, our planet is very peaceful," she replied. Now he was aware of the slightly labored quality in her voice, and he felt another bit of guilt for making her talk when it was all she could do to carry the heavy burden of their companion. "There is no physical violence, though there have been known to be a few psychic battles now and then. I'm afraid that this war business will be quite new to me. I would prefer not to have to find out about it."

"If you don't mind my asking," Rame said, "you are obviously too young to die of old age, Tirsa. Without violence, how did you end up here?"

"I am not ready to tell you the whole truth, but I will tell you part of it," she said. "I did not die of natural causes, nor did I die at the hands of someone else. I took my own life."

"You killed yourself?" sputtered Seth. "Why, if you loved your family and your world, and had such perfect communication with others, why would you kill yourself?"

"There are aspects to perfect communication that become difficult. At the time, I thought I had sufficient cause. In retrospect I am less certain. I now think that something in my head, at an unconscious level, wanted me to do it. I felt as if I were needed somewhere else. Apparently I was. I really did not want to die; I knew the pain it would cause my family and my lover, but I also knew that it had to be done. I am glad now to realize that the attempt must have failed on my plane and my family at least has my double, who perhaps lacks the fatal flaw I possess. I miss my family, but if what we are doing here can save their lives, then it must be worthwhile."

Seth was taken aback by more than one aspect of her statement. It had never occurred to him that she could be the suicidal type! But of course she wasn't; it must have been the impulse of the Chosen, reaching across the planes to tag the three of them who had to come here. He had thought his own drowning was coincidental, and now knew that it was not; similarly, her suicide would not have been her own idea, however much it might have seemed like it at the time.

Another aspect was her passing reference to her lover. Seth had somehow thought of her as pristine, untouched by emotion or affairs of the flesh. But of course she was human, with the interests and passions of the human kind. She had been forthright about this from the outset of their association, advising him that she was interested in romance but not with him. Of course she had a lover! He had allowed his foolish image of her to cloud the reality, though the reality was far more credible and admirable than the image.

Third, she had spoken of a fatal flaw that had made her think that death was the only way out. She had not died, but she seemed to believe that the flaw remained. What could it be? Certainly there was nothing he had ever observed about her that was less than admirable.

Thank you, she thought wryly, and he jumped. He had to stop thinking so freely!

No, your thoughts are naive but honest, and they become you. I would not have minded resembling either your prior image of me or your present one, though both are false.

Both false? The first, maybe; but the second image had the authority of his recent experience with her. She was a good woman, even if she chose not to believe it herself. But why didn't she believe it?

"How was it with you?" Tirsa inquired aloud. "If your dream was any indication, it had something to do with ice."

Seth had to wrench himself out of his consideration of her and reorient on his own situation. "Yes. The last thing that happened to me on my Earth was a fight. There really wasn't any reason why we were attacked, but now it makes sense. During the fight I ran from my friend who needed my help. I don't know why I ran. I hated myself for running. But I didn't stop. Now maybe I understand why." He went on to describe the way he had drowned in the icy lake.

In a few minutes the rain began again, and the group stopped talking. Seth noticed that the terrain was changing; in the distance were gray snowcapped mountains. The mountains did not appear to be a problem; in fact it seemed that their group had intercepted a path that might take them through the easier slopes. This was not a main path on the map, which was mainly topological with the exception of marked villages and the main Teutonian path. They decided to follow it, since there was unlikely to be much traffic on it, and it did go the way they needed, and they did want to make good time. There was no telling whether Vidav's condition would continue to improve. It was best to get him to whatever help was available.

"Before my dad died we did a lot of camping," Seth remarked. "I realize that many mountains may look the same to a stranger, but these look incredibly like the Grand Tetons. That's a mountain range in Wyoming."

The others gave him a curious look.

"Uh, Wyoming is a state, er, an area of land in the country, er, region I live in." Who would have thought that such an innocent statement could become so clumsy!

They kept walking. At the crest of the first hill Seth gasped in astonishment. In the valley below was a beautiful area of grass, trees, and a brilliantly blue lake. The rocky mountain peaks surrounded it. What made this astonishing was that Seth had seen an identical sight while hiking the Tetons with his dad. "This is amazing! The only thing missing are the bears."

There was a horrendous roar from behind a nearby boulder. Seth immediately drew his sword. From behind the boulder walked a grizzly bear, about fourteen feet in height and standing on its hind legs.

"What is it?" Rame yelled in unsuppressed astonishment and terror.

"It's a bear," Seth yelled back. "The grandaddy of all bears! What's it doing on your plane?"

There was no time to answer. The bear charged forward. Seth swung with his sword. The blade sliced through the bear's midsection and Seth stepped back. The bear, however, wasn't hurt; the sword had done no damage. In fact, there had been no impact. Had he missed?

The bear swung its massive paw. Seth raised his sword, but the clawed digit passed through it and came right at his face. He didn't even have time to scream— before the paw passed through his head. He had been braced for impact and pain, expecting to be smashed to the side, but felt nothing. What had happened?

Then Seth noticed his outstretched sword. Its tassel was white. He was in no physical danger. "How can this be?" he asked, mesmerized by the monstrous bear before him.

"It can't be real," Rame said as the bear let out another very convincing roar. "Its hand passed right through you. It must be an illusion."

As Rame spoke, the bear disappeared.

The faun did a double take. "When I said it couldn't be real, it was gone!"

"And when I thought about a bear," Seth said, "one appeared, only it wasn't solid, it was an illusion."

"I think that's the answer," Rame said. "Much of the surrounding land of Earth Plane 4 has collective individual magic. This region, maybe just this particular mountain, produces illusion invoked by our thoughts. Maybe one of us should think of something, preferably something that won't frighten us in the manner your big bear did."

Could this relate to telepathy? Seth didn't like the notion, because it meant that their secret mode of communication could become known. But maybe this was more general. They communicated in words, while the bear had been more like a picture. People said that one picture was worth a thousand words, but there were occasions when it was the other way around.

"Let's think of our families and friends," Seth suggested. "See if they appear."

The others nodded. Seth thought of his mother and sister and his friend Rian. They appeared, look-

ing completely lifelike. But that wasn't the limit.
Rame's hamadryad Malape appeared, and several
others that he didn't recognize. Those were surely
Tirsa's conjurations; indeed, one of them did seem
to look like an older version of Tirsa herself. Her
mother? The figures looked around exactly as if
alive, and walked here and there, but then two of
them walked right through each other without notic-
ing. They were illusions, sure enough.

The three living folk stood in silence, each one
wishing that he or she were home, but knowing that
this was not going to happen. There was no joy, at this
moment.

"We need to keep moving," Tirsa reminded them.
"I think it would be best if we wished them away."

Rame nodded. With that all the people vanished
except Seth's, and as he concentrated, those did too.

But even then, one remained, one whom none of
them had summoned. He was a large man who resembled Vidav, except that he was slightly
transparent. Seth, Rame and Tirsa looked at each
other, and then at Vidav's motionless body.

Then the figure spoke. "I am not all right. If we do
not reach the elf village in time I may jeopardize the
entire mission. The poison in the dart was not lethal; it
was intended only to stun. But it contained a bacterial
culture, and the bacteria developed into a parasitic
creature that is trying to take over my body. Right now
it is lodged in my spinal column, preventing my nerve
impulses from carrying out messages, which is why I
can hardly move. It is also battling me mentally, which
is why I couldn't reach you before, or respond to you.
The magic in this region, however, enhances the abil-

ity to transmit thought, so I am able to reach you, briefly. My body will continue to recover; however, if the creature takes over my mind ..."

The others understood what Vidav couldn't say: if his mind was taken over by a creature of Nefarious, he himself would became a creature of Nefarious. The attack of the Sateons had been more devious than they had thought! Only by this coincidental event had they discovered the real danger it posed to them. The evil sorcerer couldn't lose, Seth realized; had they drowned, he would have been rid of them, and if they survived infected by organisms that served him, they would pose no threat to him. Maybe the Teuton Empire wasn't perfect, but it certainly seemed better than Nefarious!

They walked down to the lake and trees. There were liana vines associated with the trees. They cut several and used them as ropes, binding Vidav's arms and legs securely. These might not hold him for long if he became fully active, but they should restrain him long enough to represent a safety factor.

It was ironic, Seth thought, that the physical improvement they had noted in their friend was no longer cause for joy, but for alarm. A physically perfect enemy was no blessing!

They finished the job and were about to resume their march. Seth looked up at the clouds. The storm was clearing away at last; there would be no more rain. But something twinged in his stomach. "Where is Brieght?"

The others looked up, startled. Seth drew his sword. The tassel was jet black.

For a moment he froze. When the bear had

charged him, the tassel had been white; now that all seemed serene, it was black. He trusted the tassel—but what was the threat they faced now?

No one spoke, or even projected any thoughts, because in this region those thoughts could become all too evident. The others moved Vidav's stretcher into the spreading branches of a sprawling tree, where he was concealed by the foliage. With luck he would be safe from any outside menace. Then they drew their swords and looked warily around. There seemed to be nothing.

They formed a line and walked slowly in the direction they planned to go. If that proved to be safe, they would return to carry Vidav to a new hiding place. As long as the tassel remained black, they could afford to take no chances.

There was a snap behind them. They spun around.

Two women were standing there. They must have stepped in from the side, perhaps from behind a tree, after the three passed them. They were not pretty specimens, though definitely female; their hair was bound into efficient knots to keep it clear of their faces, and they wore single-piece tunics over rather stout bodies. Their faces were set into similar looks of arrogant appraisal. They seemed to be unarmed.

This was the danger that turned the tassel black? Seth found that hard to believe. But he wasn't going to dismiss the warning without learning more. Maybe these were monsters who only looked like women, in order to lull their prey until they could get within striking range. Yet if that were the case, why weren't they beautiful? An unpretty siren did not lure many sailors to their doom!

One woman lifted her hand, making a peculiar gesture. There was a shaking of the tree in the direction she seemed to point to. Then Vidav's stretcher floated out of the foliage.

Seth stared. She was using telekinesis—or more likely magic—to lift that heavy body as if it were so much mist. No wonder these women weren't armed! With power like that, they needed no weapons.

The woman hissed—and the stretcher broke in half. Vidav dropped painfully to the ground.

That did it. The tassel was right. As one, Seth, Rame and Tirsa charged with their swords.

And stopped. They were abruptly unable to move. They did not fall, they merely froze in place, as if caught in invisible hands.

"Dx nxt xttxck xs!" hissed one of the women.

Why couldn't he understand them, since he now could understand all the human folk of this plane? Did that mean that these were not human? Yet he could almost figure it out. It was a matter of filling in the vowels.

Do not attack us, Tirsa supplied.

Now Seth felt a painful throbbing in his gut. He doubled over and fell to the ground. Tirsa and Rame were undergoing similar pain, for they too were falling. His stomach was being twisted internally until the pain intensified to a point where he could no longer breathe. The strange women were punishing them for their attempted attack! In a few seconds he lost consciousness.

* * *

Seth looked up from the table where he and his dad were having dinner. They had just finished a camping trip and were eating at a diner on the way home. Seth was only eight and his father looked young and healthy. There was no sign of the cancer that would take his life in the years to come. It was late at night and there were only a few others.

A car pulled up outside. Seth turned to look, routinely curious about everything that happened near him. Strapped to the hood of the car was the corpse of a deer.

"Daddy, look what they caught!" Seth whispered, motioning at the two men who had just entered the establishment, and then to the car outside. "Can I go look?"

"If you like," Mr. Warner replied, expressing no emotion.

He glanced at his father, for there was a strange look in his eyes. But Seth was too innocent to think much of it. He ran happily out to the car, to see the animal. He fancied it was like a stuffed toy, a pretend bear or tiger.

Stepping close to the car, he extended his hand. He touched the deer's fur. It was soft, but not warm. He drew back his hand and walked to the deer's face.

That look changed his life. The eyes of that creature burned into Seth's mind. This was no stuffed toy! The look on the deer's face—its last look—was an expression not of horror, but of innocence.

Seth moved over and saw the wound where the creature had been shot. Now he realized that it had been killed, and he had heard of killing, and seen it in cartoons; this had not quite registered on the vis-

ceral level before. The deer itself had not compre-
hended its fate. Now he understood that innocent
gaze. What could such a creature know of death?

Why had it been killed? There was no justifica-
tion! No need by the hunters to survive. They had
slaughtered this beautiful, living creature for fun.

Seth began to cry as the feeling of grief and anger
built up in his heart. He turned from the awful scene,
ran inside, and stumbled into his dad, sobbing.

Mr. Warner was quick to comfort him. He was
against hunting, but had let Seth look at the deer in
order to allow him to form his own opinion. Perhaps
he had known how Seth would react, but thought it
best for the child to find out in his own way.

Seth continued crying as Mr. Warner tried to calm
him down. He was not ordinarily the kind of child
who cried, but this vision of the deer had struck at a
level other than the physical, and it disturbed him
deeply.

"Will you shut that kid up!" a man yelled from
across the room.

"I'm sorry," Mr. Warner replied. "Seth, it's okay.
Let's get back in the car and we can talk about it."

That was one thing Seth liked about his father: he
always wanted to talk things out. But Seth continued
to cry.

"I said shut him up or I'll shut him up for ya!" The
man had been drinking. Mr. Warner quickly stood
up to leave, taking Seth by the hand.

The trucker also stood, apparently hoping for a
fight. "Where ya going so quick, wimp?"

It would take more than that to get Mr. Warner to
fight. He was strongly against violence, and hoped

Seth would turn out the same. Now was the perfect time to show the boy how to walk away from a fight. He walked toward the door.

"It's just like your kind not to fight back, dirty Jew."

Mr. Warner stopped cold. He was wearing a chain with the Star of David on it. He wore it everywhere, and was proud of his religion. His hands began to clench into fists.

Then he felt Seth's little hand trembling in fear, and calmed down. He did not say anything, but resumed his walk to the door.

The drunk would not leave well enough alone. He picked up a bottle and charged from the side. Now there was no avoiding trouble.

Mr. Warner pushed Seth away so that he would be clear of the action. He spun around and grabbed the drunk's outstretched arm. He shoved his hip into the man's gut, wrenched the arm still clutching the bottle over his shoulder, and flipped the man hard onto his back. The air rushed out of the man, and he lay still. He would be all right, but for now he was out cold.

Mr. Warner took Seth's hand again, and they walked on outside. There was no sound from the men in the diner. The two of them got into the car, and Mr. Warner began to drive. As the car pulled slowly out of the parking lot, Seth saw into the diner, through the windows, as people were clustered over the unconscious drunk, amazed.

"Seth, let me explain this to you," Mr. Warner said gently. "I know that when you are older you may have your own ideas, but for now I want you to hear mine.

First, about the deer: I do not believe in hunting, probably for the same reasons you began to cry when you saw the deer. Man does not have the right to take the life of another living creature, or even to hurt it intentionally. Animals were put on this Earth by God, just as we were. The only one who can determine life is the one who gives it." He paused, and Seth thought of those great innocent eyes of the deer, and nodded. Never again would he accept death casually, even the mock death of a cartoon.

"There are, however, certain times when defending yourself is necessary. When that man attacked me, I had to act, and then I did so to good effect, but not to any greater degree than the situation required. You should try to avoid these situations, as I did, but you should also know when a physical confrontation is necessary, and how to handle it appropriately. You do not want to become a deer, but you also do not want to become a tiger, hunting and killing others. Do you understand what I'm telling you?"

Seth thought about how his dad had tried to stay out of trouble, even walking away when the man had called him a name. How he had put the man down hard, but not killed him or tried to hurt him further once he was down. His dad might have looked like a deer at first, and like a tiger when he acted, but in the end he had been a man.

Seth nodded his head slowly. He was young, but he did understand, and that understanding was to deepen with time.

He woke to discover tears in his eyes. He had not

before dreamed of his father, since his death. He contemplated the memory, which was now fresh in his mind. That day meant more to him now than it ever had before. He realized that he still did carry his father's values, and that what his dad had told him about knowing when to fight was very important right now. Soon there were likely to be numerous deaths.

The tears stopped, letting Seth's vision return. But like a tremendous weight being pressed upon him, the gravity of their current situation returned to his attention. This time, waking was no relief from dreaming; indeed, the opposite was the case.

He was in a cave, tied at ankles and wrists. Tirsa and Rame were lying at different sides of the room. In the middle was a solid fire with something roasting on it; the smell of the meat suffused the chamber.

There was a commotion from somewhere beyond. Seth craned his neck to look. Two of the women were carrying Vidav. Peering closer, Seth saw that Vidav was actually floating; they were merely guiding him. Once he was in the cave, his body descended, and he was still.

Something nagged Seth's mind. He looked back at the fire, at the thing roasting. It was a large fowl, no, it was Brieght! There was enough plumage remaining to make their friend recognizable.

Horrified, he realized that not only had these people killed and cooked a sapient bird, they intended to eat it—and maybe to feed it to their captives.

Seth.

Tirsa! Do you realize what—?

Yes. I don't know what these creatures are, but I

can read enough of their minds to know that they intend to kill us. Rame is still unconscious, and I don't know how long it will be until he is coherent. I believe we need to take quick action. These creatures appear to be storing food, and we may be part of that food. Four of them intend to go out and capture other creatures as they did us. One intends to maintain guard here. Don't underestimate that one! She can cripple all of us with a glance.

This was a lot worse than a bigoted drunk picking a fight with a stranger! They were outclassed, and already captive. But he refused to give up. *Rame's knife is in my jacket pocket. If I can get at it I could cut my bonds unnoticed.* The creatures evidently hadn't searched their captives; perhaps it hadn't occurred to them to check for weapons they themselves did not need.

Wait for the four creatures to leave, she responded. *Our only chance is when there is only one of them.*

Seth waited and watched in agony as the five creatures tore at the cooked flesh of Brieght. He kept seeing that deer, and more than that, a friend who had been helping them—and forfeited his life in the process. It was terrible, and the hate in his body stirred into rage. He did not know what these creatures were, but he wanted them dead.

Calm down, Seth! If you do anything now, we will all end up like that.

She was right. He had to keep his head, or suffer this fate worse than death: to be mounted on a spit and cooked and then eaten. Would they bother to kill him first? Would he have to watch while they roasted Tirsa, or would she have to watch him?

Seth!

Her second warning jolted him out of it. He managed to calm himself, and to concentrate on the problem of escape. That was a better use for his brain!

The five women completed their meal. Then four of them left, leaving one to watch over the captives. Seth wanted to act, but had no idea how. He struggled surreptitiously to reach his knife, but could not do so without contorting so vigorously that it would certainly attract unwelcome attention.

After some time, the guard turned and looked at Vidav. His body began to rise.

Seth, she's going to cook him for when the others get back! Tirsa's thought was panic-stricken.

That did it. Seth risked the contortion while the woman was concentrating on Vidav, and got his fingers on the knife. He worked it into position and began to cut at the vines holding him.

Vidav's body floated slowly toward the fire. The woman seemed to be paying close attention to it, gesturing frequently with one hand. Evidently this power was not casually exercised; like a powerful tool, it had to be precisely controlled. Seth sawed at his vines, risking further motion, because he knew that time was short.

The body was almost to the fire when Seth cut his last rope. He sprang up, dagger in hand, and charged the woman.

Now she saw him. She spun away from Vidav, whose body dropped abruptly to the floor, and reoriented on Seth.

Some kind of force struck his head, jarring him backwards and knocking him off his feet. It felt like a vise being tightened around his skull. He screamed and flailed with his arms, but this did not help; the pain intensified inexorably. It was no good; he was helpless before her dreadful power.

Then, suddenly, the pressure stopped. Seth heard music. It was Rame, playing his reed whistle. He had recovered consciousness! Could his music nullify the power of these creatures?

The woman turned away from Seth and stared at Rame. The faun dropped his whistle and fell back in pain. Too bad; the magic of his whistle couldn't counter the power of the woman.

But while the woman was distracted, Seth was free. He rolled to his feet, drew back his arm, and sent the knife flying at the creature.

She heard him and turned back to face him. The vise clamped on his head again. But the knife was already in the air, and in an instant it plunged directly into her chest.

The woman's eyes widened in surprise. She looked down, saw the knife—and collapsed.

Seth went over to her, half afraid that she was going to turn into a monstrous spider or toothy alien monster in her death, but she remained human, physically. Now, without her power, she looked harmless, like the dead deer. But he knew better! He took the handle of his knife and drew it out of her body, cringing at the blood. Cannibal or not, she was human, and he had killed her, and the notion revolted him in a way that his action against the Sateons had not.

She looks human, but she's another creature of Nefarious, I think, Tirsa thought. *Her mind isn't human!*

That made Seth feel a little better. He knew it had been a choice between this creature or their lives, but he hoped never to have to do anything like this again.

When he looked up, he saw Rame untying Tirsa. "How?" Seth asked. "I had your knife."

"And you gave me yours," the faun responded, holding up the pocket knife.

Oh. Seth was just glad that his friends were back in control.

"We have to move quickly, before the others return," Tirsa said. "Where are our weapons?"

Seth looked at the ceiling and pointed up. Their swords were hanging from vines tied to stalactites above the fire. "Can you get them down with your whistle, Rame?"

Rame played his music, and it lifted toward the weapons. The vines started to twist, to release what they held. But then the fire blazed up, the flames reaching high and engulfing the swords. That was no good!

Rame stopped playing, and the fire subsided. The swords remained above. The flame seemed not to have hurt the weapons; it was more as if it was protecting them. But it was protecting them from their owners!

Rame considered. Then he began a melody, only instead of playing single notes he played chords. Seth was amazed; he had never heard this before, and hadn't known it was possible with such an instrument. But of course it was magic, and the rules were not those he had known at home.

Again the music approached the weapons, and again the fire rose, only this time it was met by a flood of water pouring down from the stalactites. Fire met water, and steam spread out from the point of contact, forming a hissing cloud. The fire could go no higher.

Meanwhile the swords were cutting themselves free of the vines. Then they floated down to their owners, even to Vidav; that one came to lie next to the still body. Seth had never imagined that playing more than one note at a time could have such an effect!

Quickly they grabbed their weapons and sheathed them. Seth took Vidav's legs and Rame took his arms. Following a path in the cave they made their way to the exit.

Tirsa, in the lead, stopped dead in her tracks. In a moment Seth saw why.

The other four women were returning.

• Nine

Hermit

Tirsa pushed them back inside the cave. "If they see us we're as good as dead," she whispered. "We could barely handle one; four would finish us."

"What other choices do we have but to fight?" Rame asked as they ran back into the cave.

"There was another tunnel leading in a different direction from the main room. I'd say that's our best chance."

Seth had to agree. Certainly they had no reasonable chance facing the four women.

They ran past the chamber where they had been held, and took the tunnel that went deeper into the cave. They had no guarantee that it wasn't a dead end, but it was a chance they just had to take.

After a few minutes they heard the sound of screeching, and of pursuit. Having to carry Vidav was slowing them down, and their magic boots were more of a hindrance than an asset here, because they could not take any giant steps in here; they would quickly bounce out of control as the boots shied away from the surrounding rock. But there was no point in taking them off; they needed those boots, outside.

In fact, now, too late, Seth realized that they might have made an escape by giant-stepping the moment they saw the women. They might have passed them by so fast that the women wouldn't have noticed. But it

was hard to think of the best course when caught by
surprise.

The tunnel divided. "Left!" Tirsa said, coordinat-
ing their motion, without pausing for thought.
Speed was more important than deliberation, right
now!

Maybe they'll split at the fork, Tirsa now thought. *That
will give us better odds. But regardless, something about this
side seemed more inviting.*

But it would be better yet if this route led them outside, because their odds against even one woman
were not good, and were worse against two.

The cave was not well lit, yet neither was it dark.
Seth was able to follow Tirsa's lead without looking
straight at her; indeed, there was no choice of direction in this tunnel! He glanced to the side, and
saw that there were small plants, or lichen, growing
along the walls. They seemed to glow, providing
some slight illumination. That made all the difference! Probably in daylight that glow would not
show at all, but in the darkness it made the walls
and ceiling clear.

They seemed to be going straight under the mountain, deeper into unknown territory. The sounds of
their pursuers were growing fainter, and Seth did not
find that reassuring; surely the women could have
caught up by now, if they had taken this passage. Why
hadn't they? Was there a dropoff into an abyss, or
something worse? They did seem to be following, but
more cautiously, as if afraid of something.

Up ahead, it looks like an entrance to another chamber!
Tirsa's thought came.

Seth looked. Sure enough, they did seem to be approaching another room, whose plant-light was brighter. Much brighter! No dropoff, at least!

Tirsa entered the chamber, slowing, shading her eyes from the brilliance. Seth followed, hauling Vidav's legs. Suddenly Vidav's body stopped as if it had run into a wall, jolting Seth's hands loose. Rame, who had been running behind, carrying the man's arms, felt the impact and flipped over Vidav's fallen body. He scrambled off, entered the chamber, and stood with the others, looking back.

Vidav's body lay in the room from feet to neck, but his head remained in the tunnel. Some force would not let the man enter completely, yet it posed no barrier to the rest of them.

"Maybe only conscious people can enter," Seth said as the others turned to gaze into the bright room. "Tirsa, Rame, help me pull him. Maybe if the three of us try it slowly, we can do it."

They did not answer. Seth turned, his eyes adjusting to the light.

This was a home of some sort. It had a chair, table, a cupboard and a crude bed. Within it stood a little man. He was old and bearded and grizzled, with what in another plane might have been considered comical clothing: a little black vest, green baggy trousers, and a green pointed cap.

"What are you doing in my home?" the little man demanded querulously, and with what to Seth seemed remarkably close to an Irish accent.

"We are all in a lot of trouble," Rame said quickly. "In a minute four women will be coming down that tunnel, and they will kill us, if we don't leave now."

"Not in my house they won't!" the man snorted.

"They can't come in here!"

"I don't think you understand, they want to dispatch us and eat us. I'm sure they will do the same to you. Is there a way out of here?"

The man scowled. "It is you who don't understand. I didn't say they won't come into my house, I said they can't. My spell won't let them even get close. Nothing evil can enter this chamber, or the rest of my humble abode."

Seth, who had been listening closely to the conversation, felt Vidav's body slide into the hallway. Startled, he looked, and was face to face with two of the woman-creatures. They had hold of Vidav's hair and were trying to pull his body into the tunnel. Already he was there up to the waist.

Seth cried out and grabbed Vidav's legs. He hauled back. Apparently it was true: the women couldn't enter this room, and neither could their power; they had to depend on their physical strength. But that was enough to pull Vidav out, after which they would levitate him back to their cooking-fire.

"Help!" Seth yelled as he struggled to haul the body back. Those women were strong!

Rame drew his sword and swung at the women through the spell wall. But they maneuvered Vidav's head as a shield, moving it so that it was between them and the blade. He could not strike without braining or decapitating his friend!

Rame sheathed his sword and grabbed Vidav's feet. With the two of them pulling, they had the edge, and were able to haul Vidav back through the invisible barrier. But again the head balked. It seemed that the protective spell considered Vidav to be evil.

"The bacteria in Vidav's mind!" Tirsa exclaimed. "It is evil! We can't get him in!"

Rame glanced back at the little man, who was now pacing nervously. "Can you turn the shield on and off quickly?"

"I suppose I could, but why would I want to? You three are all right, or you could not have entered, but your companion is evil. You'd be better off without him."

"He's not evil, he's sick!" Seth protested, still pulling against the women. "We want to get help for him, to cure him!"

"Evil is a sickness that is difficult to cure, as well I know! Who are you?"

"We are the Chosen," Tirsa said grimly.

If she had expected a reaction, she was disappointed, as was Seth. "I don't know what the Chosen is," the little man said grumpily.

"You don't know about the Chosen?" she asked, dismayed.

"I told you I don't!" the man snapped. "Are you hard of hearing?"

Vidav's body moved, as the women gave an extra pull. *If we don't get him past the barrier before the two other women arrive,* Seth thought, *they'll have too much strength for us to resist, and we'll lose him!*

"I don't have time to explain!" Tirsa said to the man. "I beg you, let our friend in immediately!"

"You can beg all you want!" he replied. "I am not letting an evil person in!"

Tirsa drew her sword. "If you don't, you will suffer

a worse fate than he does!"

"You can't threaten me! That would be an evil thing!"

Tirsa stepped toward him, orienting the point of her sword. "It's for a good cause!" But as she moved, something happened. She seemed to come up against another barrier, and could not approach the man.

She struggled a moment, then stepped back. "You're right," she said. "It would be evil, and I can't do it. Couldn't do it even if it weren't for your magic." She shook her head, as if trying to resettle her thoughts. "But it is evil of you to prevent us from saving our friend. You know what those women are like."

Now the man reconsidered. "Maybe you're right about your friend. After all, the spell did let you in. It allows only those with good conscience to pass. You couldn't even speak like that to me, if you didn't truly believe it. I'll help you."

"Good!" Rame said, relieved. "When we say to, turn the shield off and then on again as quickly as possible!"

Tirsa stood ready with her sword at the entrance. She had no doubts about attacking the women!

"Are you ready?" Rame asked Seth, and Seth nodded. Again by common consent, they did not use the mind talk.

"Now!" Rame cried, and he and Seth heaved as hard as they could on Vidav's legs.

The little man waved his hand. Hauled by their combined strength, surprising the women, Vidav's body slid in. One of the women tumbled forward, about to enter the chamber. But the man waved his hand again, and the woman's head crashed into the restored wall. She fell to the tunnel floor and rolled in agony. There was no mark on her, but she might have sustained a concussion.

Vidav was inside. But the other woman stood up, drawing a knife. She cocked her arm, and Seth was suddenly sure that the spell would not stop that metal weapon, any more than it had stopped their own swords. It tuned in on conscience, and metal did not relate at all. She was aiming not at them, but at the little man.

Tirsa stepped forward through the wall, swung with deadly accuracy and force, and lopped off the woman's head.

The head toppled and rolled into the room, while the body fell the other way. Apparently the dead woman was no longer evil, by the spell's definition.

Rame swooped down, grabbed the head by the hair, and threw it into the tunnel where the downed woman was recovering. In a moment she got up, saw her dead companion, made an expression not of horror but of disgust, and staggered back away from the room. In a moment the body and head lifted and floated after her, neither one bleeding any more.

Seth took a shuddery breath. This was the second recent killing, and he did not find that the experience grew more pleasant with repetition. He turned to Tirsa. "For someone who's not used to violence, you really came through," he remarked, with a not-too-successful effort to put the horror behind them.

"I did what was necessary," Tirsa replied, shaken. "Bear with me a moment." Then she set down her stained sword, stepped into Seth, and put her arms around him.

Astonished, he was frozen for a moment. Then he realized that she needed comfort, a sort of physical shielding from the horror of what she had done. She had done the same for him when he lost control in the Fur-Gnomes' lake. He hugged her close, not saying anything.

Rame looked at the little man. "She may have threatened you, but she also defended you," he pointed out. "She is trying to do what is right, but it is hard to judge between good and bad when your friend is dying and people are trying to kill you."

"I see that, now," the man said, looking doubtful. "But I think she is overreacting. Women do that, of course."

"Nymphs do," Rame said. "But this one is fully human, and it upsets her to kill another human being."

"Oh, is that the problem! Those women aren't human, though perhaps their ancestors were; they assume that form for convenience, so that others won't recognize them as witches. They are taking their companion back to their cave, where they will use their ointment to seal her head back on her body, and she will be as she was before. You can't kill one of them except by chopping her up and eating all of her, and of course they don't taste very good."

Seth, holding Tirsa, found this most interesting. That meant that he hadn't killed one of them either; he had just put her out of commission until the others could use the magic ointment. That might explain why the women were so eager to eat others: they feared that otherwise their prey would revert to life and return for vengeance.

"My friend will be relieved to know that," Rame said. "Meanwhile, we apologize for intruding on you; we were desperate, and seemed to have no choice."

"I understand, now," the man said. "I'm really not used to company. I'm a hermit, you see."

"If you have a mop or rag, I'll clean up the mess," Rame said.

"I have both." In a moment the faun was mopping the blood from the floor, and using the rag to clean off Tirsa's sword.

"Let's exchange introductions," Rame suggested as he worked. "I am Rame, and these are my companions among the Chosen: Tirsa, Seth and Vidav, who is unconscious."

"I am Wen Dell," said the man. "I left society when I was twenty, and I am now forty-two, if I have kept accurate count. So I may be a bit out of date on recent developments. Just what do you mean by 'Chosen'?"

"I think we are not quite certain ourselves," Rame said. "We are each from a different Earth-plane—do you know what I mean by the planes?"

"Of course!" Wen Dell said, aggrieved. "Everyone knows that!"

"It seems we were assembled by design," Rame continued. "There was a prophecy indicating that four Chosen would come at this time, and when we arrived at the capital of the Teuton Empire, knowing nothing of this, we became the Chosen. We have been charged with eliminating the threat to the planes that Nefarious represents."

"Nefarious!" the hermit exclaimed. "I have heard

of him! But I thought the Empire had a sorcerer to match him."

"It did until recently. But now Nefarious is much stronger, and no one can stand against his magic. So it's up to us, we were told. We actually know little about it, and so far have barely survived the attacks by the sorcerer's minions. Our friend, here, was poisoned and infected by one of their darts, and we fear he will die or turn against us if we don't get him to the elf village soon for treatment."

"Oh, dart infection!" Wen Dell exclaimed. "I have magic to abate that! Now I understand why he was deemed evil."

"You can treat it?" Rame asked, suddenly excited.

"Perhaps. It depends on the variety. Let me look at him." They went to squat beside the unconscious man.

Tirsa had been quietly sobbing into Seth's shoulder. Now she had recovered enough to resume activity. She disengaged, picked up her sword, checked it, sheathed it, and turned to the others. "Anything you can do, we shall surely appreciate!" she said to the hermit.

Wen Dell nodded. "I can do something, but not enough." He waved his hand. "Now the infection is stopped, but he is not cured. I have only halted the progress of the bacteria. When you reach the elf village, their sorcerer will cure him. He is stronger than I am. At least the one who was there when I last saw the village was."

"Yes, elf healing magic is stronger than mine," Rame said. "I played my whistle, but it could not help him."

"Oh, it did help him," the hermit said. "I felt that healing when I worked my magic, and built on it. You saved him from a rapid takeover by the bacteria, but couldn't stop it entirely. I have stopped it, but can't reverse it. We amateurs cannot do much against those who devote their whole lives to the sinister arts." He glanced at the tunnel through which they had come. "How did you folk get involved with those witches?"

"We were carrying our friend toward the elf village," Seth explained. "We found clear traveling along a good trail through a pleasant valley. But we discovered that anything we imagined appeared, and then the women appeared, and used their magic to immobilize us and float us into their cave. They killed and roasted an intelligent bird who was our friend, and were going to do the same to us, but we managed to cut ourselves free."

"Yes, it is their hunting ground," the hermit agreed. "The magic of the region enables them to hide their nature and seem harmless, until they come within levitating range of their prey. They were there when I first came, but they could not penetrate my defensive spell. Since I wanted no contact with the outside world, I decided that such folk would serve as an excellent barrier to intrusion, and so I set up in this deep cave near them. Of course I have nothing to do with them, and once they discovered that they could not reach me, they left me alone. I am able to conjure such food as I require, and to relax with my thoughts."

"But don't you get lonely?" Seth asked.

"Why should I?"

Seth couldn't answer that. Evidently the man could live readily enough without human companionship.

"We must move on," Tirsa said. Evidently she had heard Wen Dell's explanation about the nature of the witches, and recovered her equilibrium, and with it her poise. "But we can't risk the tunnel we came through. Is there another way out?"

"There is. But you must remain for a meal. What I conjure is not fancy, but is adequate. Now that I have come to know you, I would like to learn something of the outer world. You say the Teuton Empire is about to wage war against Nefarious?"

"Not exactly," Rame said. They weren't eager to delay, but they did need to eat, and did owe the hermit more than a token. So they remained to eat with him, while Rame told him of recent events on this plane. The hermit served a respectable meal consisting of blue soup and red bread: as he said, not fancy, but sufficient.

"I don't mean to offend you, but why would you want to leave society?" Rame inquired. "I have been something of a hermit myself, but not from choice; I was exiled from my tribe. I much prefer to be with company, male and female."

"I did not like what I was seeing," Wen Dell replied. "Too much violence, too much evil."

"That's no reason to leave," Seth protested. "You should have tried to change what you thought was wrong." He had always been a believer in the ability of people to change things, if they really tried. He had long ago concluded that it was no solution to ignore evil.

"Perhaps if you succeed in your mission, things will be better, and I will rejoin society. But perhaps not."

"You have talents that are very important in society," Rame insisted. "Your spells are of an excellent caliber. You could be of significant help to others right now, as you have been to us."

"Thank you, but I do not think I am ready for society. Please let us change the subject. Rame, why do you carry Vidav's body in that cumbersome manner?"

"Do you know another way?" the faun asked, surprised. "We lack the ability of the witch-women to make heavy objects float."

"Conjure him into your reed whistle," the hermit said matter-of-factly.

"My whistle is not quite that powerful," Rame protested. "It can move small things around, conjure food, liquid, even weapons sometimes, but not human beings."

"Let me see it." Wen Dell took the whistle and walked over to his cupboard, which now seemed to be a small room. After rummaging inside for a few minutes he emerged with a six-foot reed. "May I borrow your dagger, Seth?"

Seth handed him the new dagger Rame had conjured, and he sliced off two sections of reed. One section was smaller than any of Rame's reeds, and the other section was larger. In a few minutes he had them fastened to the sides of the original reed whistle, extending it in the manner of a panpipe. He handed this back to Rame. "Now try."

Rame put the whistle up to his mouth and played a

very compelling melody, using the two new pipes. Vidav's body quivered and disappeared.

"Uh—" Seth began, not at all sure about this.

"Will he be all right?" Tirsa asked, with similar apprehension.

"He is in a frozen state, very much like being in another dimension, a timeless one," Wen Dell explained. "As long as you have the reed whistle, you can conjure him back."

"I don't want to seem unduly ignorant," Seth said. "But could you conjure him back now, Rame? For a moment?"

Rame put the whistle to his mouth and played. In a moment Vidav reappeared. He seemed to be exactly as before. "It doesn't hurt him?" Seth asked. "I mean, he can still breathe?"

"He doesn't need to," Rame said. "For us, perhaps a minute passed, but for him, no time. Had I realized that this was possible, we would not have needed to struggle so hard to cure him, for he will not regress when conjured by the whistle."

"We could have saved some effort carrying him, too," Tirsa remarked, rubbing a hand over her shoulder where the stretcher pole had chafed. "We must thank you, Wen Dell, for this singular favor; this will make it possible for us to get our friend to the elf village with far less labor and danger to ourselves."

The hermit shrugged off the thanks. "I must warn you, however: do not conjure a conscious subject in that manner. The frozen state could do an active human being permanent damage."

Rame played once more, and Vidav disappeared again. "We thank you most appreciatively for your hospitality," Tirsa said to Wen Dell. "But now we do have to move on."

"Yes, and I thank you too," Rame said. "You have greatly enhanced my whistle!"

"I have not talked to other humans in twenty-two years," Wen Dell said. "I had almost forgotten how pleasant it could be, and now I realize how much I missed it. I truly wish you success in your mission. I think it more likely now that I will re-enter society. But wait!"

"We really must go," Seth said, fearing more delay.

But Wen Dell was already walking back to his cupboard. He brought out several metallic items. "Please take these." He handed Rame and Tirsa each a white medallion. "They are complementary to the tassel on Seth's sword. Rame, your medallion will turn black if someone is in danger from a non-physical force, and Tirsa, your medallion will turn black if someone is lying to you or your group."

"But we really shouldn't take your precious amulets!" Tirsa protested.

"I also wish you to take these," the hermit continued, handing them four rings. "I have been keeping myself busy inventing all of these amulets. Now, finally, they will be put to good use. These rings will allow you to see in the dark as if it were day."

"Hey, now!" Seth exclaimed, putting his on. "I can really use this!"

Rame conjured Vidav's ring into the reed whistle, and he and Tirsa put theirs on. "We thank you again, for your wonderful generosity," Rame said. "You have assisted us greatly, and we will not forget. We owe you."

"You do not owe me. I really have had no contact with Nefarious, but I know evil, and if you can set it back I will owe you more than I could ever repay. Now you must go, I have delayed you too long. This tunnel will take you all the way through the mountain range, and will put you at this point on your map." He indicated a spot for Rame. "About twelve kilometers from the elf village."

That was good news! They could get there by the end of the day, since they were no longer burdened by Vidav's weight.

They said thanks and goodbye once more, and this time they did get away. They started out through the tunnel.

But Seth had been too confident. The way out was not nearly as comfortable as they had hoped. It widened and narrowed erratically, and at times was so small that they needed to drag themselves through on their stomachs. Seth and Rame could do this, but Tirsa retained her fear of being crushed deep in the earth, and was unable to proceed.

Seth understood her situation, because he had shared some of her dream. She had died, or almost died this way, perhaps because of her suicide attempt, and it remained a horror for her. But they had to get through.

"Maybe you can put her in your whistle!" Seth exclaimed. "Then conjure her back once we're through the tight part."

"But she's active," the faun protested. "It would be dangerous."

"Well, maybe if she's unconscious." But how were they to arrange that? Certainly they weren't going to knock her on the head!

"I must get through myself," Tirsa said grimly.

"Maybe I could hypnotize you," Seth said. "I've had some experience with this, though hypnotism is nothing to fool with. If you were in a trance—"

"No, this is something I must conquer." She approached the narrow part and stopped. "Yet it terrifies me so! I'm afraid I will freeze up, and won't be able to move. You two must go first, so that if I can't do it, at least I won't block the way for you."

Seth exchanged a glance with Rame. No way were they going to let her go last! But how were they going to get her through?

Then Seth had another idea. "Rame, you go first, and trail your rope. Then we can tie it to Tirsa, and you can haul her through, eyes closed. I'll follow, to make sure she doesn't snag."

"I'm not a bag of feed!" Tirsa protested.

"You can crawl if you want to," Seth pointed out. "The rope will just ensure that you can't freeze and be stuck."

She considered, and decided to try it, though her face was drawn. Rame scrambled through the narrow pass, trailing the rope, and Seth fashioned a kind of harness of rope around her upper section. She was a well-formed woman, and he was embarrassed as he pulled it snug.

"Thank you," she murmured, smiling. But her lips were thin. She really was frightened.

"Ready?" Rame called from what seemed like far away.

Tirsa opened her mouth, but couldn't speak. "Ready," Seth called back.

Rame began to take up the slack. But Tirsa just stood there, paralyzed. She couldn't even start!

Seth had what he hoped was a bright idea. "Now that I have you tied up . . ." he said. Then he put his arms around her and kissed her on the mouth.

"What?" she sputtered as he broke, her eyes seeming to catch fire.

"If you don't move, I'll do it again," he said threateningly.

"I'll settle with you later!" she said darkly. Then she stepped into the narrow crevice and started working her way through.

So it was working, he thought. Outraged at his temerity, she had forgotten her apprehension about the cave. Anger had conquered fear. He had thought that might be the case, but he wished it were not so. He wished, but what was the point? She had made her attitude quite clear. He was, as she put it, an impetuous youth.

When she was safely past the constriction, Seth followed. He had to drag himself along on his stomach to navigate part of it. Tirsa was smaller than he was, but this would have been no joy for her. At least he had done what he had to do, and enabled her to make it.

Rame and Tirsa were waiting for him as he emerged from the squeeze. Tirsa was evidently still angry; she would not look at him, and made no mental contact. How well he had succeeded!

They went on. Farther along the cave floor turned to mud, which they waded through up to their knees, then their waists, and finally almost up to their necks. This was a veritable river of mud! At least they had no difficulty seeing their way, because of the magic rings, but there really was nothing they cared to see.

The mud thinned. They were thoroughly plastered. Yet even caked into shapelessness by the mud, Tirsa still looked good to him. He knew he did not look good to her. He wished he could have found some other way to make her angry—angry at something else, instead of at him. What had seemed clever at the time seemed embarrassingly stupid in retrospect. It had worked—but at what cost?

They finally slogged past the last of the obstacles of the tunnel and reached the outside forest. Seth could appreciate why the witch-women did not use this route!

Curious despite his physical and mental discomfort, Seth slipped his ring off. Sure enough, it was night time, and pitch black outside. They had used up their day just getting out, and certainly needed the rings. Quickly he returned the ring to his finger.

They left the cave, and left the mud on their clothing. There wasn't much they could do about it at the moment, and it might prove to be effective camouflage.

They reoriented with the compass and map, and started again toward the elf village. They took mincing steps, because though they could see well enough at close range, farther out the night closed in, and the boots would have plunged them into dangerously invisible territory. They were close enough now so that normal progress would suffice.

Seth kept a wary eye on his sword tassel. Instead of being pure white, it remained gray. Apparently they were in constant but not immediate physical danger.

Seth wasn't sure he liked that, but he was glad they had the magic amulets that warned them and helped them proceed.

They tested Tirsa's medallion by telling stories and seeing if it could decipher the truth from the lies. It turned out to be quite accurate; they could not deceive it.

Rame tested his medallion by having Tirsa make minor attacks on Seth with her mental powers. Seth wasn't sure just how sincere she was; it depended on how angry she remained at the way he had gotten her through the cave squeeze. The medallion also proved effective, turning gray when she tried; apparently it knew that this was not in earnest. Their friend Wen Dell did seem to be good at his magic.

After walking for about an hour they encountered a fog bank. It was nothing major but it hampered their progress slightly, because their night-vision rings weren't proof against this. Soon it got thicker, coalescing around them and becoming so thick that they had to hold hands to keep together without frequently calling. Only by constantly scrutinizing the compass could they be sure that they were traveling in the right direction. Their night vision was now useless.

Seth wished they could find a safe place to lie down and sleep. He was tired, but didn't dare relax. Once they reached the elf village, then they could rest. If only the way there wasn't so hard!

You are remarking on the obvious again, Tirsa thought reprovingly. Well, at least she was communicating with him now.

He could tell by the feel of the ground that they

were entering marshy land. He remembered how on his own plane snakes seemed to go hand in hand with swamps. Of course snakes were beneficial creatures, and he respected them—but in this fog he felt uneasy about encountering them. Did the backwards Synops travel at night?

Then he thought of something else. *Tirsa, Rame— we should be careful,* he thought. *It seems very coincidental to me that this fog bank showed up when night could no longer hamper our progress.*

I agree, Tirsa thought. *But what can we do about it? If we stop moving and stay in the bank till it clears we are an easy target for any creature more adapted to other senses than sight.*

We must keep moving, Rame thought. *Besides, my medallion is white and so is your tassel, right? We aren't in any danger.*

Seth was taken aback. He had neglected to watch his tassel, being absorbed by his effort to see through the fog. *Wrong!* he thought, alarmed. *Now it's black!* It must have changed in the last few minutes, and he had been criminally careless in not noting it. Rame's medallion indicated only non-physical danger, so that could mean—

Then he heard Rame scream, and then a thud.

"Seth, Tirsa, stop walking!" the faun called. "I've found the elf village! It's about two hundred feet below us!"

Seth and Tirsa edged over to what the physical danger was: the brink of a cliff. It was clear below the fog, and Rame had fallen only about ten feet onto a large ledge. In the distance they could see the fire lights of what must be the elf village.

Then a gust of wind passed and the faun threw himself flat on the ledge.

"What's the matter?" Seth called. "Are you injured?"

"He's afraid of the air," Tirsa reminded him quietly.

Now Seth understood. Each member of their party had his nightmare. Tirsa had gotten through her horror of the constriction of the deep earth; now Rame had to handle his air phobia. How was he going to do that? It was evident that they were going to have to go down the cliff, as there seemed to be no other route to the elf village.

"I think I can help him," Seth said. He peered down at the ledge on which his friend lay. "Rame, I know this is difficult for you, but we can handle it. I want you to close your eyes and follow my instructions. As long as you do that, you will not fall. Do you understand?"

Rame shuddered. "Yes," he replied uncertainly.

"Conjure a rope and throw it up to me. You don't need to look; just sit there and throw it at the sound of my voice."

Rame conjured a rope and managed to hurl it up to Seth. "See if you can find a tree, or something to tie the rope to," Seth said quietly to Tirsa. "We're going to need to lower ourselves down; I know how to do it."

Tirsa felt through the fog until she came to a tree that was thick enough to support anything the rope could hold. She looped it and tied a secure knot.

Seth had Rame conjure two more ropes, which Tirsa anchored similarly. Then he made crude harnesses for each of them, fitting them carefully.

"Now that you have me tied again—" Tirsa began.

"Of course not!" he said, flushing. "I only did that to make you angry."

"You did not succeed."

"I had to take your mind off that cave!" he continued defensively. "So you could, what?"

"Now is not the time," she said. "Except, perhaps, for this." She stepped close and kissed him.

Seth stood stunned. Not angry? Then what was in her mind?

But he couldn't afford to dither on this at the moment. They had to get down that cliff.

Seth had Rame conjure six more little ropes, with which they tied loops. As they did so, he instructed Tirsa in what to do. He had rappelled before, and though this was not exactly the same thing, the principle remained. Finally they passed their ropes through the loops on each of their harnesses, and threw the loose ends over the cliff.

"Play your whistle until you are sure each rope reaches the ground," Seth called. The faun did so; in fact he played so long that there was probably extra rope piled up down there.

"Are you ready?" Seth asked Tirsa.

"I defer to your judgment," she said, though she did not look fully confident.

Seth was more than slightly nervous himself, for this was farther than he had ever rappelled before. "Watch me, and do what I do," he said. "I will be below you, and will advise you if you are going wrong."

Cautiously he walked backwards over the edge, holding on to his main rope so that he did not fall, until he was standing perpendicular to the face of the cliff. Tirsa watched him, surprised but understanding. He bounded down lower, then called for Tirsa to come.

He had expected her to hesitate, but she did not. She followed his example exactly, making no errors.

They reached Rame's ledge without complication. Seth gave the faun the harness he had made for him, and threaded the ropes through the loops. "Now keep your eyes closed, and hang on to your rope," Seth told him. "I will be below you, and Tirsa will be above you. We will go down just a little at a time, together. You must stand up, and back off the edge, and walk down it as if it is a level plain—but you are not loose, and you will not be blown away. If you had been tied like this, that storm would never have lifted you. We are all together, and we will talk to you as we go."

Rame did not speak. He only nodded. He remained terrified, but he trusted them, and knew this was the only way to get to safety.

Seth started down again, and waited while Rame followed. "That's it," he called. "Hold on to your rope, keep your footing, let yourself swing out— that's it. Now move your hands down the rope, and take a step backward—yes, that's it. Keep doing that, and stop when you wish to. That's all there is to it."

Tirsa followed. They proceeded down the cliff, picking up speed as the others became more proficient. This cliff was relatively easy to rappel down, because it was not wet or slippery, and there were plenty of grooves and footholds. Seth took a few large bounds, dropping about twenty feet at a hop, but Rame and Tirsa were satisfied to walk it down. This would take more time, but was better for them.

Seth reached the bottom in about fifteen minutes, with Rame and Tirsa reaching it a few minutes later. They unhooked their belts and left the rope alongside the cliff. Seth saw that Rame's eyes were open; somewhere on the way down he must have risked it, and found that the competence of the rappelling system eased his fear. He had, perhaps, conquered his demon, just as Tirsa had conquered hers.

They looked forward, away from the cliff. Now the fires of the elf village were only a short way off. This was where they hoped Vidav could be cured. By mutual consent, they ran toward it.

Ten

Fire

"Halt!" It was an elf guard with drawn bow. The bow was small, as was the elf, but there was no telling what poison or magic was on the arrow. They stopped.

"We are the Chosen," Rame said. "We have come to—"

"Right this way!" The elf hastily slung his bow over his shoulder and led them into the village. At the central and largest fire stood the captain of the elf guard. "The Chosen are here!" the perimeter guard reported.

"Excellent!" the captain exclaimed. "We have competent quarters ready for you! But why are you so late? We feared something had happened to you."

"Yes," Rame agreed laconically.

"And where is your fourth member?"

"We have him with us. He needs immediate attention by your sorcerer. If you can make him well—"

The captain signaled to another elf. "Rouse the healer!"

In a moment the whiskery healer stumbled up to the fire, rubbing sleep out of his eyes. "There is one injured?"

Rame played his reed whistle. Vidav's body appeared.

"Sateon poison!" the healer exclaimed after one

look. "But far gone."

"Can you cure him?" Tirsa asked worriedly.

"Yes and no. I can exorcise the bacteria, but he has already suffered damage that will remain. For a complete reversal, it will require stronger magic than I can muster."

"Can you give us a referral?" she asked.

"Yes, of course. But he may refuse to help you."

"Let's do what we can here," Rame said. "Then we will seek the other healer. Who is he?"

"The wizard Rightwos. But it has been long since he practiced, and he can be surly when disturbed."

"We'll risk it," Seth said. "Meanwhile, if you will abolish the bacteria—"

"I have already done so," the healer said. "At least, I have set the process in motion. It will be several days before the last one is driven out."

"Several days!" Tirsa exclaimed. "We had hoped—" But she did not finish, realizing that it was necessary to take whatever time was required. Their mission would just have to wait until Vidav was better.

"I will watch him until the curse is gone," the healer said. "I see that you other Chosen are tired. Go to the quarters we have provided for you; you are safe here."

Suddenly Seth realized how tired he was. They had not truly rested for a day and a night, for their captivity by the witch-women hardly counted, and then it had been in a home-made lean-to in the forest, in a downpour. He was ready to drop.

"But perhaps we should clean up first," Tirsa said.

"If you wish," the elf said, as if it were a minor matter. The elves had been too polite to mention that the three Chosen were so caked with mud that they resembled so many bags of muck dredged from a polluted lake.

There was a pool formed in a loop of a small stream beside the elf village. The three stripped their clothing and waded in. They swam and ducked their heads and splashed until the pool was brown. Then they rinsed out their clothes, and the pool became black. They had to go upstream to find water clean enough to rinse away the dirty water they had made. Then, naked, they walked to the thatched shelter the elves had provided.

Inside were four beds fashioned of spongy dry moss. Seth went to the last one and dropped on it. In an instant he was asleep.

He woke in daylight. Someone had spread a coverlet over him, which was just as well, for he remained naked. He saw Tirsa sitting up, brushing her hair, whose striping had been restored after being lost in the mud.

She saw him, and tossed some material to him. "Tunic," she explained. "We didn't want to continue wearing Empire clothing anyway."

Seth sat up and put the tunic on over his head. He was just about ready to burst. He hoped there was some sort of sanitary facility close by.

"That way," Tirsa said, gesturing toward the back of the tent. Had she read his mind, or had to locate it for herself?

Both. She wasn't looking at him, but she smiled.

Evidently she had gotten over her anger with him, or whatever it had been. Had she really kissed him, at the top of the cliff? Why?

Because my perception of you has changed. Perhaps we shall have time to discuss the matter, while we wait for Vidav.

He certainly hoped so! He got up and walked in the direction she had indicated.

The elves fed them well, and in the late afternoon Seth and Tirsa took a walk around the region. The territory of the elves was well tended, with efficient little glades cultivated with tubers, grains, fruits, nuts, and herbs. Paths led everywhere, and pretty flowers bordered them throughout. There were no fences, for the elves needed none; each did his task without interfering with the task of any other elf. It was about as nice a region as Seth could remember seeing. There was even a yellow-trunked Sen-Tree standing guard at the border. Seth chatted briefly with it, to Tirsa's amusement.

But they were not really sightseeing. They were talking. "I regret embarrassing you by my description of you, when we first met," Tirsa said. "On my plane, it is no crime to be youthful or to be impetuous. I have had no reason to alter that assessment."

"But you said that your perception had changed!" he said. Actually, she had thought it, but they never referred to their mental contact directly, in speech that any other party might overhear.

"My perception of a suitable object for romance changed," she explained. "Our recent experience has shown me that you have qualities that override those I first noted. You are a natural leader, with excellent judgment, and I think commendable values.

You have been instrumental in carrying us through crises, of which the cliff was only the most recent. You are in fact a man."

"But—I thought—" He was unable to continue, flustered.

"I think I should not do this," she said. "But perhaps it is fitting that I indulge my guilt before I explain it." She put her hand on his arm, causing him to pause and turn toward her. Then she embraced him and kissed him again. This time it was no passing thing; it was charged with emotion that stemmed from her mind.

How sweet it was! "Oh, Tirsa—" Seth began, overwhelmed.

"Now I must tell you why what I have done is wrong," she said, disengaging and resuming the walk. Seth, mystified, had to go along, though his heart was flooded with burgeoning emotion. "It is not that you are younger than I, for age is no barrier to true friendship or love. It is not that you are an unsuitable prospect, for I feel you are. It is not that I am affianced, for I believe that was severed with my separation from my home plane."

"Affianced?" Seth got out. "You mean, engaged to be married?"

"I would have mentioned it before, had I deemed it relevant. It did not become relevant until recently. Now it does relate, but I think not in the way you anticipate. I told you before that I was interested in romance, but not with you. Now I am interested in romance with you. That is why I must tell you what may distress you."

"Oh, Tirsa!" he exclaimed. "If you—I can't

think what—"

She smiled. "Your impetuosity has become endearing. But I will tell you what. First let me explain the seeming mystery of my reaction to your kiss. I had already come to the conclusion that I had judged you imperfectly, and was waiting for the appropriate occasion to apologize for that. But your reaction to my attitude had been so hurt that I felt it was better not to hurt you further, and to leave it as it was. Then you kissed me, and I realized that I had also misjudged myself. Knowing that we were to be stranded on this plane regardless of the success of our assignment, I thought I would have to seek companionship with a male of this plane. I realized abruptly that I had no interest in that; I preferred to seek it with you. It was not anger which motivated me to conquer my paralysis in the cave; it was passion. I knew that I could have no relationship with you if I remained crippled by the trauma of the separation from my home plane. I said I would settle with you later; now I am doing so."

"I never dreamed—"

"You must hear the rest, Seth. Then you will decide. I was affianced, but the relationship was strained. I told you I had tried to commit suicide, but I did not tell you why. Remember, every person in my culture is what you call telepathic; we freely interchange thoughts and emotions. When we marry, we are very certain of our feelings for each other. But I did the unpardonable: I deceived my lover about my commitment. It was not intentional; I deceived myself as well. I thought I loved him completely, but after we were affianced and gave each other to each other completely, there turned out to be a reservation in my feeling. We explored it, and it turned out to be a passion for another man. I had no knowledge who that other might be, but the feeling was there, and I could not be completely fulfilled with the one I had chosen. Our union could not be perfect until this illicit passion was eliminated. My lover, naturally, was deeply hurt, but in the generosity of his nature he did his best to enable me to expunge this barrier between us. We concluded that it was a phantom passion, rising not from any actual experience with or knowledge of another man, but from the hope that such a man existed. Such things are known in our culture. So I undertook a journey alone, trying to extirpate this phantom passion. The purpose of this journey was to put me in such danger of my life that I would yield the illicit passion in favor of the licit one. Do you understand?"

"I'm trying to," Seth said, his head spinning. He had never known anything like this.

"I believed that if my choice were between death and the extirpation of the illicit passion, I would choose the latter. So I explored the wilderness, with limited supplies, alone, where the thoughts and feelings of others would not interfere. I came at last to a great declivity, from which the only feasible escape was a tortuous passage through the rock: a narrow cave. I commenced that ascent, but my physical stamina was depleted, and I was unable to draw myself through the closest constriction. I realized that I was going to perish deep in the earth—yet in that fading moment the passion that remained with me was not for my husband, but for that unknown other. Death itself would not cleanse my crime of emotion. And so I died, not with pride but with shame. In this manner I found myself on the surface of Earth Plane 4, where a passing peasant of the Teuton Empire found me and guided me to the capital. The rest you know."

Seth was silent. What she had told him was at the same time much more and much less than he might have expected. Her telepathic culture had deeper implications than he had realized, while her supposed crime was no crime at all in his culture. Ambiguity was a fact of human life, as he knew it, and he had long since understood that what counted was not so much what a person thought, but what he did. Thus a man might take delight in a vision of a pretty girl on television, but still be true to his wife. A girl might long for the most fattening pastries, but remain on her diet. A man might have the capacity for devastating physical combat, yet strive for peace, as his father had taught him. Thoughts did count, of course, but not as much as actions, in the end.

"But you see, if you were to unite with me, I would train you in mental contact, and our thoughts and feelings would be completely open to each other." She was answering his thoughts, without making a direct allusion to them. "Such ability, once invoked, cannot be banished. At present you share my thoughts and feelings, and those of the others, only when I create an ambience; when I desist, your thoughts are indeed private to all except to me. I will say that your private thoughts become you, and this has influenced me significantly. But if mine were always open to you, you would come up against the reality of my guilty passion, and you would know that

I could not love you completely any more than I could my affianced. You would find this painful."

"You *still* have that—that secret love?" he asked, surprised though she had never suggested otherwise.

"I still do. My shame remains, and death will not abate it. I can offer you everything physical and mental, but my love can never be true. This is no bargain, and I regret hurting you in this manner, but in the circumstance I believe it is necessary for you to know. I think your best course is to eschew any further emotional involvement with me, in the interest of sparing yourself greater distress later."

She offered him, by her reckoning, half a loaf, with the best part always in view but never attainable. Yet was that more than any person in his culture offered any other? On his plane half of all marriages ended in divorce, and many that survived did so because of economic or social considerations, rather than true love or loyalty. Still, true love had always been his aspiration, and she could not give him that.

Yet she had given him honesty. That was valuable in itself. She had told him her limit, and it went far to counter what she called her shame.

"How do you feel about it?" he asked.

"It is not appropriate for me to say, apart from the interest I have already expressed. I have described the manner in which my judgment of you has changed, so that I now deem you to be a suitable prospect for a serious relationship. The actual state of my emotion is not relevant to your consideration."

"Yes it is! I think you're beautiful and courageous and compassionate and intelligent—the ideal woman. But it is what you want that counts, or this is none of my business. Do you want my—my love?"

She hesitated. "I see I did say too much, so that you have been unfairly influenced."

"I was influenced the moment I first saw you! I'm young and impetuous, remember? But I need to know your real desire. Do you want my love? Or is this just a passing entertainment for you?"

She gazed at him expressionlessly. Then she nodded. "I want it, Seth."

"I—" He found himself at a loss. He really hadn't expected her direct affirmation. He had thought she would offer him the undoubted delights of dalliance, without deep commitment, being reserved even in romance. He had expected to be put astride the horns of a dilemma, whether to take what she offered or to wait for true love elsewhere. Instead he had found none. She wanted a full relationship—as did he.

She paused, and put her hand on his arm again. "I think you are not ready for this, Seth. Shall we say that at such time as you approach me, you shall not find me unapproachable? There is much that may be said for a gradual relationship, and we have much doubt in our immediate future. Our lives have already been threatened, and we have suffered discomfort."

"But—but what if I wait to—to approach you, and then one of us gets killed?"

"Even so, things must be done in their own time."

He considered that, and realized that it was true. He had no clear idea what she meant by being approachable; it might be that she just would not call him an impetuous youth again, or it might be that if he wanted her in his bed—

"I think in due course you will know what is appropriate, and when you do, so will I," she said. "I am not inexperienced in such matters, as you understand."

Seth felt himself blushing. She was right: mind-reading could be a problem at times!

Perceiving his embarrassment, she alleviated it. She extended her hand. He took it gratefully, and they continued their walk holding hands. It was the right level, for now.

Rame was busy conjuring new fruits and vegetables into his whistle when they returned. "I did not come here for this, but if I had, it would have been worth it," he said. "The elves have marvelous variants." He looked up. "What were you two doing?"

Whereupon Tirsa smiled and Seth blushed. The faun nodded slowly. "About time," he remarked.

"Do not belabor the obvious," Tirsa said, and at that they all laughed.

"How is Vidav?" Seth asked.

"Visibly improving. He should be ready to wake in another day. But then—"

"Do you have the wizard's address on your map?"

"I do, now. With the magic boots we can reach it readily. But the elves have warned me that the wizard's cure will not be easy, even if he agrees to do it."

"We shall simply have to do what we can, and hope for the best," Tirsa said.

They had another good meal with the elves, and retired at dusk. Seth expected to fall instantly to sleep, as he had before, but instead he lay awake, marveling at the day's events, especially his dialogue with Tirsa. How suddenly his hopeless love had become hopeful! Yet a dissatisfaction somehow remained. He could not quite pin it down.

Tirsa got up from her bed. She picked up her moss in a big armful and carried it over to Seth's bed. She dumped it down, straightened it, then lay down beside him, taking his hand. She closed her eyes.

The dissatisfaction was gone. Seth sank into sleep.

He woke at dawn. Had it been a dream? Then he found Tirsa's hand in his, and knew it was not.

On the following day the elf healer roused Vidav. They were all present as the man woke. "Where am I?" he asked, sitting up.

Caution! Tirsa thought to him. *There is a spy here.* Aloud, she said: "We are at the elf village, Vidav. You were poisoned by a Sateon dart, and almost drowned after saving us. We brought you here, but the poison did you harm."

"I remember the lizard attack," Vidav said. "We were in the river, and—" He shook his head. "That seems a long time ago."

"Several days," Seth said.

"We must be on our way!" Vidav exclaimed. "Every hour counts!" He got to his feet—and wobbled.

Seth jumped to help support him. "You have been very ill! You must take it easy."

"Nonsense!" Vidav said. "Our mission is too important." He took a step, and stumbled. But for Seth's support, he would have fallen. "How can this be? I'm weak!" he exclaimed, appalled.

"It is the damage left by the bacteria," the elf healer said. "It was extending itself to take over his mind, but first it captured the nervous system for the body. That system has been freed—but what remains is only a shadow of its original condition. Fortunately he was very strong, so that what would have killed an ordinary man merely reduced him to fractional strength."

"But I cannot exist this way!" Vidav cried. "Strength is my essence! Without it my life is nothing!"

"We shall take you to a wizard who can restore your strength," Rame said.

Vidav, suddenly insecure in his awful weakness, sat down on his bed. "Is it far? I do not know how far I can walk."

"Not far," Rame assured him. "Tomorrow we will take you there."

Vidav lay back on the bed, satisfied.

But in the evening, as Seth lay down to sleep, Tirsa's terse thought came. *I told no one, to preserve the secret. But we must go tonight. The spy is planning to set an ambush for us when we are away from the protection of the elf village.*

But we can't use the boots effectively at night, Seth protested.

Rame! she thought. *You have plotted the route?*

Yes. But if there is an ambush—

I read in your mind that there is an herb the elves grow that will cause unconsciousness for an hour. If Seth and I take that, and give it to Vidav, could you play us all into your whistle?

Now the faun understood what she was getting at. *I could. But we are larger than the elves, and the herb is not attuned to us. It would cause only brief unconsciousness in us—perhaps no more than five minutes. Even with the boots, it will take me several hours to reach the wizard's castle.*

But time is frozen within the whistle, is it not? So we would not need more than the instant it takes to put us in, and would wake soon after being taken out.

That's true! Rame thought, surprised.

The spy does not know that. He thinks we will have to walk together down the route the elves told you, and he has a spell to nullify the boots. You must go alone, and take a different route.

But that will take much longer!

Only till dawn. Then you can use the boots to full effect, and soon be there.

True, Rame agreed. *Is the spy watching now?*

No. He plans to rouse at midnight to set his trap for us, and deliver us to Nefarious without the elves' knowledge.

Then I will go pipe Vidav into the whistle, and return for you. Keep me informed if the spy wakes.

I shall.

Rame got up quietly and left the house. Seth and Tirsa lay where they were, eyes closed, holding hands.

You are some woman! Seth thought appreciatively.

Do not state the obvious. But she gave his hand a squeeze.

Soon Rame returned. *Will the spy hear if I play here?*

Not if it is not loud.

Here is the herb. Rame handed each of them some hard little berries.

They took them and chewed them up. Seth wondered how long/

/it would take to—but the air had changed. It was now cool and dank.

Seth found Tirsa's hand in his. She remained asleep; she had taken her dose after him, so would recover later, if it had the same effect on her. It might have more of an effect, because she was smaller than he.

It seemed to be about midmorning, and they were beside a foul river. No—it was a grimy moat, for there was a decrepit castle on the other side. The wizard's castle! He sat up for a better look.

"Ah, they wake," Rame said from behind. He and Vidav were standing, evidently surveying the situation.

"Why didn't you take us on inside the castle?" Seth asked, shaking clear the last wisps of fog left over from his unconsciousness. Now Tirsa was stirring, and he took her hand again and squeezed it.

"The wizard wouldn't let me in," Rame said. "I called, and said I represented the Chosen, and needed help, and he called back 'Go away!' I never even saw him; he was just a voice."

"The elves said he might not choose to help us," Seth said. "They must have had experience with him."

While they talked, Tirsa had recovered. "Perhaps I can get through to him." Then she concentrated, and they heard her mental call: *Wizard! We must meet with you!*

There was an impression of someone's jaw dropping. *Who calls me?*

We are the Chosen, sent by the Teuton Emperor to nullify Nefarious. But we have suffered by the attack of Nefarious's minions, and need your help.

Show yourself!

We are standing outside your moat.

There is only a satyr there, a creature of mischief; I know the kind. Desist with your tricks; I'll have none of them.

Then I will show myself mentally, she responded. She sent a thought of such complexity that Seth was amazed; it incorporated her origin on another Earth plane, and her assignment as one of the Chosen, and her presence here before the old castle. It was as if she had thrown off her cloak and stood naked, only more so, for she valued her mind more than her body.

Enough, woman! the wizard replied. *I believe you! No creature of this plane possesses such power of the mind except Nefarious, and his is not that type!*

A few minutes later the drawbridge was cranked slowly down, and they crossed to the castle. There they were met by a wizened man, old and stooped. "I am Rightwos, once a wizard of repute, deposed long ago by Nefarious and reduced to this state," he said. "His minions still pass by, tormenting me with idle atrocities, apparently just for amusement. I thought the satyr was of that number."

Seth saw Tirsa glance at her medallion. It remained bright. The wizard wasn't lying.

"I am not of that type," Rame said. "But I comprehend your concern. I left my kind because of their attitude, and now consider myself to be a faun. I should have realized that you would have had cause to distrust satyrs."

Quickly they explained their situation, and Vidav's problem.

"My powers are diminished," Rightwos said. "Age and the injury done me by Nefarious have left me with more memories than actual magic. But I can still do some things adequately if not well. I may be able to help your friend—but the way available to me is not one you may wish to use."

"If it restores my strength, I'll use it!" Vidav said.

"It is the firewalk."

Vidav paled. "I don't like fire."

"Neither do I," Rightwos said. "But it retains its elemental power, and this we need. Neither the Sateons nor their poisons can stand up to it. Magic fire is that much more potent against their works. You must walk through the enchanted fire to which I will take you, and conquer it, and in so doing you will abolish all the evil done you by the Sateon poison. It is the only way."

Vidav looked as if he were about to faint. "I can but try," he said tightly.

"The site is not far from the castle," Rightwos said. "I will show you the way." He walked briskly enough, but the others had to mince their steps to prevent the magic boots from carrying them far ahead.

They came to what looked like an ancient volcano crater. The floor of it was level, but smoke vented from crevices, and it looked dangerous. In the center was a continuous jet that reminded Seth of a gigantic upward-pointing blowtorch. The heated air shimmered around the translucent fire.

"That is the curative flame," Rightwos said. "Ordinarily it would burn you, but my spell will enable you to survive it. The legacy of the Sateon poison will not." He gestured, and a cloud formed around Vidav, quickly dissipating. "You have but to walk into it, and stand until its color returns to normal. At that point your strength will return. But I must warn you that though it will not harm your flesh, it will hurt exactly as if it is destroying you. My magic is no longer strong enough to shield you from the pain, only the actual damage."

Vidav swallowed. He started walking toward the flame. It was strange, seeing the man so nervous, but Seth thought of his own recent fear of water and ice, and knew what his friend was feeling. When a thing kills you, he realized, you do tend to be wary of it.

The others followed, unable to help their friend in this particular thing. No one else could do it for him.

Then Seth noticed that the tassel on his sword was darkening. "Um, I think there is danger—"

There was a burning hissing sound behind them. "Curses!" the wizard exclaimed. "Firefish!"

"What?" Tirsa asked, turning to look. Seth did also. He saw a streamer of fire extending across the edge of the crater, but it seemed to have no origin.

"Another of Nefarious's nuisances! They can't cross my moat, but now they've trapped me in the open. This is going to be difficult."

"What are firefish?" Seth asked, alarmed. All he saw was the extending line of fire. It had ringed them already, and now was thickening toward them.

"They are demon fish that swim through air and squirt fire from their mouths," Rightwos explained. "They feed by burning their prey; they absorb the nutrient smoke and fumes. Fortunately they are readily stopped, for they cannot tolerate water."

"Great!" Seth said. "Where's the nearest water?"

"In the moat."

And the firefish had just cut them off from the moat. The crater, of course, was completely dry.

"Rame!" Tirsa exclaimed. "Can you conjure water?"

'Yes, I did to counter the witch-women's flames," the faun replied. "But I can't bring enough to do much, and it would only fall at our feet."

"A jug of it."

"A jug of it," Rame agreed. He put his whistle to his mouth, and in a moment had a narrow-necked crockery-jug.

Seth took the jug and pulled out its stopper. A fine stream of cool water poured out. He advanced on the ring of fire, but it did not retreat. Maybe the firefish didn't believe the jug really contained water.

He swung the jug, and a thin stream of water emerged. It sailed out to intersect the ring—and fell through it without much more effect than a small hiss of steam.

The ring of fire did not break; it healed over as fast as the water passed. "You aren't accomplishing anything," the wizard said. "The fish form the ring by squirting fire continuously; when one squirt ends, another squirt begins, from another fish. Your water cut through a fire-squirt, but those are constantly being replenished anyway. You have to score on the fish themselves to be effective, and they are adept at dodging. A body of continuous water, like a lake or a moat, is a perfect barrier, because the water's effect extends above and below for some distance. But a splash just isn't enough."

"Maybe if we made a temporary moat," Tirsa suggested. "A channel of water in a circle, and we could stand inside."

"That would take time, and a lot of water," Seth pointed out. "We'd have to pour it out bottle by bottle, or splash by splash, and it might sink into the hot ground or evaporate before we completed the job. Meanwhile, those fish are closing fast." Indeed, they had to keep walking toward the central column of fire, to avoid the closing circle.

If Vidav had been nervous before, he was highly agitated now. His eyes flicked between one fire and the other. His hands shook. There was sweat shining on his face, though the heat of the fires had not yet affected their party. "Trapped!" he muttered.

"Come on," Tirsa said. "I'll scoop out a channel, and Rame can conjure more jugs of water. It may hold them off until we can figure out something better. Perhaps rain will come."

"No good," Rightwos said. "They can't cross even a small moat, but they can fire across it for a meter or more. We would have to make a large circle to get out of their range. We have neither the time nor the water."

"I could excavate a big channel in time," Vidav said. "If I had my strength."

"You can have your strength, if you step into that curative flame," Rightwos pointed out.

Vidav gazed at it. They were now quite close, and its heat prevented a nearer approach. "I can't!"

"I'll do it!" Seth cried. "Enchant me so that my

flesh can withstand it, and I'll—"

"No. I exhausted my limited power for that enchantment when I did your friend," the wizard said. "In any event, you are not ill; you have no great strength to recover. The curative fire would not change you."

Seth realized it was true. He had been impetuous again, to no purpose.

"But maybe the woman can help," Rightwos said. "If she links your minds, the foolish courage of the one may transfer to the other."

Immediately they were linked. *Draw from us, Vidav!* Tirsa thought. *We will face the fire with you.*

Seth felt Vidav's agony of spirit. The memory of the flames that had killed him overlaid the current scene. He felt the remembered pain, and knew that the fire was going to kill him. He couldn't face that again!

Seth had a healthy respect for fire, but it hadn't killed him. Ice had. He could face the flame, knowing that an enchantment protected his body from real harm, if not from the sensation of harm. *I will take that walk with you, in your mind,* he thought.

Tirsa feared the deep earth, though not as much as she had. She too could face the fire. *I will too,* she thought.

Rame feared the air, the power of storm, but not fire. *I too!* he thought.

Don't leave me behind! Rightwos thought. *This may not be magic, but your mental contact is a wonderful thing. I know that the fire will give you pain and restoration. You may not believe, but I do. I will face that pain with you.*

Behind them the firefish closed in, constricting

their ring. Now the heat was both front and back; there was no escape.

If it's a choice between fires, I'll take the clean one! Vidav thought, gaining courage from their support. He leaped into the central column.

The fire surrounded him, burning away his clothing in a moment and cutting through the skin. Horrible pain flared all around his body. His skin cracked, his eyes glazed, and an inferno roared into his lungs.

Involuntarily, he tried to jump out. *No!* Seth thought, though he was hurting the same way, and wanted desperately to escape it. *We must stay and conquer it!*

Stay! Tirsa echoed, though her hair was frizzing and burning.

Stay! Rame agreed, though his hoofs were melting.

Stay! Rightwos thought, his beard turning to ash.

Vidav stayed. The fire passed through his skin and into his underlying tissue, making every muscle knot. It ate into his internal organs, giving him the worst possible sickness. It consumed his brain, causing explosive hallucinations. Finally it ground through his bones, turning them to seeming charcoal.

Then the pain faded. Vidav stood whole and invulnerable within the column of flame, and his strength was back. He was naked but exultant.

But we are frying! Seth thought, for though he stood outside the column, the fire ring was close at his back, burning him. It was the same for the others; they had nowhere to go. It was also too late for any moat; there was no room for it.

Vidav leaped out of the column. He picked up the

jug of water. He tossed it into the air, and as it came down, he clapped his two hands into it, on either side.

The jug was smashed inward. The water in it exploded. A spray of it flung up and down and outward, drenching them all and saturating the close ring of firefish.

There was a soundless scream. Suddenly the fish were gone, and the ring of fire flickered out. The explosion of water had caught the fish by surprise, and if it hadn't killed them, it had certainly dismayed them and broken their concentration. There was no chance for them to form a new ring before their prey escaped.

"That was great, Vidav!" Seth exclaimed. "Only your strength could have done it!"

"It was little enough, after you saved me from the Sateon poison," Vidav replied. "I knew you had risked your lives for me, and endured much discomfort, and were suffering the agony of the flame with me, giving me your strength. I had to give you mine, and the debt is far from repaid."

"I wonder how Nefarious knew to send this particular scourge to this place at this time," Rightwos said as they walked back toward the castle. "You had gone to such an extreme to elude his spy in the elf village, yet he knew precisely where to strike to take out not only you, but me. That cannot be coincidence."

"The Emperor said that Nefarious can detect those who use magic," Rame said. "We four were Chosen because we have no inherent magic; we use magic objects, but that is not the same, and he can't detect that."

"True," Rightwos agreed. "He knows where I am, because of my magic. He would have destroyed me long ago, except that I am now harmless to him, and he prefers to revel in my humiliation. He lets me play with my golems and work my little enchantments as if I were still a great wizard, knowing that I know how far these tokens fall short of my prime. He can't detect what I do in here, but it doesn't matter; he knows its limits. He should not be able to detect the invocations of your objects, unless—" He broke off, looking thoughtful.

"Unless what?" Seth asked, getting an ugly notion of the answer.

"Unless he planted them!" Rame exclaimed. "The spies Tirsa spotted at the capital—they could have put magic tags on those artifacts! Did you check for that, Tirsa?"

"No, I didn't think to," she confessed. "The whole situation was so new, that I just identified them and watched them, without delving further into their memories. How stupid of me!"

"None of us thought of it," Seth said quickly. "We were so busy training, after being wrenched from our home planes, or home forest in Rame's case, that we couldn't explore every possibility."

They arrived at the castle. "I will inspect all your artifacts, and determine whether any have the stigmata of Nefarious," Rightwos said. "This much I can readily do; I am long conversant with the stink of his works."

Inside, they got to work on it, after Rightwos found a tunic for Vidav, to replace the clothing he had lost in the flame. The three others had not actually burned; it had been only sensation. The magic tassel on Seth's sword was clean, as it should be; it was Rame's gift. Rame's whistle was clean. The gifts of Wen Dell the Hermit were clean: Rame's medallion that warned of non-physical danger, Tirsa's medallion that identified lying, and their four rings for seeing in the darkness. That reminded Rame to present Vidav's to him. They could not check the magic tent and stove, for they had been lost in the raging river. That left their boots. Vidav's were gone, but the other three were wearing theirs.

The boots had the stigmata of Nefarious: all three pairs.

"So wherever we went, he knew!" Seth exclaimed in disgust. "We avoided his spies, only to have him send new ones! He knew when you arrived here, Rame; he waited only to see what you were up to, and punish Rightwos for trying to help us!"

"It is his way," Rightwos agreed. "He derives pleasure from watching cornered rats scurry here and there in futile efforts to escape before he destroys them. You may be sure that something nasty will lurk for you the moment you leave the protection of this castle."

"He may have outsmarted himself," Seth said.

"How so? I can protect you here, but only within the castle, which is a bastion against hostile magic. I can give you charms against particular threats, but nothing which Nefarious could not readily overpower. I fear this is a trap for you that will effectively nullify your mission."

"Because he thinks he's got us bottled up—and he

doesn't," Seth said. "By the time he realizes his mistake, we'll be far away, and he won't know where."

Tirsa cocked her head. "Do you know something we don't?"

"No, I've just thought it through a step ahead of you," Seth said. "And, with luck, two steps ahead of Nefarious. Look, he can't track us, just our magic boots, right? So if we take those off, we lose him."

"I think you have omitted a detail," Vidav said gruffly. "His minions will be watching this castle."

"And when those boots leave it, they'll follow," Seth agreed. "And when, after toying with the fugitives for a while, they close in for the kill, they'll find those boots being worn by walking golems—while under the cover of that distraction, we will have escaped unnoticed and be on our way."

Tirsa's jaw dropped. "Why, I believe it could work!"

"Can you provide us with boots like these?" Rame asked Rightwos, removing his as if they were unclean.

"Not as good as those, but without the stigmata, yes," the wizard agreed. "The boots I fashion will take you only ten paces for one."

"That will do!" Rame said. "Ten paces undetected is better than thirty that give us away!"

"But if the minions of Nefarious are watching the castle, they should see us depart it anyway," Vidav said. "They would not be so stupid as to stop watching Rightwos just because his guests depart."

"I can help you there!" the wizard said eagerly. "I have a spell to make you undetectable. Invisible, inaudible, unsmellable—for a time. It would not be effective against Nefarious himself, of course, but his minions are lesser creatures, and relatively stupid. It would fool them, if they believed you had already left anyway. By the time it wears off, you will be well away."

"He will know we are coming, but he won't know how or when," Vidav said with gusto. His spirit had returned with his strength, and he was his old self again.

"Aren't we forgetting something?" Tirsa asked.

Seth looked at her. Her striped hair was shining with its original luster, and she was beautiful. "What?"

Yet again you belabor the obvious! She thought in response to his appreciation. But she also responded verbally. "Nefarious will know where we started from—here—and where we are going—there. He should have no trouble checking the most expedient routes between, and his minions will set traps along all of them. Escaping this castle would be but a temporary reprieve; we would surely be snared again, long before we posed a threat to him."

The others nodded gravely. They had allowed their enthusiasm to overwhelm their common sense. Tirsa was right: it was apparent that they could not even get close to Nefarious, let alone do anything to him.

But Seth was youthfully stubborn, and who cared how Tirsa saw him? "There has to be a way!"

I love it—and you care. "There is surely a way," she said. "We have but to find it."

Vidav looked at them. "I follow your words, but your thoughts are obscure. Did something happen while I was ill?"

We are considering whether to love each other, Tirsa thought, sharing the thought with them all. *He is enthralled by a pretty body, while I am intrigued by youth.*

"Oh." Vidav obviously wasn't quite satisfied with that explanation, but let it pass. "Is there any feasible route that Nefarious would not be watching, or have his minions on?"

"One," Rightwos said. "But you would not care for that one."

"If it's a good route, that's safe for us, we're interested!" Seth said. "What is it?"

"Through the ice."

Seth stared at him, feeling a chill reminiscent of that ice. What could the wizard be talking about?

• Eleven

Ice

"Nefarious's castle is in the northern reaches," Rightwos explained. "It is protected by a glacier so massive it is called the Mountain of Ice. It is considered impassable; storms are almost continuous, and the terrain constantly shifts as the ice moves. The only access is a road from the south, kept clear of ice by the sorcerer's magic. Beside it are many bounteous fields that yield excellent harvests, but it is known that at any moment the whim of Nefarious could bury those fields in snow and ice, and all attending peasants with them. All who approach along that road are verified by magic; no enemy of the sorcerer can pass unless in chains or worse."

"Or worse?" Tirsa asked.

"Some are blinded or stripped of their limbs, or otherwise restrained. Some are put under horror spells that make them long for death. No potentially dangerous enemy is allowed near Nefarious."

Seth gulped. "How is it that Emperor Towk sent us out without telling us this?"

"That is an interesting question. Surely he had some reason."

"Decoy!" Vidav exclaimed. "Here we are talking of using decoys to distract the sorcerer's minions from us; we must be decoys to distract Nefarious from the Emperor's real attack!"

"But who would be fool enough to go along with that?" Seth asked. Then, immediately, he answered his own question. "People from other planes, or the backwoods, who don't know the situation. Innocents who believe what they are told."

"The Emperor gave us no truth-medallion," Tirsa agreed. "Yet I fathomed his mind, and found no such deception there."

"Maybe he didn't know," Seth said. "The best decoys are those who think they're the real thing. So if the Empire strategists tell the Emperor one thing, and plan another, that keeps him honest, and maybe leads the spies astray too. The Emperor has what on my plane is called 'deniability.' If something goes wrong, he knows nothing about it."

"I was never quite sure about the Empire," Vidav growled. "Now I think I know why."

"The Empire is imperfect," Rightwos said. "Yet it is better than what Nefarious plans. It is better to support it."

Seth looked again at Tirsa's medallion, where it hung on her bosom. It remained bright. No lies, here. "So what do we do?" he asked. "Go on and be good decoys, until Nefarious catches us and tortures us to death? Or quit now?"

"I do not like the Empire much," Vidav said. "But I like quitting less."

Seth agreed wholeheartedly with that! "So why don't we go ahead and astound everyone by completing the mission? Maybe the Empire's other thrust will turn out to be the decoy, and we'll be the one that succeeds."

"But to do that, to even make the attempt,"

Rame said, "we have to come at Nefarious from the one direction he won't anticipate, because it's impassable. The north."

"But how can *we* pass it?" Tirsa asked.

"I have no experience with ice," Vidav said. "But after facing the fire, I have no fear of the opposite! I could forge through it at an excellent rate."

"The distance you would have to travel is approximately five thousand kilometers," Rightwos said. "Even with the boots multiplying your speed tenfold, you could make only three hundred or three hundred and fifty a day, because of the violence of the terrain, and storms would slow you further. It would take you at least fifteen days to get there, and Nefarious would know that, and be waiting for your arrival."

"But you said he would not expect that!" Tirsa protested.

"I said he would not be watching that route," Rightwos corrected her. "Because he has no need to. He knows that you will come from the south, which is the most direct and navigable route, and that if you try the north you will either perish in the effort or take longer than two weeks to get there, which means he need have no concern."

"No concern?" she asked, irritated. "Does it matter when we arrive, so long as we surprise him?"

"Two weeks from now he will have made his move to nullify the Teuton Empire, so that there will be no barrier to his assumption of power on the plane," Rightwos explained. "Thereafter your effort will be irrelevant. Emperor Towk will be dead and the Empire will answer to new leadership. Even if you killed

Nefarious, you would not be able to reverse the damage; you would only hasten the onset of the anarchy and chaos that will destroy all four planes."

Tirsa paled. "But if we cannot make it in time through the ice, and not at all by the southerly route, how can we accomplish our mission?"

"By being good decoys," Rame said. "We'll have to hope that while Nefarious is watching us, the real Chosen are getting through."

"If we can't, how can they?" she demanded.

Rightwos nodded. "An excellent question, to which I have no satisfactory answer."

"We *have* to do it!" Seth exclaimed. "I don't care if we were supposed to be dupes, the only way we can be sure of saving our frames is by doing it ourselves."

"But if the only way is through the ice, and that's too slow—"

"I know how to make it faster."

She gazed at him. "But your phobia—"

Seth gulped. "Yes. But Vidav walked into the fire, and I can walk into the ice." Yet he wasn't sure he could.

We will be with you, her thought came, echoed by the others. *You helped me, and Rame, and Vidav; we will help you similarly.*

Seth hoped that would be enough. He dreaded the notion of heading into five thousand kilometers—that would be about three thousand miles—of arctic wilderness, though before his death he had enjoyed winter sports of all types. He could ski well, and skate well, and had tried his hand at ice-boating. That was how to make it faster: to use the tools of winter sports to speed up their traveling.

"But we don't know how to do those things," Tirsa said, picking up his thoughts and speaking for the rest of them.

"You can do it—if you link minds with me while I do it," he said. "That way I can teach you instantly."

"Why not teach me," Rame said, "and I will carry the rest of you in my whistle, until I arrive? That way you need have no fear of the ice."

"Because you couldn't make it three thousand miles alone, even with boots," Vidav said gruffly. "You will need my strength and endurance. I have not been much in snow, but I know this: it is like mountain climbing, in that you need more than one person, tied together by a rope, so than when one falls, the other saves him."

"True," Seth said. "And several are better than two. I can teach you to ski and skate, but there is expertise I cannot teach because I won't know what is required until I see the situation. I must go too, even if I wish I could avoid it."

"Better than a rope linkage is a mental linkage, so you can act as one throughout," Tirsa pointed out. "There will be times when storms prevent you from seeing or hearing each other, and perfect coordination will be necessary without reference to the physical senses. Therefore I too must go."

They looked at each other and nodded. They were a team; they had to do it as a team, each contributing his ability to the whole.

"Then let's get planning," Seth said. "Even with the best equipment and training, we will be hard put to it to get there in time. We must know exactly what we're doing."

To that they readily agreed.

Next day they set out. The golems wearing their boots went out first, heading directly toward Nefarious's castle a week's march distant. Then, when Rightwos indicated that the way was clear, Rame went out, wearing his new boots, masked by the spell of undetectability. He hurried north until hidden within a deep forest, at dusk. Then he played his whistle, and Vidav appeared, asleep. Rame said the spell the wizard had given him, and Vidav woke.

Vidav had a huge pack. He lifted Rame onto it, and put a strap around the faun. Then he forged on northward, carrying Rame, who slept. He avoided populated regions, following the route marked on Rame's map. The land was relatively open here, and soon it became tundra, with wide desolate spaces that were ideal for rapid straight-line travel. Vidav pushed his boots to the utmost, and made almost the velocity that one of the others might have made with the original thirty-pace boots. They were gaining on their schedule, and there was no sign that anyone knew where they were.

Vidav hiked all night, for he had the hermit's ring and was well rested. Indeed, he enjoyed indulging his strength, having so recently recovered it. At dawn he paused, about six hundred kilometers farther north than Rame had whistled him out.

Rame woke, and played his whistle, conjuring food for his friend. Vidav ate as he walked. Then the faun gave him one of Rightwos's potions, and he fell immediately to sleep. Rame played his whistle, and Vidav disappeared. Once more the faun traveled alone, it seemed.

In this manner, in two days and nights they traversed fifteen hundred kilometers, and were at the fringe of the northern barrens, well ahead of a normal schedule. Furthermore, two of their number remained well rested.

But once they came to the snows, it was time for the full party to manifest. Rame whistled them out, and woke them. At this point Seth became aware that their plan was working; to him and Tirsa the transition had seemed an instant. They had taken the potion, and then woke at the fringe of the barrens.

"Now we can use the sled," Seth said. Rightwos had used his magic to build items to Seth's specification; the wizard's magic might be reduced, but he had been formidable in his day, and even his minor remaining magic was quite an asset for routine chores. What might have taken several days manually had been done in several hours magically. Rightwos had conjured wood and metal of the appropriate shapes, and the four of them had worked as a team to assemble the units. Tirsa's ability to link their minds had helped greatly; Seth had not had to explain much, he had simply visualized each item and its place in the whole.

Rame played the sled into solidity. It was crude, for Seth had had to work from memory and no particular expertise at construction, but it had clean runners and a solid surface, with handholds along the sides and a mechanism to steer it in front. If they found themselves at the top of a long snowy slope, this would slide them down it handily.

Rame and Vidav got on, lying flat. It was their turn to rest, for Vidav had gotten little in the whistle—he had progressed seemingly instantly from night to night—and Rame had not had the best of it riding on the bobbing pack. Seth and Tirsa took the cord, hooked it to their belts, and started forward, hauling it. The sled moved well, even as they lengthened their stride in tandem and moved ten paces for one. So they were traveling at the predictable speed, but providing two of their number good rest. By shifting off, they could travel much of the day and night, effectively doubling their average pace.

I become increasingly impressed with you, Tirsa thought as they moved. *I regret I do not have more to offer in return.*

Who cares about your mind? he returned jokingly. *Your body is enough.* Not that he had touched her body; her interest was what really counted.

If only that were so! Yet she was pleased.

The terrain became colder and rougher. A chill wind came up, cutting slantwise at them. They were wearing warm suits so that they were not cold, but it still wasn't fun. Then they came to a frozen lake. "Ideal!" Seth exclaimed.

He had to wake Rame briefly, so that the faun could conjure the sail they had fashioned. Seth mounted this on the sled, and angled it to take advantage of the wind. For this purpose a side wind was fine; Seth tacked against it. The sled began to move, driven by the air. Fortunately Rame had returned to sleep immediately; he would not have felt secure about depending on air.

"This is marvelous!" Tirsa exclaimed as they picked up speed. "I was sure you knew what you had in mind, but somehow I could not quite believe it! We are having a free ride!"

"Just so long as this doesn't work into a storm," Seth said, watching the sky warily.

There was no storm, but they did come to the end of the lake and had to resume hauling. Nevertheless, they had gained more time, and Seth's nervousness about the ice had hardly manifested. It wasn't ice that scared him, he realized, it was thin ice, and being in icy water; this was thick ice, and therefore safe. Maybe he would get through all right!

Then they came to mountainous country, and were unable to haul the sled efficiently. But they had given their companions several hours of deserved rest, while making excellent progress. Rame whistled the sled away; it was time for the boots again.

Now the going became more difficult. There were steep slopes and twisting gullies that Seth didn't trust. They had to use the ropes. They tied themselves in a line, and Seth led the way, poking ahead of him with a metal-pointed stick he had packed for the purpose. Tirsa kept them mentally linked too; they marched in step, so that the boots would not jerk them about if one stepped while another paused. Seth wasn't sure how long this would work; there was bound to be a place where speed was impossible.

Sure enough, he soon found a filled depression; the covering of snow made the surface even, but he could not plumb the bottom of it with the pole. They had to wait while he poked to the side, finding firm footing. Now they were losing time, as he had known they would somewhere along the way. It was their average speed that counted, and anything could destroy that average—if they got careless.

They made it to the top of a ridge, and there ahead was a long curving slope down. Now it was time for the skis.

Rame conjured four sets. "Follow me," Seth said. Tirsa kept them linked as he set off downslope; it was as if all four of them were Seth Warner, all competent skiers, though Rame and Tirsa had never skied before, and Vidav's experience was limited. They were making good time again—until they came to the foot of the slope.

Now they faced another ascent, and the snow was too deep for the boots; they sank in up to their thighs. "Conjure the snowshoes," Seth told Rame. Soon they were trekking up on the snowshoes, taking several paces at a time; the magic boots coordinated well enough, once they got the hang of it.

"Without your expertise, we would be only half as far as we are," Tirsa told Seth.

"Don't belabor the obvious," he retorted, and they laughed. The snow was cold, but his heart felt warm in her presence.

Near nightfall they came to a bleak, level, snowswept plain. It extended as far as the horizon, and the footing under several inches of loose snow seemed secure. Rame conjured the sled, and Vidav hauled the three of them on it, so that they could eat and sleep without stopping their forward progress. They were gaining on their schedule again.

When they lay down, Tirsa wordlessly embraced Seth. Bundled as they were in their winter outfits, it didn't mean much physically, but as a gesture it was wonderful. Yet he remembered what she had said about her secret passion, which had not been for her fiance of her home plane, and was not for Seth in this one. To love this woman could be asking for heartbreak.

It seemed to be what he was destined for, however.

In this manner, constantly changing off, they proceeded for several days. Sometimes they skated along a winding frozen river, linked by Tirsa and guided by Seth's experience with skates. Sometimes they used hammers and pitons to climb steep icy cliffs. Mostly they just slogged along through the snow, roped together. If any of them had considered the rope unnecessary, this changed when the snow gave way beneath Tirsa, who was taking her turn leading, and she disappeared into an icy cave. The other three braced and held, and Vidav hauled her back up. Shaken, they proceeded around the cave, saying nothing, but the point had been made.

One night, when they slept on the moving sled, nightmares came. But this time they recognized the source, and resisted them more readily than before. Nefarious, aware that they had escaped his trap and were on their way, was trying to take them out mentally, and not succeeding. That was a good sign.

Then the storm came up. Rame was terrified, for this was too much like the one that had almost carried him away. Seth felt nervous, but was able to handle it; it was icy water that really got to him.

They had two choices: either build a snow igloo to hide in to ride out the storm, or keep moving. They knew they couldn't afford to stop moving; the storm might last for days, and that would ruin their schedule. But it was dangerous to keep moving; they could be swept over some cliff to their deaths.

"This is where we need your strength, Vidav," Tirsa said. "We must each be strong enough to plow on through the storm the way you can."

Vidav nodded. They had drawn on Seth's expertise with skis and skates, and on Rame's ability with the reed whistle; now they would draw on Vidav's strength. They put spikes on their boots, and held poles with which to brace themselves. Then Tirsa tied them in with Vidav's strength, and each had the ability to forge onward at what would otherwise have been superhuman force.

The storm did its utmost. Rame got blown off his feet, because his boots were not as secure as his hoofs would have been. Tirsa, next in line, simply hauled him in hand over hand until he was secure, while Seth and Vidav braced to support her. "I think I am losing my fear of the air," the faun remarked.

Another time the wind started them all sliding down a slope—in the wrong direction. "Hup!" Seth cried, mentally as well as verbally, and as one they jammed their poles down into the snow and stopped the slide. After that they used their poles like pitons, jamming them in as anchors, and kept traveling upslope. It was slow, but it was a lot better than nothing. The storm had been unable to stop them.

They came to a valley where large animals grazed. Tirsa did a doubletake. "How can they graze in snow?"

"They look a bit like caribou," Seth said. "They probably sniff out moss on the rocks beneath the snow, and eat that. They should be harmless if we leave them alone." He remembered his camping excursions on his home plane; he had been aware that the human party was intruding in the domains of the wild creatures, and had been careful not to do any avoidable harm. It had become a habit. Only when the creatures attacked did his attitude change. Here in this fantasy realm of Earth Plane 4 a number of the wild creatures did attack—but a number did not.

They were on skis at the moment, traveling fairly well on fairly level terrain. They headed for the region where the caribou weren't grazing, so as not to disturb them.

"Seth—look at your sword," Tirsa said urgently.

Seth looked—and saw the tassel turning dark. Oops—danger! But where was it? He saw nothing threatening here.

"Maybe something is coming," he said. "We had better find some cover." But there was nothing.

They moved on—and the tassel turned black. "We seem to be heading right into it," Rame commented nervously.

"The snow is solid here, and not deep," Vidav said, ramming his pole down hard. It struck rocky soil. There were no hidden pitfalls here.

Tirsa brushed something away from her face. "We'd better get on past here quickly."

They tried to keep moving, but something was wrong. Tirsa was becoming agitated, and Seth felt cold down his spine. Vidav was turning his head this way and that. "Cold wind!" he remarked.

"There's no wind," Rame said. But he too looked uncomfortable.

"Well, *something's* cold!" Tirsa said. Indeed her lips were blue, and a webbing of ice was forming across her furry hood.

"It's as if the wind is cutting right through our clothing," Seth said. But he had to agree with Rame: there was no wind. The day was calm.

"What are spiders doing here?" Tirsa asked, with a flurry of brushing at her face.

Seth began to get a glimmer of something. "Let me look." He peered into her face.

Sure enough, it was framed by what looked like cobwebs. "Must have been a nest of little spiders in the suit," he said, hoping that was all there was to it. "Now they're running about, leaving their little lines so they won't fall."

"I'm infested with spiders?" she asked, alarmed.

"Something like that." Now he saw one: a tiny white eight-legged creature. "Let me move it away for you." He removed his glove and put his hand up to intercept the spider, who was descending a bit of line. He didn't want to hurt it.

But as his finger touched the white body, a jolt of cold went up it, numbing it. He jerked back.

Rame came close. "What is it?"

"Is there any type of spider on this plane that can generate cold?" Seth asked, flexing his hand to restore feeling.

"Yes, I've heard of the arctic ice spider," Rame said. "It quick-freezes its prey. Not only does that immobilize the victim, it keeps the food fresh indefinitely. But that spider is rare, and it stays away from warm creatures because it can't stand the heat."

"Suppose there were a lot of them in one place?"

"Then I suppose they could immobilize larger

prey, and could collectively go after—" Rame broke off, looking uncomfortable.

"Suppose Nefarious had a spider farm or something," Seth continued relentlessly, "and bred thousands or millions of such spiders, and dumped them into the northern reaches just above his stronghold?"

Vidav overheard that. "No wonder he doesn't fear an approach from the north!" he exclaimed. "The spiders will freeze any living thing that passes through!"

"That was my thought," Seth said. "And I think we just blundered into it. I know I've got them down my back."

"How can we get rid of them?" Tirsa asked, her teeth chattering.

"Heat," Rame said. "They can't endure heat. So if we make it hotter than they can stand, they'll retreat."

"But our bodies aren't hot enough!" Tirsa said. "Not in this snow, with so many of them. I can feel them numbing my skin all over!"

"Fire!" Seth exclaimed. "*That* will be hot enough!"

"I can't conjure fire," Rame said. "Or wood to burn; I didn't think to whistle any into storage. Our food won't burn well; it's too moist."

"That pocket knife I gave you will strike fire," Seth reminded him. "But the wood is a problem." Seth looked desperately around. There were no trees here, only snow. "The moss!" he cried. "We can fetch moss! It should be pretty dry, under the snow."

"You mean what the animals eat?" Rame asked.

"Where do we find it?"

"Where the caribou are; *they* know where it is."

They turned and headed for the herd. The animals spooked at their approach and bounded away, but the marks of their prior grazing remained. Seth and the others poked through the snow there, and came up with handfuls of spongy frozen moss.

"Clear a place!" Seth said. "Once we start it burning—"

They swept a place clear of snow, baring the frozen ground below. Rame brought out the knife, with its flint and magnesium rod, and a few scraps of paper, and struck some sparks. Soon a scrap caught, and he used it to heat a piece of moss. The moss was porous, and the flame licked through it and started it burning. This became the base for a larger fire, as they carefully heaped more moss around it.

"But there's not enough for a big fire!" Tirsa protested, shivering so violently she was almost dancing.

"Rame!" Seth said. "Conjure some moss into your whistle—then conjure it out again."

The faun nodded. He played his whistle over a mound of moss, and the moss disappeared. Then he played again, and it reappeared—and as he continued playing, another mound appeared, and another. Soon it was piling up high. Then he conjured that larger pile into the whistle—and brought it out again. Now he could pipe it out by the peck. Their problem of fuel had been solved.

The fire blazed high. They crowded around it, but still they were cold. "The ice spiders are inside our suits!" Tirsa said. "The suits protect them from the fire!"

"We'll have to get them out," Seth said grimly. "Take off your outfit, Tirsa."

Without hesitation she stripped. He skin was blue with cold, but it was now warmer outside her suit than inside it. She stood naked by the fire, slowly turning to warm each side. "Ah, that feels so good!" she said.

They took the items of her clothing and held them close to the fire, turning them inside out. The little spiders danced out and scrambled away. As each piece was clear, she donned it again: panties, bra, socks, shirt, furred trousers, jacket, hood and boots. They worked hardest over the outer pieces, because they had many more nooks for spiders to hide in; nothing could be skimped.

Then Seth stripped similarly, and they toasted his clothing at the fire. Then Rame, whose natural fur was now buttressed by unnatural furs, and finally Vidav, who had been able to hold out longest against the cold. They were all clean, and warm.

"But how are we going to travel?" Tirsa asked, her cheeks now rosy instead of blue. "The moment we leave our fire, they'll be back!"

That problem had occurred to Seth. "We'll just have to take the fire with us," he decided. "We can put some dirt on the sled, to protect it, and put the fire on that."

"But this isn't sledding country," Rame pointed out. "We're using skis."

"We can still haul the sled behind," he said. "It may slow us, but it's necessary. This may even be an advantage, because Nefarious will never expect us to get through in time."

"*Will* we?" Tirsa asked pointedly.

"We've got to!"

She didn't argue.

But it wasn't easy. Whoever left the immediate vicinity of the fire got quickly infested and had to return, strip, and get deloused. That meant they had to spend more time stalled than moving. They couldn't do it while traveling; the sled bumped over the rough snow, and it was impossible to run along beside and hold out items of clothing without getting them reinfested as fast as they were cleared. When they came to a downhill slope they all piled on the sled, around the fire, and rode down—but then there was the uphill haul. It was soon evident that they were not going to make it in time, this way.

"Oh for some firefish!" Tirsa said with irony.

"You know, that might work," Seth said. But of course Rame hadn't conjured any firefish into his whistle.

Rame looked at his map. "We are not far from the castle," he said. "In fact, it should be right beyond that mountain range." He pointed to a towering range ahead of them. "If we could just move at top speed, we could pass it in a day and be there in time."

But they couldn't move at top speed, or even at moderate speed, because of the spiders. If they tried, they would all be dead of the cold in short order. Nefarious's last ploy seemed to be his best; they could not get through in time.

"There's got to be a way!" Seth exclaimed angrily.

Rame pored over the map. "There may be. There's a river that supplies water for the castle, and to irrigate the surrounding farmsteads. It draws from the glaciers of the north, but magic keeps it liquid. It tunnels under the mountain range and comes out right at the castle reservoir."

"We could sail down that river!" Tirsa exclaimed. "Fire and all!"

"No. I said it tunnels. It's an underground river."

Seth felt a chill not of the weather—the same one he had felt when he learned of this arctic route, only worse. Cold, dark water, under the ice. . . .

"Well, we have a water-breathing spell Rightwos gave us," she said. "We could swim—" Then she realized how this was affecting Seth. "Oh."

He tried to say something brave, but could not. The very notion of entering such a river appalled him! It had killed him once; how could he risk it again?

"Seth," she said earnestly. "This is the only way. But you don't have to do it directly; Rame can pipe you into his whistle—"

"No," he said with difficulty. "I've done some scuba diving. This is similar. I've got to do it. In fact, I should do it while you and Vidav ride in the whistle."

"I think we shall do it ourselves, or not at all," she said. Then, in a private thought: *Seth, we know this is dangerous, and that we may not survive it. Perhaps it is time for you and I to—*

What? he thought, alarmed.

To clarify our understanding, she continued. *I so much regret that I cannot commit to you completely, but want you to know that if there were any way for me to be free of that other passion, I would gladly eradicate it. I think you're a fine young man, fully worthy of any woman, and it is my hope that in some manner it will become possible for—*

Here I am, being cowardly, and you are telling me how wonderful I am!

You are not being cowardly, you are facing your legitimate fear. You helped each of the rest of us to get through our fears, lending your strength to us, and now we shall lend ours to you. But what I mean is that in case I don't have opportunity later, I must tell you now that it is my hope to find a way to abolish my fault and commit to you completely. To be able to tell you I love you.

Seth stood as if rocked in a storm. This wasn't at all the way he had imagined romance to be, but of course he had never before had a relationship with a mature telepathic woman. Tirsa said or thought exactly what was on her mind, lucidly, sensibly, honestly. There was no evasion, no softening, just the truth. When she had had no romantic interest in him, she had said so directly; now she said the opposite, and he could believe it. But she had not used the term "love" before, when speaking of herself. Even if this wasn't a complete commitment, it was an impressive one.

Well, he thought, *I don't have to wait to tell you I—*

No, she thought. *You must not, until I can.*

But—

For now, this. And she sent him a mental kiss of such encompassing passion that it was as if the world imploded, turning him pleasantly inside out.

After a moment he recovered his equilibrium. He was standing in the snow, amazed that it hadn't melted around him. Rame and Vidav were poring over the map; either they had not been aware of his mental dialogue with Tirsa, or they were politely ignoring it.

"I can do it," he said. For now his vision of dark icy water was overlaid by the feeling Tirsa had put there: her wish to love him. He had fear, yes, but he also had love, and his horror of dying under the ice was balanced by his delight in living with what she offered. Perhaps she had done this deliberately, in the manner he had kissed her in the cave, timing it appropriately. It was a nice thing, and nice timing.

"Here," Rame said, touching the map. "It has to be here, in this basin."

"I agree," Vidav said. "We must go there and dig, and we shall find it."

Seth looked at the map. The spot they marked was only a few miles from where they were now camped. It was certainly feasible.

They trekked to it. For this hop, they tried a new ploy: Vidav hauled the sled, stripped, while the other three rode by its fire and held blazing torches on long poles. These they held near Vidav, passing them up and down his body to drive away the ice spiders. It worked tolerably well, but was not comfortable for him. They knew this, because they were linked to his mind; his sensations of cold guided their torches. But the ride was jerky, and inevitably they came too close and burned him, and there were also places their long-range torches couldn't effectively reach. Only his great strength carried him through.

Tirsa extended her mental awareness, tuning in on the water below the snow. "It is here," she said. "Rivulets percolating down through the porous earth and rock, forming pools and slow-moving streams below. But I can't fix on it precisely."

Rame brought out his whistle. "Maybe I can help."

He played, and the melody was pretty but faint: the water was good but not copious. But as they moved, the whistle became louder. Finally it became almost deafening: they had found the main river.

By the time they reached this spot, Vidav was almost dead on his feet. He collapsed in the snow, and they hauled him onto the sled and carefully burned away all the spiders, and then put salve on his burns, and dressed him in decontaminated clothing.

Tirsa watched Vidav, while Seth and Rame started digging. They soon cleared a round region of snow, and were faced with the frozen ground below. How were they going to get through that? Vidav might have the strength to break up the rocklike ground, but he had done his part and had to recover.

"The fire!" Seth said. "We don't need to move it any more. It should melt the ground, or at least soften it enough so that we can dig it."

They moved the fire to the ground, and added more moss, so that it blazed high. Its heat radiated out, melting the snow and turning the ground to mud. They had to scrape the mud away so it wouldn't drown the fire. Gradually the fire sank, forming a pit. Then, suddenly, it dropped into a wet hole and sizzled out.

"Oh, no!" Seth exclaimed. "We've lost our digging tool!"

Vidav sat up. "That's because you've found the river!" he pointed out.

Seth felt foolish. Of course! The fire had melted through, and fallen into the underground water. They no longer needed it.

Rame played his reed whistle again. The notes

were true. This was what they wanted.

Seth gazed into the dark pool, and shivered. Then he thought of Tirsa's love, and felt warm again. It might be death, a second time, but he was going to do it.

Rame whistled, and a package appeared. This was another of Rightwos's gifts: fish pills. They would be good for only one use, for the wizard lacked the power to make replenishable fish magic. But that should be enough. Once they were out of the water, they would be on their own.

What would they do then? Seth had little notion. He did not like the idea of killing a man, but he saw no other way to stop so powerful and unscrupulous a sorcerer. Probably they would simply sneak into Nefarious's home and strike him down any way they could. What about the sorcerer's guards? Well, Rightwos had provided a sleep potion that might help.

The whole thing seemed uncomfortably uncertain, now. But if the river carried them through as it should, they would arrive at night, when the defensive guard should be down, and at least a day before expected—if Nefarious thought they would make it at all. So they had a chance.

"We have a chance," Tirsa agreed.

They took the pills, while Tirsa kept them mentally linked. They hoped that they would be able to retain that linkage throughout, because they had no idea exactly how long or rough their trip down the river would be. How would one know where another landed? Suppose there were dangers; they wanted to be able to warn each other.

Seth found himself breathing rapidly. His neck

itched. He felt dizzy. What was the matter?

We're growing gills! Rame thought, more accustomed to the ways of magic than the others were. *Get in the water!*

That made sense! Seth scrambled out of his clothing and jumped in, discovering that his fear of icy water was gone. In fact, the water felt good. He ducked his head under and exhaled, blowing out all the air. Then he took in water through his mouth, and it passed on out through his gills, and he was breathing again. He discovered that he no longer had to breathe in and out; he just had to keep the water flowing into his mouth. That was easier to do if he moved, so he started swimming—and discovered that his hands were webbed.

The others were with him. They looked like themselves, but with gill-slits along the sides of their necks, and the webbing on their hands and feet. They had become fish-men.

Fish-MEN? Tirsa thought.

Seth looked at her. She wasn't a mermaid, for she had legs instead of a tail, but she definitely wasn't male. Even with the fisheye lenses of his new eyes, that was too obvious to be belabored. *Fish-folk,* he thought, correcting himself.

We had better move, Vidav thought.

They moved. Vidav had recovered from his chill ordeal, thanks to his immense reserves of strength, and now led the way. They swam single file down into the dark stream. Deep down, they found the main current, and it helped carry them along. This channel was lined by ice, but Nefarious's magic kept the water liquid.

Seth privately reveled in his freedom from the fear of icy water; that nightmare would no longer haunt him! Just as Vidav's experience with the healing fire abolished his fear of fire, so that he had hardly reacted even when burned by their torches, this fish spell had ended Seth's fear. From now on, he was sure, he would be able to go through the ice without concern.

Their fishy eyes enabled them to see in the darkness, and they were able to swim well, though not as well as a true fish could. The nether river did not constrict; instead it grew larger, as more water flowed in from icy tributaries. It was an artificial river, intended to fill the reservoir, so it had no twists or confusions. This was almost too easy.

My thought too, Tirsa agreed. *Surely Nefarious has not left this avenue unprotected.*

But they really had no choice except to proceed. They swam downstream, making good time. Seth judged that they were already passing beneath the mountains, and would soon emerge beyond. If they made it unobserved—

They did not. Suddenly there were tentacles in the water. Some huge squidlike creature was here, grabbing for fish!

Retreat! Vidav thought, drawing the knife he wore. Knives were the only weapons they had been able to take along, for this final leg of the journey. Rame had his whistle, but that was inoperative under water.

They tried, but the current bore them on, and the best they could do was remain in place. The tentacles sought them out. They slashed with their knives, but the tentacles were not soft but hard; they seemed to be armored. There were many of them, reaching in now from all directions.

It's got me! Tirsa thought despairingly.

Seth struggled furiously to reach her, but the tentacles caught him too. In a moment he was being dragged through the water, helpless to hold back. The evil sorcerer *had* put in a defense, and they had fallen prey to it.

They were captives of the monster. Was this the end?

• Twelve

Nefarious

Seth found himself hauled out of the water. Immediately the spell faded. He choked as his gills closed up and his lungs tried to resume their function—full of water. He heaved out the water, took in some air, and heaved out more water. The tentacles obligingly suspended him upside down, facilitating this. In a short time, objectively, but long subjectively, he was fully human again.

Then tentacles set him down on a platform beside the water. He was naked and shivering; what had been comfortable for fish was not so for warm-blooded folk! In a moment his companions joined him, in similar condition. The tentacles withdrew.

"I think Nefarious was ready for us," Rame said bleakly.

Indeed, there was a noise, and a door lighted in the wall. It slid open on an elevator. They had either to wait here and shiver, or to try to make a break for it through the icy water, or to step into the elevator; there was nowhere else. Since the other two choices promised cold disaster, they stepped through the door.

The elevator closed, and moved up. The others were startled, but Seth sent a reassuring thought; he was used to this sort of thing. It brought them to a warm room where clothing was waiting: four completely different outfits. One was exactly like the clothing in Seth's home plane: trousers, shirt, jacket, shoes, and associated items such as underwear and socks. Another was simply a pair of shaggy green pants, similar to those Rame had seemed to wear in the forest.

"Why, that's a three-quarter sarong!" Tirsa exclaimed. She picked up the long band of red cloth and wrapped it around herself. Evidently this was her normal mode of dress. Seth now realized that she had seemed slightly diffident about donning what Rightwos had provided; that clothing had been alien to her normal experience.

Seth went ahead and donned the clothes he recognized, and Rame and Vidav did the same. How had the sorcerer known their home-modes?

There is something strange about this, Tirsa thought, answering his thought. *Nefarious seems to know much more about us than he should.*

Soon they stood dressed. Vidav wore what struck Seth as a military outfit, with gray trousers tucked into heavy boots and a belted jacket extending to the knees; it was almost like a Civil War officer's uniform. Rame wore trousers and little else; his hoofs were free. Tirsa—

"My appearance bothers you?" she inquired.

"Uh—" For her three-quarter sarong, as she called it, did cover three quarters of her torso. All but the upper right quarter. He had seen her fully clothed, and he had seen her naked, but somehow this compromise made her more striking than either. Yet it was evidently the standard garb of her culture. "I, er, like it." That was a somewhat guilty understatement!

Obviously women cannot read minds on your plane.

Now he was blushing. He kept getting caught by her mind-reading, even though he had pretty much learned how to do it himself. He read her mind—and encountered amusement. She had anticipated his reaction, and felt no shame. Her culture had no secrets and no hangups about sex.

"Hello."

The four of them jumped. There stood a man behind them, of middle age, handsome, in a bright white cloak.

"Nefarious!" Tirsa exclaimed.

The sorcerer smiled. "So it is true: you can read my mind." His gaze passed coolly across them. "Attack me."

Dumbfounded, Seth was motionless. "You know we came to—"

"It will be easier if you satisfy yourselves at the outset that you have no chance to do me harm," Nefarious said. "Do your worst, Chosen."

Let's take him at his word, Seth thought. *He may be overconfident.*

Then, acting as one, they attacked. Vidav leaped at the sorcerer, swinging a fist at his head. Tirsa dived for the knife she spied at his hip. Rame swept up his reed whistle to conjure their weapons. Seth held back, waiting for his opportunity.

Vidav screamed and fell back without touching Nefarious. So did Tirsa. Meanwhile a sword appeared, conjured from the whistle. Seth grabbed it and hurled it at Nefarious's chest.

His aim was true, but the sword never got there. It bounced. In a moment it was flying back at Seth. Had he not been moving when he threw it, so that his body was no longer where it had been, his own weapon would have skewered him.

It's no good! Tirsa thought. *I can see it in his mind: he is invulnerable to anything we can do. His magic protects him from all physical threats.*

What happened to you and Vidav? Seth thought.

Nightmare horrors! The earth was crushing me much worse; I would have died before I could touch him.

And the flame consumed me, Vidav added. *The closer we get to him, the worse it is.*

Nefarious smiled, unruffled. "You are reading my mind, I believe. I cannot read yours, but I trust you are satisfied: you can neither harm me nor conspire successfully to harm me, physically or magically. You may continue trying if you wish, but it will be easier to converse if you desist. You are no threat to me."

Now Seth read the man's mind directly, and found verification. Nefarious had absolute confidence in his security, and it seemed justified. He had the most potent magic on the plane, and it protected him absolutely, awake and asleep and wherever he went. They had never had any chance against him.

Disgruntled, they desisted. "Excellent," Nefarious said. "Now we shall eat, for I am sure you are hungry. Then we shall settle in comfort, and I will explain why I summoned you here in this timely fashion."

"Summoned us!" Vidav exclaimed angrily. "We are the Chosen!"

"Indeed you are," the sorcerer agreed. "Chosen by me. I have been most eagerly awaiting your arrival. Had you not come today, I would have had to fetch you in tomorrow, for the critical time is near. But please, let the business wait an hour, while we get to know each other better."

Tight-lipped, they followed the man to the elevator. They entered, standing close together, not making any further attempt on the man's life. What a reversal!

The elevator brought them to a small dining hall, where places for five were already set. In fact, the banquet was set out too: roasts and puddings and wine and salads and soups. In fact, Seth realized, the cuisine was different for each place, according to the standards of the plane from which each guest derived. How could the sorcerer know them so well, when they did not even know each other's customs?

Rame hesitated, still holding his whistle. "Go ahead, play it!" Nefarious said to the faun. "Or read it in my mind: if I wanted to be rid of you, I have no need to poison you. I could do it more readily by magic. This food is safe."

Rame did play, and Seth did read it in the man's mind: there was no threat here. Still, it was hard to believe: they had come to kill Nefarious, and the sorcerer knew it. Why was he treating them like honored guests? Seth tried to fathom the answer from the man's mind, but could not; Nefarious's conscious thoughts were only of the welfare of the visitors, and it wasn't possible to read unconscious thoughts.

So they ate, ill at ease, but resigned. There was no question that they were in the power of the enemy, so it didn't seem worth agonizing over at the moment. But if any opportunity came to change things, they would act instantly.

Seth had a good meal, but somehow never tuned in on exactly what he was eating. He was too busy watching the others with their strange repasts, and wondering what was going to happen to them. He saw Vidav drink his soup from the bowl, and sip his wine from a spoon. Tirsa mixed bean curds with dark jelly and ate them delicately with S-shaped chopsticks. He saw her glance at his fork as if it were a barnyard tool. They came from different cultures, all right! But it didn't matter; they were a team, and they knew each other in ways that hardly mattered at the dining table.

They finished with dessert. Rame had what looked like a candied slug, while Vidav chewed on something like wooden nails. Seth looked at his chocolate cake, saw Tirsa shudder, and decided he could live without dessert. By mutual consent they did not share their thoughts at this point; it could have made one of them get sick.

After the meal they adjourned to a pleasant open court with a fountain in the center. Chairs were around the fountain, and light came from a crystalline arched ceiling. Exotic plants bordered the pool, their nodes angling to spy on the visiting party.

"I will speak to the point," Nefarious said. "You could read it in my mind, but I think it best if I simply present it my own way, while you verify it. Let me start by clarifying that you are not decoys; you really are the Chosen. You may have been told that you were brought here by prophecy to eliminate me as a threat to the Teuton Empire. That is only partly true. There is a prophecy, but it does not specify the side the Chosen are to assist. In his arrogance, Emperor Towk assumed you would help him. My magic is more penetrating than any the Empire can muster, so I saw further into the prophecy."

Seth read his mind, and found no dissembling there. He glanced at Tirsa, who nodded.

"It also does not specify the manner that the Chosen are to participate," Nefarious continued. "The Emperor assumed that you were to kill his enemy, but that is only one interpretation of many, and not the most sophisticated one. It could be that the Chosen's destiny is more positive: to help one side, rather than hinder the other."

Still he seemed to be speaking the truth, but there were levels and levels in the man's mind that Seth could not fathom. Tirsa had a similar doubt. She reached into her pocket— Seth had not known that her spectacular wraparound had one!—and brought out her medallion. She put its chain over her head, so that the medallion hung at her bosom. It glowed white.

Nefarious smiled. "I must advise you that the magic of Rightwos is not as potent as mine. You can not trust that device in my presence. Note: Black is white."

It was an obvious lie, but the medallion remained bright.

"You are beautiful," Nefarious said to Tirsa. Now the medallion turned midnight black.

Rame coughed. The sorcerer had certainly made his point: the medallion had given the lie to an obvious truth.

"You are ugly," Nefarious said. And the medallion turned bright red.

They stared. They had not realized that it was capable of color!

"It isn't," the sorcerer said. "No, I am not reading your minds; I simply know what you must be thinking at this stage. That simple amulet is very limited, but my magic can transform it to whatever I wish." He glanced at it, and abruptly it was a giant white spider.

Tirsa stiffened. But then the spider became a tiny yellow bird, which flew to Nefarious's hand. The chain on which the medallion had hung became a thin green snake, its mouth clamped on its tail. It let go, and slithered into her lap and on to the floor, where it disappeared in a puff of smoke.

"Read my mind," Nefarious said. "That is the one talent you have which is not subject to my power; you can trust it."

Impressed, Tirsa nodded. So did Seth. They had underestimated this man phenomenally!

"The prophecy says that the influence of the Chosen will be decisive," Nefarious continued. "That is all it says. Since it is apparent that I cannot prevail in my quest for ultimate power without assistance, I assume that the Chosen will decide the issue in my favor. Actually, I have been able to fathom the prophecy to a small additional extent: in the original language, which was poorly translated, it said that *one of* the Chosen would be decisive. But I do not know which one."

He leaned back, his eyes meeting each of theirs briefly. "And this is why I arranged to bring you here. Oh yes, it is true; verify it in my mind! I lack your ability of mind-reading, but I have managed to develop the ability to send a mental signal. I realized that if one of the Chosen were to help me, I would have to make sure that all of the Chosen were of my own choosing. Since they had to be from the four separate planes, this was difficult, but not impossible. So six years ago, when my research indicated that there was a key nexus spanning the planes, I sent the most powerful signal I could, to touch the potential Chosen and attune only those who would be useful to me. Exactly in what manner that signal had effect I do not know; I only know that it reoriented the situation in whatever slight way was necessary to set apart the four I required. It may be that you are aware of that change."

Suddenly it registered. "That was when my father died!" Seth exclaimed. "It changed my life—"

Black rage clouded Vidav's face. "When I was passed over with prejudice for appointment to the board of planning, destroying the dream of my youth, no reason given, so that I had to go instead into the combat pool—"

"Six years, that was when something first made me realize that I was a faun rather than a satyr," Rame said. "From that point on, I questioned the ways of Clan-Satyr, despite the warnings of the Elders, until finally the rift became open and I had to leave. That early realization was to cost me everything I then held dear, though the mischief was long in the fruition."

"When I felt the first stir of that illicit passion," Tirsa said, "I dismissed it as girlish fancy, being just fourteen at the time, but somehow it persisted long after I thought it gone. That was the root of my failure in life."

Nefarious nodded. "That was my signal, seeking

each of you, changing your lives in dramatic or subtle manner, but with similar force. That marked you as Chosen, though you did not know it then. More recently my second signal actually brought you here."

"But it was sheer coincidence!" Seth protested. "I ran afoul of punkers, and fell in a frozen lake, and drowned. That doesn't make me anyone special!"

"So Emperor Towk may have suggested," Nefarious said. "But his information is incomplete. There was no coincidence to the selection of Chosen, no chance; you were Chosen six years before, and recently Called. The circumstances of the Calling may have seemed coincidental, but had you had a wider perspective you would have known it was not. You were destined to come to me, and now you have. The Emperor was foolish enough to think that you came to facilitate his side, but that was not the case. My minions tracked you throughout, seeking to capture you and bring you to me without harm; as it happened, you proved to be elusive. So I tried herding you instead, and this turned out to be more effective."

"Herding!" Vidav exclaimed angrily.

"By allowing you to depart Rightwos's castle in peace, and distracting you with dream-sendings which I trust you found interesting. At last you did arrive. This is the hour of reckoning."

Seth, reading the man's mind, still found that bewildering complexity of thought, but truth as far as it was possible to grasp the pattern. He felt as if he were a grade-schooler tackling the concepts of calculus, knowing they made sense, but unable to fathom *how* they made sense. Nefarious was dangerous in a far more complex way than they had thought. They were not just magically overmatched, but conceptually too.

"I think we have a score to settle with you," Vidav said grimly.

"Do you?" Nefarious shrugged. "Let's explore this for a moment, as it may facilitate understanding. You say you were passed over for an appointment, which I gather would have been a prestigious thing, so that you had to undertake lesser work. I gather that you were qualified and should have had the appointment, and would have done well for yourself and your culture there. Now I ask you: had you had that appointment, would you have had any interest in coming to this frame?"

"I had no interest as it was!" Vidav growled. "I was married, with a child—"

"Happily?"

"That is not relevant!"

"I believe it is," Nefarious said. "You were Chosen because you were fit for the office, and part of that fitness was the developing problem of your existence on your plane. The loss of your aspired appointment made it possible for you to give up that life, and the unsatisfactory marriage. It remained only for the second signal to free you for the new life here."

Vidav glared at him, but did not argue.

"Now let us try whether you are the one I require," Nefarious said. "I do not know in what way I need the help of one of you Chosen, but perhaps it is in the form of a virtually indefatigable warrior."

"I am not going to help you!" Vidav exclaimed angrily.

"I am being open with you, so I will explain what I am doing," Nefarious said. "Though I lack your ability to read minds, I am not as yet clear with which one of you that talent originates—I can send certain emotions, as I have demonstrated, and can block out certain qualities of character. I am now going to block out what you call your conscience, your preconceptions of right and wrong. You will be obliged to fall back on more basic values, and I think you will find it worth your while to join me."

"Never!" Vidav snapped.

Nefarious gazed at him, and made a seemingly negligent gesture with one hand. Vidav's defiant manner relaxed.

Vidav! Tirsa thought with alarm. *Don't let him enchant you!*

Vidav glanced at her. "You are beautiful, but your judgment is distorted," he said.

Seth read Vidav's mind—and found there a complete change of attitude. The man cared nothing for their welfare, only his own. The enchantment had taken over.

Seth! We must stop this instantly! Tirsa thought. *He has the power to corrupt us by force!*

The three of us must act together, Seth thought. *Go for him: one, two, three!*

They leaped as one for the sorcerer—and fell writhing to the floor as the terrible visions overcame them. They were helpless against Nefarious's power.

"Fools," Vidav remarked mildly. He had been aware of their effort, but had not budged.

"What is your salient desire?" the sorcerer inquired.

Vidav considered. "Power," he said, as the remaining three of them crawled back away from the sorcerer, bedraggled.

"If you join me, you shall have it," Nefarious said. "You shall be my chief lieutenant, supervising the conquest of the Empire. Anything you need or wish, whether great or whimsical, you will simply take. My subject Domela, who likes you very well already, will be your concubine, for you and she are now on the same side. Or you may take any other female or females you desire, at any time."

"Excellent," Vidav said.

"However, we have not yet determined whether you are the Chosen One. What have you to recommend you to this trust?"

Vidav was surprised. "I thought it was obvious. I have unparalleled physical strength and endurance and constancy in my chosen pursuit."

"How would physical strength assist me in a magical effort?"

"Why, I assume there would be a need for physical effort too, in the actual storming of the battlements, the transport of supplies—"

"No. My magic will handle that more expeditiously. I do not plan to waste good troops foolishly storming battlements! I will simply demolish those defenses with a spell, and send a poisonous fog to kill all those who seek to resist."

Vidav pondered the matter. "Then I may not be of much use to you."

"I agree. I think you are not the One." He looked away from Vidav, and the man abruptly became tense again.

"How could I have—" Vidav said.

But Nefarious was already focusing on Rame, and the faun's aspect abruptly changed from incredulous to submissive.

Don't let him do it to you! Tirsa thought desperately, but it was already too late; Rame's mind was different.

Seth, well aware of the foolishness of any further physical or mental effort, resumed his seat and watched. They were up against superior power, without question—but there had to be some way to get around it! If only he could find that way, in time!

"What is your salient desire?" the sorcerer inquired, exactly as he had before.

Now Rame pondered. "To have my powers of magic restored, and amplified, so that they are limitless," he replied.

"If you join me, you shall have virtually limitless powers of magic," Nefarious said. "Limited only by the limit of mine; I cannot give you more than I myself possess. But you will have access to the ancient texts, so that you may by study and practice increase them to whatever extent you are able. Your nymph Malape will be at your side; I can free her of her attachment to her tree."

"That's good enough," the faun said.

"What do you have to recommend you to this trust?"

Rame considered. "I understand the ways of the wild magic creatures of this plane, and can enlist their support for you. I also have an excellent reed whistle, which can conjure many useful things."

"I have no need for the support of wild creatures,

nor the reed whistle, as my magic is superior," Nefarious said. "All creatures will be my slaves."

"Then I have nothing sufficient to offer you."

"I agree." Nefarious's gaze left him. Rame, like Vidav, looked appalled as his conscience returned.

The sorcerer gazed at Tirsa, who gazed back defiantly. But then she melted. She could not hold out against his power.

"What is your salient desire?" the sorcerer inquired a third time.

"To be free of my illicit passion," she replied without hesitation. "So that I can love truly."

Nefarious smiled. "If you join me, I will grant you better than that. Your passion will remain, but will no longer be illicit. I am its object."

Tirsa's jaw dropped. "Why so it is! I never realized!" She stood and walked toward him. "All these six years I tried to extinguish it, without understanding its nature. Let me love you, Nefarious!"

Seth watched, appalled. How could she do this with the enemy? Yet she had told him of her passion, and its persistence. What a logical yet awful thing!

The sorcerer lifted a hand, and she halted as if stunned. "Not yet. I must ascertain whether you are the One. If you are, not only will you love me, I will love you."

"Oh, I am the One, I am!" she breathed, reaching for his hand and kissing it. "I have the origin of the power to read minds, and to enable others to do the same. I can open the minds of your enemies to you, so that you can never be betrayed. The one power you lack will now be yours, through me!"

Now Nefarious considered. "All this, and beauty

too," he murmured. "Yet I think I can have it all regardless, by making you my slave and returning your conscience to you. Rather than see your friends suffer, you will do whatever I ask."

"That is true," she agreed. "You can have it all without granting me any status. Only allow me to love you."

"I think not. I really have no need of love, when I have power, and I would not trust a person with your power of the mind with too much freedom. You see, you might discover how to influence *my* mind, and become the true master."

"That is possible," she agreed sadly, and Seth realized that the sorcerer had neatly avoided a very real trap. "Then do whatever you feel is necessary, only let me be close to you, in any capacity you desire."

"Perhaps, for my temporary pleasure only," he said, and looked away from her.

Tirsa's expression congealed into a mask of rage and horror. Suddenly she was Woman Scorned, and helpless to do anything about it. But she was also completely disgusted with herself. She had learned the origin of her illicit passion, and found it to be worse than she had imagined.

Now Nefarious gazed at Seth. Seth tried to avoid the man's eyes, but could not: he simply refused to take the cowardly way out. So he met that gaze/

/And his reality changed. Suddenly the principles that had guided him seemed inapplicable. What had seemed important on his home plane had no relevance here; he was in a different world, with different rules, and if he was to survive, he had to work with the current situation. He did want to survive and prosper; nothing else mattered.

"What is your salient desire?" Nefarious inquired. It was a reasonable question.

"To be home again," Seth answered. Then he had to qualify it, for his prior life really had little meaning for him now. "That is, to be able to go home—to cross the planes at will, and be where I choose to be."

"If you join me, you shall have the power to cross between the planes," Nefarious said. "I have not chosen to cross myself, because I have business here, but I was able to send my signals across. It is but a matter of exchanging identities with your alternate persona there. With some preparation, you will also be able to arrange for visits to the remaining two planes, and to return to any at any time."

"That seems sufficient," Seth said, for he realized that this was a very special power. No prison could hold a man who could move between planes, and no information could be denied him, if he managed the transitions aptly.

"What have you to recommend you to this trust?"

Again, the question was reasonable; nothing was given without its price. "An objective perspective," he replied. "I have a logical mind, and can reason things out, and come at the truth without bias, now that I am free of the distortion caused by conscience. There will be many instances when you need to make a correct judgment, and this I can do for you."

"Why, when I shall have complete power? I will define what is correct, which will be whatever is in accordance with my will."

"Not so," Seth said. "When you invoke magic, you must follow its rules precisely, or it will be ineffective or counterproductive. When you appoint subordinates, you must select the best for the particular position, or your interests will not be well served. You cannot do it all yourself; you must have an apparatus that magnifies your impact by adding to it the effort of correct tools. When you come to a difficult decision, such as how much of your resources must be allocated to which tasks for maximum effect, you need a concurring opinion. Just as the distance of an object can be judged because you have two eyes instead of one, providing by their interaction the perception of depth, you need two minds for effective judgment. Without this balance of perspectives, you will inevitably go astray, and your efforts will in the end come to nothing, or perhaps lead to your destruction."

Now Nefarious considered. "A most intriguing concept! I had not thought of this, but I believe it is true. I have made errors in the past, that set back my progress; I wish to make no more. But I am not sure that your mind is the best for this purpose. Can you give me an example where your perspective would have profited me?"

"Your attempt to bring the four Chosen to you was clumsy," Seth said. "You allowed us to meander all over the plane. For example, your Sateons were supposed to capture us, but they almost killed us by driving us into the river where we could have drowned. Where would you have been if that one of us you needed had died on the way? As it was, we survived as much by chance as by skill."

Nefarious nodded. "How would you have arranged to bring in such a group?"

"I would have sent a spy to represent himself as a guide. In fact, he would have believed exactly that, so that his secret mind could not betray his nature. But he would lead the party not to a secret entrance, but to this chamber, where you would be awaiting us. One simple betrayal, eliminating virtually all risk."

The sorcerer pursed his lips. "I like your approach. It is true; I have been muddling along, when I could have proceeded more effectively. I believe you are the One."

"I am the One," Seth agreed. "But I shall not serve you."

For the first time, Nefarious was startled. "What?"

"As I informed you, I have perspective. I can see that it is not to my long-range interest to serve any will but my own. Therefore I shall not serve you."

"I can destroy you!" the sorcerer said angrily.

"And with me, your only hope of long-range success. That would be the second of your serious errors with respect to us. Your first was to tell us of your direct need for the Chosen, for that provided me with the power of information which I am already exploiting. Your judgment may be flawed, but not to the extent of making that second error at this time."

The three others were gazing at him with amazement. He was surprised himself; he had never before been this logical or direct. It had always taken him time to come to fundamental revelations. Evidently his conscience had inhibited or distorted his judgment.

Nefarious looked at him appraisingly. "How is it that you can defy me, when my magic governs your mind?"

"I think you would have difficulty comprehending the answer." Indeed, it had come to Seth himself only as the question was asked. It made such phenomenal sense that he marveled that he had not understood it before encountering the sorcerer.

"Tell me anyway," the sorcerer said grimly.

"It is my heritage, and the image of a dead deer."

"What nonsense is this?"

"I warned you that you would have dif—"

"Tell me!"

"My heritage is that of a minority group that I believe has no parallel in this plane," Seth said. "There are precepts that we learn earlier and understand better than others, because of our awareness of a very long history of pride and error and persecution. Even those of us whose ties with this group are loose, which group some call a religion and some call a race, retain the awareness of its origin and nature. We remember, for example, an episode we call the Holocaust, in which perhaps a third of our number on the plane were destroyed. We remember how the members of other groups chose to pretend that this horror was not happening, or did not concern themselves about it because it did not seem to affect them personally. It did affect them, and in time, to protect their own interests, they had to wage a savage war to destroy the hostile power responsible for the Holocaust. In that war as many of them died as our total dead, and they knew that they should never have tolerated the presence and growth of that evil power. What they had taken to be in their short-range interest had proved to be against their long-range interest.

"They soon enough forgot that lesson, and went on to other misjudgments and other wars, but we who had suffered most did not forget. Each of us, I think, has had to answer for himself the question 'Why did it happen? How can it be prevented next time?' For there is always a next time, no matter how far away the last episode is or how safe we seem to be; the millennia of persecution have taught us that. Others may tune it out, but we dare not; we must always be vigilant, for it is our only hope of survival. And so I too thought it out, and came to my own answer, and it is this answer that now enables me to see the illogic of serving you. In the short range I might benefit, but in the long range I would find such benefit meaningless. As it is written in a book you would not understand, what does it profit a man to gain the world, if he lose his own soul?"

"Soul?" Nefarious asked sharply. "What is that?"

"A concept it would require volumes to explain," Seth said. "But I use it figuratively. It applied to me in this way: I concluded that I could not live my life rightly while ignoring distant wrongs. I realized that eventually those distant wrongs would come to affect my own situation. It did not matter that I did not approve those wrongs, and was not responsible for them; I still had to be aware of them, and to do what I could to guard against them, even if all I could do was to prepare myself intellectually. This was not an ethical conclusion, but a rational one: the toleration of distant wrongs was bad for my long-term survival. This boiled down to the realization that it was my best policy to do what I judged to be right, at all times, because this was appropriate usually to my short-term comfort and always to my long-term survival.

"The image of the dead deer confirmed this judgment, for it gave a direct personal touch to a cold objective concept. The deer had been slain only for sport; there was no fairness about it. In the short range, might had made right; the hunter with a gun had brought down the innocent animal. But in the long range this is a facet of disaster. The hunter was doing at close range what mankind is doing at long range on my plane: destroying the ecological balance. In time there will be no wild life, and no wilderness; there will only be man. Then it will be too late for man, for the planet needs diversity and balance of life. Without it, man will suffocate, having destroyed all that sustained him, as a parasite run amok destroys its host and dies itself. So I knew, even without conscience, that the slaying of the deer was wrong, and it was a thing I had to oppose when I was able to. Now I am able."

Seth looked levelly at Nefarious. "You will not be good for this plane, so I will not serve you, and therefore you will fail. Your power of magic cannot change that."

"So you would have it that I would be best off simply to destroy the four of you now," Nefarious said.

"No. You would be best off to renounce your plan of conquest and turn your energies instead to positive things, so that the four planes can be saved."

Nefarious smiled. "I think not. I prefer to do it my way. Tirsa."

Tirsa looked at him, disgusted. "Any feeling I had for you is gone," she said. "Your invocation of it extirpated it. You will have to force me to do your will."

"And so I shall. You will do my will because otherwise I will torture your friends to death in front of you." Nefarious lifted a finger, and abruptly several Sateons entered the chamber. They surrounded Rame and Vidav, holding spears to their necks.

"I feel it fair to advise you that you are making a mistake," Seth said. "You have nothing to gain by such a ploy, and perhaps a good deal to lose."

Nefarious's smile had no trace of humor. "When you become my adviser, I hope to make no more such mistakes. Which of the two remaining males is more important to you, Tirsa?"

Tirsa didn't answer. The sorcerer looked at her. Then her aspect changed, and the defiance drained away. "Rame. I have known him longer, because he did not spend time unconscious from poisoning."

Nefarious glanced at the Sateons holding Rame. "Make him hurt, slowly."

One lizard-man held the faun from behind. Another lifted a clawed hand, set the claws at Rame's forehead, and began to draw them down. Four channels of blood appeared as that hand slowly moved.

"I warn you again," Seth said. "You are making an error that may cost you your power."

"And you are surely ready with another lecture on the long-term disadvantage of using force to achieve a short-term objective," the sorcerer said contemptuously.

"It is more specific than that. I strongly suggest that you heed my caution."

"I can wait." The claws were now coming to Rame's eyes. The faun neither flinched nor made a sound; he had the courage of his convictions, now that his conscience was his own.

Tirsa broke. "Don't!" she cried, and it sounded like a whimper.

The claws stopped moving, but did not withdraw.

"Open Seth's mind to mine," Nefarious said. "Give us a direct linkage, of the kind you have given your associates, so that I can do directly what I do indirectly through the eyes. His mind subject to mine, with no inefficiency."

"Oh, Seth, I'm sorry!" Tirsa said, tears coming to her eyes. "I love you, and will lose you, but I can withstand neither his magic nor his cruelty."

"Do what you have to do," Seth said. "He refuses to heed my warning, so brings his destruction on himself."

"I must give you credit for an excellent bluff," the sorcerer remarked, unworried.

Then he felt the presence of Nefarious; their two minds were completely open to each other. *Now you will do my will,* the sorcerer thought. *You cannot resist, for your mind is part of mine.* Indeed, what the man had done with his magic before, he now did with his mind, absorbing the essence of Seth's mind into his own. The magic had been potent on a temporary basis; this was far more effective, and permanent. Tirsa herself only connected them; she had never actually merged the minds she linked. Nefarious was like a juggernaut, feeding on everything, fitting it into his own framework, establishing connections of his own that would prevent this forced union from ever being dissolved. He was a conqueror who took the best elements of the conquered country and incorporated them into his system, so that they served him truly. After this, Tirsa's participation would no longer matter; Nefarious and Seth would always have mental contact, and the will of the master would be served implicitly.

I tried to warn you, Seth returned as this process occurred. *I did not feel it was fair to trick you, for an advantage gained by trickery may be similarly lost.*

Your tricks have no relevance. I have crushed your independence. . . .

Not exactly.

Nefarious glanced at Tirsa. "Desist; you are done." He glanced at the Sateons holding Rame. "You also. Depart."

Tirsa hid her face, ashamed. The Sateons left the chamber. Rame found a handkerchief and wiped up the blood on his face. Vidav simply glared.

"Now, Seth," Nefarious said pleasantly. "What was it you wished to warn me about?"

"Your drive for power is at an end," Seth said. "You will turn your energies to positive matters, seeking to make this plane the best possible one for all who are part of it."

"And why should I do that?"

"Because when you absorbed my mind, you absorbed my values too. You now have what will pass for a conscience."

"That is absurd!" the sorcerer snapped.

"You forgot that full mental mergence is a two-way street. Before, you used your magic to deprive others of their conscience and will; this time you allowed me to give you more than you intended. You cannot eradicate what is now part of your own mind."

"This is nonsense! I retain full free will!"

Seth shrugged. "Then do something I wouldn't

do. Torture Rame."

"Seth!" Tirsa cried, appalled.

Nefarious looked at Rame. He took a step toward him, lifting his hand. Then he paused, startled and dismayed. "Oh, no!" he breathed.

Tirsa stared. "You mean it's true?"

Nefarious fell back. "It *is* true! I cannot do it!"

Seth nodded. "I think, until you get used to this, you had better accept our guidance. We have lived with conscience all our lives; it is natural to us. In time it will become natural for you. But at present you will have to ponder every act you take, to discover whether it is in accord with your new values. It will be more efficient if you accept our word without question."

Nefarious's face worked. "Yes—it will."

"Or perhaps simply instruct your top lieutenants to obey us as they would you. Then you can retire until you are comfortable with your own thoughts."

Dazed, Nefarious lifted a finger. A man appeared, evidently of high rank. "These folk will take charge of my affairs," he said. "Obey them as you would me."

The man's eyes widened. "Sir?"

Nefarious simply looked at him. Seth knew that he was exercising his magic, making the man's will disappear. "As you direct, master," the man said. He turned to the Chosen.

"Take us to a residential suite," Seth said. "Have a map of the premises prepared for us, and inform subordinates that we are to be treated with respect. Have your military and economic directors report to us in one hour for briefing."

"This way, sir." The man led the way.

Seth sat up, and saw the sun streaming in. "Ouch! We overslept!" he exclaimed. He tickled the woman beside him. "Come on, we have business!"

Tirsa stirred. "Well, if you hadn't kept me up so late last night . . . " she grumped.

"Well, it *was* our anniversary, you know."

She grabbed him and hauled him down for a kiss. *I know, lover! You thought you were still seventeen!*

"Well, I'm only twenty-two now," he protested. "And you're—"

"Never mind," she said, hitting him with a pillow. *"I love you!"* she added in both speech and thought.

"Do not state the obvious," he replied—and got whammed with the pillow again, before they went down in another kissing and tickling bout.

Then she focused on her closet, and one of her intriguing dresses floated out and came to her. Seth concentrated on his own clothing, and it floated similarly close. He still rather enjoyed the magic they had learned, even if it really didn't speed things up much.

This was their vacation, and it was good to relax, even if they both loved the work they were doing. Both the empires of Nefarious and Teutonia were fading as prosperity and peace spread across the frame, but it required constant work to keep things on-course. Tomorrow they would get back in harness.

In due course they conjured themselves to the deep forest. Three children charged out of the cave beneath a huge tree. "Mommy! Daddy!" the girl with striped hair cried. "See what Funny can do!"

"That's Fauny," Tirsa corrected her as she hugged her.

"Sure, I know! And I'm Thirsty! Look!"

For the little girl with goatlike feet had a little reed whistle. She played a note, and a mudball appeared and plopped to the ground.

Seth shook his head. His daughter was Thirzi, but enjoyed confusing it.

Rame hurried out. The four lines showed as faint scars on his forehead; he wore them as a badge of honor. "Malape won't let her do that inside the cave," he explained, embarrassed, as he shook Seth's hand.

Seth squatted down to talk with the other boy. "Where's your dad, Domey?" he asked.

"That's Dummy!" the boy protested.

Seth smiled. "No, I think I had it right the first time. You were named after your mother."

"I guess." The lad idly squeezed a pebble between two fingers. The pebble crumbled to sand. Even at this age, no one called him "dummy" without smiling.

At that point a man came forging rapidly through the forest, covering ten paces at a step. "Daddy!" Domey exclaimed.

"Domela insisted on a last moment cleaning of the house," Vidav explained as he picked up his son. "So she sent me on ahead, with the boots."

"Let's go climb Lape's Tree!" Thirzi said, tiring of such long-winded explanations.

"No you don't!" Seth said, catching her before she could scramble away. "You have to go to the other plane to visit your Aunt Ferne, remember?"

"Oh, yes!" she agreed, remembering. "Can Funny and Dummy come too?"

"Not this time. Maybe one day we will know how to let anyone cross between planes, but right now it's just me—and you, when I carry you. We still have a lot to learn about magic."

"Well, hurry up and learn it!" she told him. Then, mentally: *I love you, Daddy.*

Seth almost dropped her. *When did you learn mind talk?* he demanded, amazed.

Mommy wanted to surprise you, she thought cheerily. *Did I, Daddy?*

You sure did! Then he hugged her. If only he had known what a wonderful life he was going to, despite a few bad moments along the way, that night he fell through the ice!

- **Author's Note**

I suspect you are wondering how collaborations come about. Well, it varies, but I think this one is unusual even within the genre of collaborative novels. I assume you have read it before coming to this Note, so you will know that it is a fairly standard adventure fantasy with, I trust, some touches that will make you remember it and perhaps think a little. It is what is known as a juvenile genre novel, featuring a main character in his teens, and it does not dwell unduly on sex or bloodshed.

I am Piers Anthony, and my work may have been known to you before you encountered this novel; I think I need no special introduction. My collaborator, Robert Kornwise, has had no novel published before, so I will tell you something about him, and about the stages of this collaboration. Let me phrase this as a story, as if he is a character in it.

Rob was a handsome youth whose description might be similar to that of the main character of his novel, Seth Warner. He was tall—six feet three or four inches—and muscular. He had brown hair and serious brown eyes whose effect was ruined by his frequent laughter. He smiled often. His nose was long, and really not his favorite feature, though his sister called it "interesting." His sister also called him "Robby," which bothered him in public but perhaps not privately. He tried various hairstyles, but finally settled on short and clean-cut, so that he could get out of the shower and shake it dry quickly.

Rob started this novel, I believe, at the age of fifteen, encouraged by his English teacher, Judy Hite. Many teenagers (and many who are older, too) have the aspiration to write, to make a story come to life, and to be published. It is a desire I understand; I went through it myself, though I was twenty before I got serious about it, and twenty-eight by the time I made my first sale. Often the hopeful writer is a misfit: someone who doesn't get along well with the existing system, so retreats to his private fantasy world. This was not the case with Rob. He was popular in school, with many friends of both sexes. He was a good student, and athletic, and interested in music. In fact, he took classes in the Okinawan form of martial art, Ryu Kyu No Te, literally "hands and feet"; there is a picture of him in his high school yearbook executing a kick. Rob did not speak of this directly to me, but my own experience with Kodokan Judo, a different martial art, helped me to understand his interest. A serious martial artist does not swagger around picking fights on the street; the first things he learns are discipline and respect, and this was Rob's approach. Neither did he just dabble in music; he played three instruments: saxophone, harmonica, and the synthesizer. He was also an amateur composer and songwriter. You can see these interests in his novel; to that extent he was writing about what he knew. He wrote the novel outside of class, for his own enjoyment. He had an interest in mythology, and I think it shows in the setting for the fantasy, with a satyr as a major character, and his magical reed whistle.

Some people turn inward because of a bad family life. There is more division, misunderstanding, and outright abuse in our society than we care to think about, but often it is hidden, buried within the family, a guilty secret. It would be understandable that a teenager would turn to his private world to escape such a situation. This may have been true with me, though I was not abused; fantasy became more sustaining in certain respects than reality, and I cannot be certain that situation ever changed. But this was not the case with Rob. His family life was close and supportive, and he returned the favor. His father had multiple sclerosis, and Rob was always at his side when needed, and did the same for his mother. "If you were able to draw a picture of what you wanted as a son," his father said, "it would have been a picture of Rob." He even got along well with his sister—any teenager with a sibling will appreciate how tough that can be!—and indeed regarded her as his best friend. He loved to tease Jill, because she always fell for his jokes, though she was two and a half years older than he. Sometimes he would jump out of some dark place and scare her, just to hear her penetrating scream. She couldn't stay angry with him long! When younger, they used to pretend they were "Cheerios," rolling along the floor and giggling as they sang out "Cheer-i-oooo!" Or he would pretend he was a fisherman, and she was his pet fish named "Okie" whom he caught and threw back into the water, over and over. Or they might be twins with super-powers. They would read each other bedtime stories, or write songs together, or make forts and haunted houses. They would exchange secrets about their boyfriends, girlfriends, love life and all, to their parents' frustration. No, his interest in writing did not stem from any alienation within the family.

Sometimes the larger environment is restrictive. When I was cooped up in the city, I dreamed of the country, and I dreamed of the city when I was in the country. A person might write about his dream of a better land, one he might like to visit. But Rob was not restricted; he may have had the best of both, living in Michigan but not in the big city. He didn't like homework (who does?) but would read things on his own, and was politically and socially aware. He loved to camp, hike and canoe, to get away from it all, but I don't think he had any aversion to his regular life. He liked building fires, making tools, and just plain *living*. He revered life, and when he found a spider in the house he would gently take it out and set it free. When he found a hurt animal he would adopt it and nurse it back to health. So I think he was writing about what he knew as much as about what he dreamed of; he extended his experience of the country into a complete fantasy land, but he was not dependent on it psychologically.

The truth is, he did not finish his novel. I think this is the liability of too full a life; there are many calls on one's time, and the long hours with a computer can become tedious, even though the story being developed is not. He read my novels, yes, I was his favorite author, and wanted to do the same. So he started in, but the distractions of a busy life made progress slow. His friends commented on the ongoing text, correcting his spelling (no one worth his salt finds spelling easy: I speak as one who was an original speller almost from the start) and making suggestions. Then disaster: a full chapter was lost through a computer foulup. Computers are like that; they wait until you least expect it, and gobble up your material. It was his longest and perhaps most significant chapter—gone beyond recovery. That sort of thing can make even a veteran writer ponder the meaning of life.

But chapters can be rewritten, galling as it may be to have to do it, even if they can never be restored precisely as they were. I think in time Rob would have gotten down to it, but I can't blame him for waiting. There were, after all, so many other things to do, and he was sensitive to the needs of others. His sister Jill went away to college, an English Major at the University of Michigan, and he visited her there, and talked to her when she was in the throes of adjusting to their father's illness and her new life away from home. Activity at school was constant. He organized a band, and he hoped to be a disc jockey on the school radio, and he worked at a nature center, and he set up his own computer sales business with a friend. He had boundless energy, and was constantly getting into new things. He liked creative games and individual sports; he and his friends would play simulated adventure games they created themselves. He enjoyed computer science fantasy games too, and loved to create his own. He was able to "lucid dream" and kept a dream journal. He had, he felt, two "out of body" experiences.

He cared about people, too. He had friends everywhere, but also a quick temper which he was

handling better as he got older. There were things
that made him angry, such as prejudice and racism,
liars, cheats, thieves. He hated poverty, disease, injus-
tice, and things which divided people, religion being
guilty of that, too. Drunk drivers, bad drugs, alcohol,
smoking, nuclear war. He was a strong advocate of social justice. He wanted to be a politician or a judge, or
an FBI agent, or even just a policeman who enforced
the law and helped others. Anything but a comfortable idiot! He wanted to change and make changes.
He was impatient with conventional education; he
knew it was important to learn, but at times school
seemed repressive and more like a prison. But he valued the excellent teachers, and was challenged by
good projects.

So it continued, with his busy life, as winter came.
In early December he went on a skiing trip with some
friends, for he was into winter sports too. Thursday
night, December 4, 1987, he phoned his sister, as he
so often did, staying in touch. "Jill, I love you," he
concluded. Friday he started home. He was in the
passenger seat, wearing his seat belt, while the vehicle was waiting for a light. Another vehicle struck
them from behind, traveling at something like fifty
or sixty miles per hour. The collision was such that
apparently Rob's vehicle bounced around and was
struck again, on the right side. The passenger side.
He received a blow on the right side of his head, that
didn't look too serious; it was just a laceration of the
scalp. But it was far worse than it looked; he had sustained a massive injury to the brain, and he was dead.
He was sixteen.

* * *

On January 26 Rob's friends wrote a letter to me, in care of a publisher, asking me to read Rob's unfinished manuscript. I received it the following month, and answered with a quick card, agreeing to look at the novel. The truth is, I was not eager to do this, for my time was exceedingly pressed. I had answered a total of 221 letters in January, and was getting ready to move, and was about a month behind on my writing schedule. I was soon to get a secretary to help with the correspondence, but still, things were jammed. About the last thing I wanted to do was read amateur fiction, which normally has high hopes and execrable execution; I was all too likely to be stuck with the chore of trying to make some positive comment on awful fiction, so as to avoid hurting feelings. But I remembered something.

When I was sixteen, in 1950, my closest cousin, fifteen, died of cancer. He had been a cheerful boy, bright, popular, with everything to live for, in contrast to me. Suddenly he was gone, while I remained, at Westtown Friends' School where we both were students. It seemed like a mistake; obviously I should have been the one to go. That shock, and the continuing questions it generated in my mind, changed my life. At first I couldn't accept it; I dreamed that it had been a confusion, that he had only been ill, and had recovered. I papered it over, as it were, and went on with my life; my roommate of the time says I hardly mentioned the matter. After all, I had known Ted in life as a child, his strengths and his weaknesses. I remembered when he had talked me into pulling him on his wagon; I struggled, but hardly made progress. Then I saw that he was holding the brake tight, laughing. I was a poor sport; I quit in a huff. I shouldn't have; it was a joke, and he was a fun person. How could such a *human* boy die? It didn't make sense. But I visited his family, serving in a manner in lieu of a brother for his younger sister, and I slept in his bedroom and saw all the little artifacts of his life as he had left them. I saw the terrible grief of his family. It was as if a giant hammer had come out of a clear sky and smashed it, leaving only the pieces. Where was the justice in this? I never was able to resolve this question, and remain an agnostic today: I cannot believe in a God who allows this sort of thing, and I don't know what rationale remains, but I hope that in some way it is justified. To an extent, my life and career have been an effort to compensate. To find some meaning in what seems to be the horrible unfairness of the universe. Now there was *déjà vu*, as another good boy that age was dead. No, I could not turn this request down.

In March the manuscript arrived. It was about 21,000 words long, consisting of Chapters 1 to 8, with #5 missing. I read it—and found that it had potential. This put me in another quandary.

What the friends of Robert Kornwise wanted, of course, was publication, as this would be a fitting memorial for their friend. I understand this well; my own claim to immortality consists of the body of my published work, where my thoughts and dreams are displayed. Death may be part of the natural order, but it remains a nasty business. There are things worse than death, and one of them is death out of turn: the death of a child. I had a hint how this felt, too, for my wife and I lost our first three babies: two stillborn, the third living for an hour. At least we never knew them; our suffering was relatively minimal. Even so, it haunts me: what might our son and two daughters have been, had they had their fair chances in life? I take enormous joy in our fourth and fifth children, Penny and Cheryl, but I can never quite forget those others, struck down in their complete innocence without having any chance at life. So Rob's friends were right, and they had come to the right person, for I had no doubt of my ability both to complete the novel and to get it into print. I have two overwhelming advantages that beginners lack: over twenty years' experience as a novelist, and name recognition that makes publishers take me seriously. Oh yes, I could do it, and do it well. But I still was not eager to take on such a project.

Why not? There was a complex of reasons, some legal, some technical, some monetary, some ethical, some emotional. Let me take these in order. Legally I could not simply take Rob's manuscript and make it my own. Original fiction is protected by statute deriving from common law; it has an inherent copyright, and belongs to the author, until a certain number of copies are published. Normally a publisher takes out an official copyright at the time of publication, keeping the literary rights tight. I was not about to pirate Rob's novel.

My technical reasons related to the state of the text: it was incomplete, and would require a good deal of work for completion. It was also amateur, with problems of spelling, syntax, and development. I could correct these, but in the process I would have to change virtually every sentence, in addition to creating new scenes from whole cloth. Thus the original author's words would be lost. In the process of rescuing it, I would be destroying much of its original nature. I remember the ironic joke: the operation was a success, but the patient died. I was loath to do that.

The monetary situation was formidable. I am a highly successful writer who can command six figure advances per novel for my individual work. But not for my collaborative projects, which was what this would have to be: that is, a shared byline. My collaborations range from a quarter to a tenth as much in advances, which is the publisher's guarantee, and a fair guide to how a novel will do commercially. I normally split the money evenly with my collaborator; that seems only fair. That cuts it in half again. No, I do not save half the work; it can take just as much time to do a collaboration as an individual novel, because of the difficulty in agreeing on scenes and meshing styles. In this case, I would have no input from the collaborator. But even if I kept all the money myself, such a project would be at a loss of perhaps 75%, compared to what I could get for a solo Piers Anthony project. I don't want to seem overly mercenary, but that gave me pause for thought.

That leads into the ethical considerations. About the only way I could consider it at all, was to do what I didn't like, and keep all the money. But that is manifestly not fair to the other party. Oh, I know, some amateurs are so eager to get their names into print that they will give up all the money, and indeed, even pay for publication. Vanity publishers thrive on that: for several thousand dollars they will publish a few hundred copies of anyone's book. The writer can then proudly show off his (often abysmal) novel and get his name into one of those paid-listing author's directories, pretending he is an author of note. There are Ph.D. mills that do much the same for those who want phony doctorates. But I won't touch this sort of thing. What, then, was I to do in this case, where Rob's folks had no interest in any money from the project, but only wanted a memorial for their son? Indeed, they had not asked me; this project had been initiated by Rob's friends, to whom I have dedicated it, who wanted to fulfill his dream of publication. Would anyone understand that I was not being greedy, but merely trying to cut my loss so that I could justify taking the time for the project? It wasn't just the money. I have been demurring while publishers have been eager for my material, as the editors at Avon, Berkley and Tor can confirm. Should I delay things yet more?

And the emotional level. I knew that if I did this project, I would have to come to know Robert Kornwise well—knowing that he was dead. I would be confronted again with the desolation I had seen when my cousin died. Death is not some distant specter to me; it is a close companion that I would prefer to see go elsewhere. I have written often of death, and Death is a main character in one of my novels. I did not relish the prospect of another experience like this.

But when push comes to shove, my conscience governs, and I do what I have to do. I agreed to do the novel. I tackled and compromised on the problematical considerations. Sanford Kornwise, the executor of his son's estate, gave me notarized authority to work with the novel. I scheduled a time to work on it, following the novel I was then amidst, *And Eternity*, and made notes for the completion of the manuscript. I concluded that though I would have to change just about every sentence to some degree, and to write new material that was unlikely to be the same as what Rob would have written, or *had* written, in the case of Chapter 5, I would save as much as I could of his text. Thus I modified by addition: virtually everything he wrote is here, and his characters and story line are intact. I deleted almost nothing; instead I amplified and clarified, doing what I believe he would have done, had he lived and grown and reviewed his text himself. I tried to keep the spirit of his story. Often the finished text was quite close to the original.

I did keep the money, but not in an ordinary way. I decided to do this as a low-budget project, so that the money would not be a factor for some time. I wrote to the publisher Underwood-Miller, explaining the situation and asking whether they would be interested in an Anthony/Kornwise fantasy novel. Tim Underwood agreed that they would be interested. I did not ask for a contract, only that willingness to look. The fact is, I could readily sell the project to a more commercial publisher, but Underwood-Miller is a small genre publisher dedicated to really nice hardcover volumes, with acid-free paper and quality bindings, and that was the kind I wanted for this. An edition that the family and friends of Robert Kornwise would be glad to have in their homes. We did not discuss money, but I had sold a novel to U-M be-

fore, for an advance of $2,000, and it seemed to me
that this would be appropriate for this one. I donated
$1,000 to the fund set up in Rob's memory, in effect
sharing the advance as in a normal collaboration.
Probably U-M's hardcover edition will be licensed for
five years; after that I will be free to sell the paperback
rights to one of my regular publishers for a much
larger sum.* So I started by paying out money, but
later I expect to get more back. In this manner I have
tried to balance the concern I have for doing right by
all parties involved, with what success I may never be
sure.

There was no compromise on the emotional aspect. I simply went through the novel, fleshing out
Rob's text, trying to know his mind—and it was a
good mind, compatible. He had a good feel for the
dynamics of story-telling, and he had some serious
things to say along the way. That dead deer—that
strikes right to the heart of it, his deep respect for
life. I hurt with him, and for him, for he was as point-
lessly killed himself. The pain was not in having to
complete unfinished work, but in trying to feel what
he felt, while knowing that he was dead. In knowing
that I could not complete his story his way, because I
am a different person, with different experience; no
matter how hard I might try, it would be to some degree untrue. Even as I edited my text, I saw errors I
had made; I think now that he intended Tirsa to be

---

* Publisher's note: The license was indeed for five years, but
Baen and U-M reached a separate agreement shortcutting
U-M's period of exclusivity.

younger than I had her, and I had reversed the two medals the hermit gave Tirsa and Rame: he was supposed to have the truth-showing one. I was also constrained by the need to make the novel commercial: that is, one that many people would enjoy reading. Something always had to be happening. I could only hope that if Rob could see what I did, he would approve. I knew it would be worse when I came to the Author's Note, and it was. Letters from his father, his mother, his sister, his teacher, his friends, telling of him, loving him, and suffering. I drew from them all, trying to make him come alive for the audience for his novel, you who are reading this Note, as he came alive for me. Then I had to tell you that he was dead.

I am not able to describe all of what I learned of Rob, because some of it might embarrass others whom he helped, and because he was modest and would have been embarrassed himself to be praised for his successes or for doing things he felt were only common decency. Yet perhaps I can come at it obliquely, by telling not what he did but what I know he would have done. When my daughter Penny was younger there was an episode involving a group of students her age. She wanted to participate, and this group was open to all; we encouraged her to join. But she was hyperactive and dyslexic, and children can be cruel about any such differences. They so arranged it that Penny was denied without proper reason, apparently because she was different. After trying several times to join, she came home on the bus in tears, rejected. I was outraged by this, but we did not make an issue because it seemed pointless to force her acceptance into a group that evidently didn't want her. So she never joined. Today, as an adult, she works for an agency that helps outcast or runaway children; she understands. But if Robert Kornwise had been a member of that group, he would have stood in protest on the spot, and shamed the others for their attitude, and she would have been accepted. He did not seek quarrels, but there were some things he simply didn't tolerate.

This, then, was the background of this collaboration. It is Rob's novel, even though I made his 21,000 words into over 75,000. The chapters he did are 1 to 4 and 7 to 9; I replaced the lost Chapter 5 with two of my own, and then concluded with three more. Some elements of his chapters I added; some elements of mine were based on his notions, so it should be very hard to tell exactly who wrote which words. But there need be no mystery about it. Here is the opening paragraph of the second chapter, which was quoted in his school yearbook, so that you can see what it was and what I did with it.

Seth was acutely aware of the hot sun beating down on him in his heavy winter clothes. Lifting a hand to his face, he felt a long stinging gash but did not remember being hit. The ice must have cut me when I fell through, Seth thought. Lying on his side he opened his eyes. A pearl white beach stretched out under him, in length, it stretched as far as he could see. The beach led up to a brilliantly blue ocean with small rippling waves. About fifteen feet behind him was a tremendously thick jungle. Although Seth was no botanist, nothing looked remotely like a Michigan landscape. If any-

thing, it was more like a tropical rain forest. The bark on the trees was not brown. A good number of them were blue, green, or white. There was also a peculiar yellow tree which appeared to have no bark at all, and was somewhat disturbing to look at. Most of the leaves were larger than what he was accustomed to seeing. Not quite green, they were almost emerald with veins of incandescent pink and violet. The overall effect was dazzling.

As you can see by looking at my Chapter 2, I did things to it. I broke it up into smaller paragraphs, I modified words, I changed sentences to add drama, I added comments. But it remains his text. This is typical of the way it went. This is Rob's novel, as it might have been had he had opportunity to revise and complete it himself.

There are ironies. The protagonist is evidently Rob, as he expected to be in two years (remember, he was fifteen when he started writing), but he changed the family in the manner that writers do, so as not to embarrass living people. His sister became younger than he, instead of older, and his father died. This should not be taken as any ill will toward his real father, just a divergence from the starting point, perhaps occasioned by his effort to relate to the fact of his father's illness. My novel *Shade of the Tree* similarly excluded my wife; she likes to say that she gave her life for that novel. I made Ferne resemble Rob's sister Jill, as she was when younger. But perhaps some of Jill's spirit came through in Tirsa, too. In the novel, the father is dead; in reality, the father lived—and Rob died. There was an accident in a motor vehicle in the novel, a rear-end collision—and a similar one in life, far more serious. It was as if he foretold his own death, mistaking only the nature of it: a car collision instead of drowning. It reminded me of my own auto accident, at the age of twenty-two, sailing off a six-foot drop-off at 40 miles per hour and rolling over. It might have killed me, but only bashed my shoulder and knocked me out a few seconds, thanks to the luck of the draw. Thus I lived to complete the novel of the one who died. In the novel, Seth died, but lived on in another world. In reality, Rob died— and I hope lives on in a world like the one he made for *Through the Ice*. I wrote the happy ending; I had to do it, for Rob, so as to be able to picture him there. Perhaps the greatest irony is that he never knew that he was to work closely with me, and to become a published author, after his death.

When I queried Tim Underwood about this project, I learned that he too had suffered a death in the family. His brother had been gunned down in the night by an Eskimo while camping near the arctic ocean, a decade before. There didn't seem to be any reason for it; apparently it was just because he and his girlfriend were there. "The living need memorials," Tim wrote, "as valuable symbols, to replace what is missing." So he too understood, because of his own experience. Thus Rob's friends chose to query the right author, and I chose to query the right publisher—none of us knowing the background that made this particular project personal. Rob's friends queried me because I was Rob's favorite author; I queried U-M because I knew them and liked their attitude toward books. Coincidence, perhaps.

There is of course no obligation, but if any reader

wishes to contribute to the memorial fund I mentioned, the address is the Robert Kornwise Memorial Fund, c/o Adat Shalom Synagogue, 29901 Middlebelt Rd., Farmington Hills, Michigan, 48018. This is a yearly function open to all, of topical interest, which may be directed toward young people of Rob's age.

Through the Ice is a memorial for one who died young. The final irony is that I wish it had never happened. I wish he had lived instead.

FREE SAMPLE

Call now for your free sample of Piers Anthony's personal newsletter and a catalog of Anthony-related books and gift items.

CALL TROLL FREE
1-800-HIPIERS